Cheers for

Nice Girls Finish First

"*Nice Girls Finish First* is a hoot! This book is funny, enter-taining, and heartwarming—a well-written, fast-paced story all wrapped inside one little book cover . . . *Nice Girls Finish First* is a top-notch story for a summer beach read, and one not to be missed."   —*Romance Reviews Today*

"*Nice Girls Finish First* is the perfect story for you to toss into your beach bag and enjoy on a lazy summer day."
                                                —*Writers Unlimited*

"Readers cannot help but be drawn into the two women's struggles, and cheer them on. This is a writer who will make you smile whenever you see that she has a new book re-leased."   —*Huntress Reviews*

. . . and American Idle

"Laugh-out-loud funny with characters that will win your heart."   —*New York Times* bestselling author Suzanne Brockmann

"Even more fun and much smarter than reality TV . . . A hi-larious, heartbreaking, and ultimately uplifting modern ro-mance."   —Susan Wiggs, author of *The Ocean Between Us*

continued . . .

Seven Ways to Lose
Your Lover

Alesia Holliday

BERKLEY SENSATION, NEW YORK

THE BERKLEY PUBLISHING GROUP
Published by the Penguin Group
Penguin Group (USA) Inc.
375 Hudson Street, New York, New York 10014, USA
Penguin Group (Canada), 90 Eglinton Avenue East, Suite 700, Toronto, Ontario M4P 2Y3, Canada
(a division of Pearson Penguin Canada Inc.)
Penguin Books Ltd., 80 Strand, London WC2R 0RL, England
Penguin Group Ireland, 25 St. Stephen's Green, Dublin 2, Ireland (a division of Penguin Books Ltd.)
Penguin Group (Australia), 250 Camberwell Road, Camberwell, Victoria 3124, Australia
(a division of Pearson Australia Group Pty. Ltd.)
Penguin Books India Pvt. Ltd., 11 Community Centre, Panchsheel Park, New Delhi—110 017, India
Penguin Group (NZ), Cnr. Airborne and Rosedale Roads, Albany, Auckland 1310, New Zealand
(a division of Pearson New Zealand Ltd.)
Penguin Books (South Africa) (Pty.) Ltd., 24 Sturdee Avenue, Rosebank, Johannesburg 2196, South Africa

Penguin Books Ltd., Registered Offices: 80 Strand, London WC2R 0RL, England

This book is an original publication of The Berkley Publishing Group.

Copyright © 2006 by Alesia Holliday.
Cover art by Nerly Walker.
Cover design by Monica Benalcazar.
Text design by Kristin del Rosario.

First edition: July 2006

Holliday, Alesia.
    Seven ways to lose your lover / Alesia Holliday.
        p. cm.
    ISBN 0-425-20994-6
    1. Dating (Social customs)—Fiction. I. Title.

PS3608.O48467S48 2006
813'.6—dc22   2006007494

PRINTED IN THE UNITED STATES OF AMERICA

10   9   8   7   6   5   4   3   2   1

This one is for Cindy Hwang,
who is simply amazing.

And for Lani Diane Rich, Michelle Cunnah,
and Barbara Ferrer,
because I wouldn't be sane without them.

Finally, and always, for Judd, Connor,
and Lauren,
for loving me when I'm crazy.

ACKNOWLEDGMENTS

Thanks to Cindy Hwang, who (among other things) convinced me that a raunchy puppet show was the way to celebrate the holidays. Because who needs a boring, normal editor? And for all those other reasons. You know what I'm talking about.

Thanks to Leslie Gelbman, Leis Pederson, Paola Soto, my talented cover artist, Nerly Walker, and most especially to the incredible people in production, who worked so hard to get this book out on time. Thanks also to the wonderful Berkley sales and marketing team, for taking my books to my readers. And of course, to the amazing booksellers, who work so hard for the love of books.

Thanks to Steve Axelrod, the human equivalent of Prozac, for more than I could ever say here. Thanks hugely to Lori Antonson, who is absolutely amazing.

Thanks to all of my friends and family who put up with me being incommunicado for so long on deadline; to Jenny Crusie and the Cherries for laughter and conversation and research help; to my support group in the PASIC chapter of RWA. You're the best!

Finally, thanks to Lani, Michelle, Eileen Rendahl, Whitney Gaskell, and Beth Kendrick at the Literary Chicks. You set the bar high, ladies. I'm proud to be your friend.

Dear Reader,

Thank you for joining me on another crazy adventure!
I hope you have fun with Shane, Annie, "Awful Ben," and
the gang. For information about my books, my truth-is-
stranger-than-fiction online journal, and to sign up for my
private members-only mailing list, please visit my website
at www.alesiaholliday.com.

Happy reading!

Alesia

Chapter 1

In case you've ever wondered, desperation smells exactly like purple passion fruit warming body oil. Fruity and a little rancid.

I stood next to the sixty-four cases of virulently purple bottles and wondered again why I'd ever thought moving to New York was a good idea. Then, soul-searching moment for the day over, I called for answers. "Solstice? Why do we have sixty-four cases of this stuff? I asked you to order sixty-four *bottles*, not cases."

Solstice wandered into the cramped back room, weaving her way around the stacks of boxes and racks of delicate silken lingerie, biting her lip and blinking.

Solstice—real name Susan—was my assistant manager. (Midwesterners who migrate to the city tend to rename themselves. I'm not really sure why. Adopted personas manifesting as symbols of surreal expectations? Or just the grown-up version of announcing, "My new name is Princess Jessica," over your breakfast cereal?)

Solstice twirled a strand of blue hair past her multiply pierced ear. You shouldn't judge a book by its pierced and tattooed cover, but her overall look was a cross between Goth grunge and flower child. Which somehow, on her, worked.

"Um, huh? What stuff?"

I sighed and rolled my eyes, praying for patience—or at least the restraint not to grab her by the beaded camisole and shake her. "The *stuff*. The DreamGlow passion fruit warming body oil. Didn't you notice when the delivery came that it was a little bit more than our usual order?"

Solstice glanced at the boxes. "Oh, yeah. Well. I was kind of on the phone when it came, dude. Why'd you order so much?"

"*I* didn't—I just said—oh, *forget* it." I rubbed my temples, hoping that DreamGlow had a vendor-friendly return policy. It would take five years for us to sell sixty-four cases of that stuff. And I was racking up the screwups pretty fast lately, for somebody who wanted to own her own boutique someday. We won't even go into the brilliant "buy matching lingerie for your pet" idea. Evidently only a few high profile celebs think dressing up their dogs is a good idea.

Of course, the seven-dollar-and-thirty-four-cent balance in my savings account isn't helping with the business-owner dream, either.

Luckily, Mrs. P. was taking some time off. Maybe I could fix it before Sensuality's tiny whirlwind-of-energy owner came back to work. At seventy-three, she had more energy than I did, even on one of my triple latte days.

The front door chimes rang. "Helloooo, dears! I'm baaa-*aack*. Did you miss me?"

Solstice grinned and rushed out to meet Mrs. P. and, probably, tell her all about the overflowing bounty of body oil. I clenched my teeth and did a slow ten-count, then trudged after her. Mrs. P. was the closest I'd come to family for a long time. I hated to let her down.

Again.

Even reeking of passion fruit–flavored desperation, I had to smile when I reached the front of the shop. I'd spent the past four years turning Sensuality into a shopper's paradise—lingerie in a rainbow of rich fabrics and textures, quirky and unique gifts, and a carefully selected assortment of products to help today's busy woman celebrate her own sensuality. The walls were painted with a warm and glowing shade of darkest peach, and the lighting was the closest I could get to candlelight without invoking that pesky fire code. All designed to make the shopper look and feel her best in our store.

(Okay, I sound like our website. So sue me. I designed *that*, too.)

It was the closest I'd ever come to having something of my own, and I didn't want to lose it. At least, not until I was ready to leave on my own terms, walking straight from here to my very own boutique.

"Uh-oh. Shane's got that dreamy look on her face again. Either she's dreaming up a new promotion to make my store even more successful, or she got lucky last night!" Mrs. P.'s voice broke into my reverie, and I felt the tips of my ears turn red as she and Solstice giggled. She was the exact age Grandma would have been, but the contrast between Gran's homespun homily and Mrs. P.'s city sophistication was like apples to apple martinis.

No "housecoats" here. My boss was a tiny, white-haired walking fashion statement. Today she favored a gossamer sapphire blue overshirt with an emerald green dress. She couldn't wear her beloved high heels anymore, per doctor's orders, so she'd ordered a few dozen pairs of sneakers to be specially designed, heavy on the bling. She wore the pair embossed with green Swarovski crystal peacocks today.

I glanced down at my jeans and simple tank top and wondered when my sense of style for the business would carry over into my personal style. Or, really, when I'd *gain* a sense of personal style.

Any. At all.

"Shane never gets lucky, Mrs. P., she lives for the store, don't you know?" Solstice said, making me cringe. "If I had that cute, all-American thing going on like she does, I'd get lucky all day long."

I walked over to the best boss I'd ever had and gave her a big hug, shooting a scowly face at Solstice over Mrs. P.'s shoulder. "How was Florida? Was your sister in St. Augustine glad to see you?"

Mrs. P. hugged me back, then laughed. "I think she was glad to see my backside walking out the door, honestly. She acts like an old woman, and she's two years younger than me! Just because I wanted to walk all around the city and the Fort for a bit, you'd think I'd dragged her on a forced march." She set her enormous purse down on the sales counter, bright eyes scanning the room for changes, problems, or the tiniest speck of dust, knowing her.

I folded my arms across my chest and grinned at her. "Um, a 'bit' of a walk? This wasn't one of your ten-hour days, was it? In the hot Florida sun?"

She wouldn't meet my gaze, but I could see the corners of her lips twitching. "Let's just say that the sight of the alligators ripping their lunch apart at the alligator farm, combined with the hundred-degree heat, may have been a bit much for her. I may not be invited back for *years*."

"Like, why'd you go to Florida in September, anyway? Isn't that a winter thing to do?" Solstice said, moving to the side of the door to let three women enter the store. Tourists. All of them clutching cameras and shopping bags. I did a mental eye roll, due to the lofty superiority of my almost four-year tenure as a New Yorker.

As tempting as it was to use the shoppers as an excuse to avoid mentioning the body oil problem, I put on my responsible store manager hat and motioned Mrs. P. to follow me into the back room. "Solstice, you'll stay and help these ladies find what they need, right?"

"Sure," she replied, meandering over to the one carrying the most shopping bags. Solstice may be on a different plane of existence from most people most of the time, but she has an uncanny knack for parting shoppers from lots and lots of money. Which is why she's assistant manager.

Mrs. P. brushed by me, carrying her things, and looked around with a distracted air. "Right. Well, Shane, we need to talk. I'm afraid we have a big problem."

"I know. I just got here and found the boxes. Don't worry at all; I'll fix it. I'm sure DreamGlow will be glad to take the return. It's all unopened, and it's not like we kept it hanging around for eight months and then tried to send it back. I'll—"

She cut me off, looking puzzled. "DreamGlow? What are you talking about?"

"The body oil. We got sixty-four *cases* instead of sixty-four bottles, and I'm really sorry, but I think there was a mix-up with the order." I never, ever blamed Solstice for anything when talking to Mrs. P., because I was in charge and should be the one to take the blame.

At least, that's what Good Shane thinks. Bad Shane wants to sit on the floor and screech that it's not my fault. Maybe with a little kicking and floor-pounding thrown in, for good measure. Repressed toddlerhood trying to rear its red-faced head?

I shoved the silly pop psychology out of my head and focused on Mrs. P.

She waved her hand dismissively. "Oh, no problem. Stuff like that has happened to me more times than I want to count. No, this is a really *big* problem. My darling Lizzie needs help."

"Lizzie, your niece?" I asked. *Lizzie, who makes movie stars and pop princesses look like amateurs when it comes to shopping?*

I'd heard stories about Lizzie, but had never met her, which was fine with me. I had zero in common with a trust-fund socialite.

Mrs. P. dumped a pile of royal blue satin garters off of a chair and sat down. "Yes, my only niece. My late brother's girl. She's in a terrible pickle, I'm afraid."

I leaned against the corner of the desk and looked at her. "What's wrong?"

She sighed. "She's involved with an awful man, and she can't find a way to break up with him, the poor girl. She's too delicate for direct confrontation."

The Lizzie Winstead-Smythe I routinely saw on Page Six seemed to be about as delicate as an out-of-work fashion model at a sample sale, but I figured it would be better not to mention that.

"Well, I'm sorry she's in a bad relationship, but—um—I guess I don't understand what that has to do with me." I said.

"You have to fix it," she said, perched on the edge of her chair and smiling up at me.

My mouth fell open a little, but I snapped it shut. Last time I checked, fixing Mrs. P.'s niece's love life was *so* not in my job description. Dealing with an overstock on body oil? *Check*. Lizzie's bad boyfriend? *Not so much*.

I tried to explain this in a tactful way. "I don't—I'm not sure I understand—"

She made a little *tch tch* sound. "Of course you understand. You see, I know all about you. You're the Breakup Artist."

And here I thought passion fruit body oil was all I had to worry about. . . .

Chapter 2

RULE 1: *The client must never, ever break up and tell.*

I stared at Mrs. P. in shock. "How did you ever hear about that? And it's more of a hobby than anything. Anyway, I'm retired. No more breaking up people for me."

"Why not? And of course I heard about it. I hear everything. Your friend Annie said you've almost made a career out of convincing poor, deluded men that they really want to break up with their girlfriends, just so the girls don't have to go through the confrontation of doing the dumping."

"Well, *career* is a strong word. I—"

She waggled her finger at me. "Don't deny it. I heard about that boy in high school who smashed your car with a baseball bat when you broke up with him."

I scowled at the memory. "I loved that car. And the Breakup Artist thing was kind of self-defense, after that," I said defensively. "It's easy enough to convince a guy that he wants out of a relationship, and it's all happy times when he thinks it's his idea."

She chortled. "Sure, if you're willing to live with the humiliation of everyone thinking you got dumped."

I shrugged. "That's the only flaw in the concept. But what's more important, eating a little humble pie or avoiding the trauma of dumping a guy who may outweigh you by a hundred pounds?"

Mrs. P.'s gaze sharpened, and she pursed her lips. "Is this something that happened to you, Shane? Did somebody hurt you?"

"What? Me? No, no. I'm just talking theoretically," I said, not meeting her eyes. Anyway, it never did happen to me. And it had never happened to Annie's mom, either, on the regularly occurring occasions when she threw her husband out.

Almost never.

Mrs. P. broke into my thoughts with a harrumphing noise. "Solstice told me you got that idiot boy who calls himself Smokey to dump her in two days."

She stood up and crossed over to me, then touched my arm. "You have to help Lizzie. I can't bear to see her be unhappy. One last breakup for old time's sake, and *then* you can retire."

"Right, except the last friend I helped with a breakup wound up marrying the guy, and guess who was *not* invited to the wedding?" I'd learned my lesson in a big way that time. Never, *ever* help friends break up with friends. Especially never admit to your girlfriend that you think her boyfriend is a skanky loser, even after he hits on you at the New Year's party. I cringed at the memory, thinking of the bad Karma points I'd racked up when I heard about Jocelyn's divorce, six months later.

She didn't seem impressed with my arguments. "Minor details, dear. My Lizzie really needs help, and you're the expert. If you help her get rid of this awful Ben person, I'll—I'll—I'll *pay* you! Four, no *five* hundred dollars." She beamed with triumph.

Unfortunately, Mrs. P. knows how much I could use the extra cash, since she's the one who signs my tiny paychecks. She's not exactly *cheap*, but frugal takes on a whole new meaning when it comes to her.

"Weeellll, I guess I could probably at least talk to her . . ." I said, weakening. "But I'm not taking any of your money until I find out if I think I can help. I don't really feel all that great about taking money from you for something like this, anyway. How about—"

She cut me off, her pink cheeks glowing. "Done! And of course I'll pay you. This is above and beyond your duties here. If it doesn't work out, you can just give me my money back. A guarantee, if you will." She collected her purse and headed for the door. "I'll call Lizzie and have her come down to the store to meet you as soon as possible. Thank you so much, Shane. You're a lifesaver."

After she'd gone, I sank down on the chair she'd vacated, groaning a little. "What the heck have I gotten myself into? I'm going to try to make 'Awful Ben' break up with Lizzie the shopping maniac, or else I have to give Mrs. P.'s money back." I started laughing a little wildly. "A kick-her-to-the-curb guarantee."

Mrs. P. popped her head back into the room. "Oh, and you have to do it within thirty days, before Lizzie and I leave for Provence. Thanks again!"

Thirty days? Great. Just great. Well, if all else fails, I can drown him in passion fruit oil and then hide the body, right?

"Are you kidding? You agreed? I thought you learned your lesson after Jocelyn and Chad!" Annie stared at me like I was nuts, her red, curly hair standing out wildly in all directions as if even her hair follicles were in shock.

She and her hair follicles were probably right. After all, I'd moved in with Annie's family during my junior year of high school when Gran died. It's not like anybody knew me better.

I slouched back on the mismatched pillows piled on one edge of our turquoise, velvet, flea market couch. "I know, I know. But she gave me the helpless face and, well, what was I going to do?"

Our across-the-hall neighbor, Michel, laughed at me from our teensy red and white kitchen, where he was opening the evening's second or third bottle of wine. "Right. And the five hundred bucks probably didn't hurt, either." Michel Lanier (I loved saying that: Mee-shelle Lon-yay) was an aspiring fashion designer who had an insane amount of tall, dark, and dangerous going on, with killer green eyes and dark, wavy hair. The hint of a real French accent he'd inherited from his Parisian mother didn't hurt, either. Women shot dagger looks of envy at me whenever he went shopping or to a bar with me.

I loved every bit of it.

"Shut up, or I'll tell people you drink wine with screw-off tops," I grumbled, trying not to smile.

Farren, Michel's lover, roommate, and sometime-partner in mocking me, snickered. "Ooooh, nasty girl. That would kill him. What would his friends at fashion design school think? The horror of it all. They'd revoke his gay card."

I raised my eyebrows in pretend shock. "You people have *cards*?"

Farren was an aspiring soap (excuse me, daytime drama) star, who wasn't much taller than my own five foot eight, but had silky golden brown hair and the kind of sculpted good looks that you only saw carved out of marble in museums or hanging out at the city's top gay clubs. Bad news for the hetero team, great news for Michel. They'd been together for five years, which was longer than any relationship I'd had with anybody except my childhood dog, Sparkle Toes. (My very awkward ballerina phase, don't ask.)

Farren also wore a rare kind of calm grace that sucked you in like a gravitational field of serenity. Anyone in his orbit gained peace merely from contact with his shimmering tranquility.

He smelled really, really great, too.

(I'd begged him for his secret after my several futile attempts at *Yoga for Really Dumb Dummies* had failed. He'd just smiled, a little confused, and sort of verbally patted my head and moved on.)

Annie shoved Farren's feet off of the coffee table and started to open cartons of Chinese food, still shaking her head. "This is a bad idea, Shane. You don't shit where you eat, so to speak. What happens if you can't get him to go for it? What happens if precious Lizzie the Wonder Niece turns out to be a bitch and makes your life a living hell?" She pushed her curls off her forehead and glared at me. "What *then*, huh?"

I leaned forward and grabbed an open carton of veggie fried rice. "Since when are you so bitter? 'Precious Lizzie the Wonder Niece'?"

She sighed and quit frantically ripping open packets of soy sauce and hot mustard. "I know. I'm sorry. It's just that I had a totally hot prospect today—at least a nine and a half on the DPM—and I blew it. Or, actually, *Nick* blew it, by coming in and acting all boyfriendy."

Michel walked in carrying actual wineglasses, instead of our usual plastic cups, and the newly opened bottle of Shiraz. "Pardon me for being dense, but I thought he *was* your boyfriend, *chérie*. And who could *possibly* rate a nine and a half on the Damp Panty Meter? Did Ewan McGregor stop by the record store?"

Annie stuck her tongue out at him. "No, this was a hottie of the nonceleb type. And Nick isn't my boyfriend. He's just somebody I date sometimes," she said.

Michel plopped down next to Farren, and handed him a glass of wine. "*Sometimes* meaning for the past six weeks? When are you going to admit you and sweet little Nick are a couple?"

I chopsticked up another mouthful of rice. "Forget it, Michel. Let's just not go there tonight. Annie only falls hard for the User-Losers. Nick's a nice guy, so he doesn't get her tingle on."

Annie narrowed her eyes and stared me down. "Yeah, six weeks, and he never even tried to kiss me yet. He just feels sorry for me because I'm the fat girl. Anyway, we were talking about you, if I remember correctly, not me. Do you have a plan for this Lizzie and Awful Ben?"

"You are not the fat girl. You are voluptuous!" Farren protested. "You are an angel descended from the heavens, a goddess of plenty walking among the denizens of a hell where stick figures reign supreme."

We all stared at Farren for a moment, and his cheeks pinked up a little. "Auditioned for an off-Broadway show— *Ophelia's Lusts*—today," he muttered.

We had a group eye-rolling moment.

Annie shook her head mutinously. "Goddess my ass. I'm an unrepentant diet dropout, and I know where that puts me in the city social ranking. Somewhere below the rats in the subway."

I sighed, not wanting to get into the "size fourteen is not fat" conversation again, and dropped back to our previous topic. "No, I don't have a plan for Lizzie yet. I need to meet her first and find out about the guy. I like to conduct sort of a 'client interview,' " I said, laughing even as the words came out of my mouth at how pompous they sounded.

Farren and Michel looked at each other, then both turned to stare at me, then back at each other again.

"Are you thinking what I'm thinking?" Farren asked.

"Oh, most definitely," Michel said, before he turned to aim a serious glance my way. "Shane, did you say *client*?"

"Well, 'client' is overstating it by a long shot. I need to meet the person who wants me to—*encourage*—her boyfriend to break up with her. Then we talk, and I—"

"They *meet*," Michel said.

"They *talk*," Farren said.

"Like a *consultant*," they both said, at the same time.

"A *paid* consultant," Michel said, nodding his head.

I was getting tired of the twin talking heads act. "Okay. I'll bite. What are you talking about?"

"We've been talking a lot about Michel starting a fashion consultant thing to help raise money for his design business. We've even plotted out the way he'd advertise and take clients; the whole deal," Farren said, bouncing up and down on his chair.

"Exactly," Michel added. "Why wouldn't it work for you?"

I looked from one to the other, still not getting it. "Why wouldn't *what* work for me? I don't even wear shoes that go with my outfit most days. How could I be a fashion consultant?"

Michel smacked himself in the forehead, while Farren rolled his eyes. Even Annie looked disgusted. Michel spoke up. "Not a fashion consultant, you dunce. A *breakup* consultant. At least if you did it for total strangers, you wouldn't have to worry about the friendship or work thing. And you could earn money for your boutique."

Annie sipped her wine, staring off into space, then she put her glass down on the table, suddenly looking excited. "You know, that's so stupid it just might work. How much is your boss paying you? Five hundred? You could make that your minimum, for the basic breakup, then escalate your rates for increasing levels of difficulty," she said. "I need to get some paper and a pen, so we can figure this out."

I stared after her as she ran toward her bedroom. "Are you nuts? You just told me I'd be a fool to get involved in the Lizzie-and-Awful-Ben problem, and now you want me to run a *business* breaking people up?"

She came rushing back in, brandishing a pen and pad of paper. "Yeah, but that Lizzie thing is still a bad idea, given the connection with your boss. But breaking up total strangers is brilliant! You can earn money by helping women out. You'd be like a cross between Donald Trump and Mother Teresa."

We all took a moment to consider the hideousness of *that* visual. *Would the Donald's hair even fit in one of those nun hats?*

It took another couple of bottles of wine, but somehow I

agreed to taking the Breakup Artist public. Borderline drunkenness edges out fear of karmic repercussions, right? And it was for a good cause, right?

And this need for chronic reassurance isn't a sign of perpetual insecurity or a really down-deep feeling that this is a bad idea, right?

Right?

Everybody raised their glasses, and Michel proposed a toast: "To Awful Ben. May his quick and profitable downfall be the beginning of a lucrative business!"

"To Awful Ben!" I grinned my most evil grin. My grin faltered for a moment—Awful Ben didn't stand a chance against the Breakup Artist.

What if he's not so awful after all?

I paused, biting my lip, then shrugged.

I can't worry about that. Anyway, isn't self-interest the new black?

I pasted a defiant smile back on my face and drained my champagne glass. After another twenty minutes of toasting and laughter, Farren and Michel stumbled off to their apartment, clutching their gift bottles of passion fruit body oil.

It never even occurred to me to think of that old expression "famous last words."

That came *weeks* later. And by then it was too late.

Chapter 3

My philosophy of the art of the breakup is simple, really. Getting dumped is painful. It hurts. There's never a day when you wake up and think, "Hey! I wish someone would crush my heart under his heartless shoes today!" (Not that shoes have hearts, but you know what I mean.)

Guess what? I figured out pretty early on that guys feel exactly the same way. I know, I know. They're guys! They're supposed to be tough. But the first boy I ever broke up with started crying.

Then he smashed the hood of my very first car with a baseball bat.

Quick thinker that I am, I figured out pretty fast that guys have strong emotions, too. (Also how to make the ex-boyfriend's parents pay for my car repair so I wouldn't press charges, but that's another story.)

So, unless you're a complete egomaniac with some sick need to hurt another person, why ever break up with anybody? Especially when it's so simple to convince him to break up with you.

Really, guys are pretty easy to read. Especially single guys. They want to avoid commitment, they want their buddies to see them out with hotties, they want to have fun, and they want their space. Oh, and they want to succeed in their jobs. A clever person can make a few tweaks in any one of these areas and achieve just enough discomfort in the average male that he will be rushing to give you the "I'm not ready for commitment" or "It's not you, it's me" speech, version 13B.

Of course, since this is the goal you were aiming for in the first place, it works out great for everyone—as long as you're strong enough to survive the avid curiosity and often fake sympathy from those who think you got dumped. People can be cruel, heartless, and uncaring.

Even the ones who AREN'T related to you.

Never forget: if you let people in on your breakup strategy, you're headed for trouble.

After I drank the exactly two and one-half mugs of coffee that Annie'd left for me in our ten-mug coffeemaker, I grabbed my purse and ran out the door, actually excited about the idea of being early for work for a change.

Which is really sad, if you think about it. Here's a hard truth: next, I'll be like one of those women on the train with her fingers glued to her BlackBerry, Wall Street Journal *under one arm, skin pasty pale from working all hours.*

I stopped in the hall, trying not to hyperventilate. I wasn't even a business owner yet, and I was already overworked and pasty. Tiny molecules of shredded business plans were undoubtedly turning my brain into mush at that very moment. I needed—I needed—

I needed to take a deep breath and just say no to lunacy. Shaking my head, I locked the deadbolt with my key, then turned to go, and then I stopped in mid-turn, and looked down in shock. I'd had an epiphany, right there in the dingy hallway.

Except my epiphany looked a lot like a brown and yellow, smushed-in face, curly haired, curly tailed, mutant miniature sheep.

The sheep looked up at me and barked. Okay, *dog.* It was either a dog, or the sheep-mutation process had turned its baa into a bark. I looked up and down the hallway for some sign of its owner or any stray vat of radioactive gamma rays.

"Hello?" I called, looking back and forth, which was kind of stupid, because the only other tenants on our floor besides me and Annie, and Farren and Michel, had been the scary hairy guy down the hall, and he'd moved out a few days before. I looked back at the sheep and it looked up at me, sort of sideways, in a halfway-hopeful, "do you have any doggie biscuits" sort of way.

I knelt down and used my softest voice to say hello, hoping not to scare the poor thing. It looked pretty skinny under that ratty, curly coat and probably didn't weigh more than ten or fifteen pounds.

"I'm sorry, little guy, but I'm determined to be early for work, and you must belong to somebody, right? Hey, what's that?"

A frayed cord was tied around its neck, with a cheap metal tag attached. The dog sidled closer to me, looking off down the hall but sneaking sideways glances to make sure I didn't have a rolled-up newspaper or a demon cat, probably. "No, sweetie, no *Wall Street Journal* yet. Although if you caught me a few days from now, I'd probably already be on the downward slope to business-owner drone. Yes, puppy, I don't make any sense at all. Come on, precious. Come to Shane."

I stayed almost perfectly still, mumbling nonsense in a sing-song tone, and finally it—or she, actually, as I discovered when I picked her up—*she* climbed right up on my knee and put her head against my chest. Before I could move, she let out a little gaspy sigh and shuddered against me, as though her entire tiny body were exhaling stored-up exhaustion.

Then she turned her head up and looked at me full-on, and I could see the hope in her eyes. I gently lifted the metal tag, only to discover that it had no writing on either side. But as she turned her head, I saw a folded piece of paper taped onto the other side of the cord. The tape slipped right off, and I unfolded the slip of paper with one hand, and read the two sad little words: FREE DOG.

I muttered a couple of choice words about people who abandon their dogs, feeling a headache start behind my eyes. I didn't have time for this. Not today, not this week, not this year. I had a new business to start and a new life to chase after.

She made a weird snuffling sound, and I carefully lifted my hand to touch her wild corkscrews of fur, then gently rubbed one silken ear when she leaned her head into my hand. When her little curly pink tongue slipped out to give my finger a tentative swipe, I realized my second hard truth of the morning: I was a goner.

I stood up, lifting her against my chest. First, she needed a bath. Then, I'd think about everything else.

Like a fantastic new use for a big stack of *WSJ*s.

Two hours later, the puppy was clean and smelled more like DreamGlow vanilla-spice body gel than like *eau de* stinky dog, and I'd found an old belt that never, ever should have been used as anything *other* than a dog leash (pink fringe, anyone?). The essential toilet functions had been performed in the appropriate places (outside), and she'd snarfed down some leftover chicken and slurped down a bowlful of water.

Now she was sleeping in what she apparently believed

was the dog bed (inside my closet, on top of a fuschia faux cashmere scarf Annie's mom had given me).

Snoring, actually. In a four-hundred-pound-man-with-emphysema kind of way. The walls were literally shaking from the force of the snores coming out of her tiny smushed-in face. I stared at her, midway between appalled and impressed, and tried to figure out what the heck kind of dog she might be.

The curly hair suggested poodle, the curly tail might be . . . that dog from *Men in Black*? Pug? And the general starved-thing look, combined with the vaguely deerlike shape of the head, had to be some kind of Chihuahua, I bet.

Or else she was a very rare example of a ferociously expensive inbred new species.

She chose that exact moment to snort, roll over, and fart, then make a snuffling sound and burrow further into the scarf, all without opening an eye.

Clearly, she was a talented girl. But I was leaning toward the Chihuahua-pug-poodle mutt thing. A poopugawawa. A pugawawapoo. A Chihugapoo.

"That's it! You're a Chihugapoo. Okay, my little Chihugapoo, don't eat my shoes. I have to go to work. I'll get you some food on the way home. Be a good dog," I said, wondering if she understood a word I was saying.

She opened one eye at the words *good dog* and gazed up at me with blissful doggy contentment and fell back asleep. I tiptoed to my bedroom door and carefully pulled the door closed behind me, wondering how long she'd been alone.

Then wondering how long I could keep her. Could a person who didn't even remember her own mom suddenly go all maternal over a mutant sheep?

But I had to get to work, or I'd never be able to afford puppy chow.

I finished stocking the new display and fitted the sign with its graceful lettering on top:

25 PERCENT OFF PASSION FRUIT BODY OIL
ACT NOW—SUPPLIES ARE LIMITED!

Turns out that DreamGlow's return policy sucked.

For about the eightieth time, I checked my watch. Lizzie was an hour and a half late for our meeting. I figured either she wasn't that desperate to get rid of Awful Ben, after all, or he'd offed her and dumped her into the Hudson.

Would that count toward me getting the cash? Technically, they'd be broken up. . . .

I shook my head to try to dislodge my poverty-induced lapse in ethics and moved on to the new Body by Boris camisole display. Boris's designs were hot, hot, hot, which mystified me, since I thought they were the ugliest trend since the brief Eighties Retro phase that had swept the city for a couple of weeks back in March. "Leg warmers? What were they *thinking*?" I muttered.

Just then the door chimes rang, and I glanced up briefly,

then did kind of a double take and a full-on stare. This *had* to be Lizzie. She was haute couture from the roots of her perfectly straightened and colored hair to the tips of her stilettos. I felt like the oversized country mouse in comparison to her size-two splendor, and barely resisted the urge to run to the bathroom to check my teeth for hayseed.

She imperiously swept her gaze around the store, right across and over me, then stopped and glanced at me again. "You couldn't be Shane Madison, could you?" she demanded, rolling perfectly enunciated vowels past perfectly collagened lips.

I raised an eyebrow, my backbone suddenly making an appearance. "Why couldn't I?"

She looked me up and down. "Well, but *really*. I thought Aunt Estelle meant someone who had . . . experience. Have you ever actually had the opportunity to break up with *anyone*?"

I blinked, feeling my throat close up on me. There's a reason they call it backstabbing. Decent backstabbers do it behind your back. Lizzie's full-frontal skewering made my face get hot and my eyes feel suspiciously like tears were hovering.

If I'd ever been any good with confrontation, I wouldn't have needed the Breakup Artist, right?

When I thought I could form words that wouldn't tremble, I stepped toward her and held out my hand. "I'm fine, thank you for asking. You must be Lizzie," I said, in a mostly steady voice. She brushed her fingertips against mine, evidently too shocked by my gargoyle-like appearance to muster up a real handshake.

I took a deep breath. I *had* to ask. "I hope you don't mind me asking, but how could somebody like *you* possibly have a problem breaking up with anybody?"

Her eyes narrowed, and I hastened to elaborate. "I mean, you must have had tons of guys after you, right? Lots of practice?"

She smiled. "Of course I have, but . . . it's complicated. Furthermore, it's none of your business."

I shrugged and turned away, summoning up some of the courage her initial attack had flattened. Then I took another deep breath and a calculated risk.

"Fine. Break up with him yourself. I don't need the hassle, anyway."

She stalked over to the side of the table and glared at me. "Oh, what*ever*. He's the brother of one of my sorority sisters from school, and she'll make my life a living hell if I break up with him. She's been dying to be part of my family for years."

I can see why. All that warmth and friendliness just sucks a person in, I thought, at least having enough of a sense of job and self-preservation to keep from saying it out loud.

Lizzie threw her hands in the air. "Look, I made the trip down to this dump to hear what you had to say. It's not like a man would break up with me *voluntarily*."

I rolled my eyes. "Of course. What was I thinking?"

She ran a finger across the tops of the folded clothes on the table, then looked at me, narrowing her own eyes. "I know Aunt Estelle made some kind of deal with you, so there must be something in it for you, too, right?"

As much as I hated to admit it, she was right. I needed the extra cash—hey, I needed puppy food now—plus I didn't want to let Mrs. P. down. If I looked at it as a favor for Mrs. P. instead of for Lizzie the evil-but-snooty toothpick, I could focus long enough to get rid of Awful Ben. Anyway, it's not like I wouldn't be doing the man a *favor*. Unless he was an axe murderer, he probably didn't deserve Lizzie.

Capitulating, I motioned for her to follow me to the back room, stopping on the way to ask Solstice to watch the front. I cleared a space on a chair for Lizzie, then sat down myself, and grabbed a notebook from the top of my desk. "Now, about Awful . . . er, *Ben*. What's he like?"

She brushed imaginary specks of dust off her skirt, wrinkling her nose with distaste. (I guess the aristocracy doesn't slum it in the back rooms of stores very often.)

"He's fine," she said, then blinked. "I mean, he's *not* fine. He's horrible. I'm sick of him. He's horrible with all that pleading for me to love him forever," she said, shuddering. "I really can't bear the clinging and neediness."

I felt a twinge of empathy, in spite of myself. I wasn't much for clinging and neediness, either. It's not like Dad hadn't told me often enough that big girls stand on their own two feet. At least, whenever he happened to be off the ship or had a free weekend to come visit me. It's hard to cling to somebody you never see.

Anyway, I hadn't had much to worry about in the "clinging men" department lately. At least not in the eight months, three weeks, and six days since I'd had a relationship last longer than one date.

Not that anybody was counting.

"Right. Clinging, neediness," I said, jotting down notes. "Anything else? What does he do?"

She waved a hand, in a gesture eerily reminiscent of her aunt. "Some sort of advertising. He really likes it, for God's sake. Has no ambition outside of being a good ad man, like *that's* some source of pride."

She grimaced. "In fact, I think he cares more about that stupid job than he does about me," she said.

I stopped writing and looked up at her. "Um, but you just said he was clinging and needy. Now he cares more about his job than you?"

I was getting that twinge again. The "maybe I'm not getting the full story" twinge I got sometimes when Solstice called in "sick" the day after a big concert.

She lifted her chin. "So? What about it?"

"It seems a little contradictory, that's all."

"Look, I didn't come down here to be analyzed," she snapped. "Are you going to tell me how to make him break up with me or not?"

I gazed at her for a long moment, then nodded. Even if Awful Ben wasn't so awful after all, I was doing him a favor by helping him get rid of Horrible Lizzie, right? My title as Queen of Self-Justification intact, the genesis of an idea started to form.

Guys who live for their jobs all have one particular kind of Achilles' heel. "Where exactly does he work?" I asked, then carefully wrote down the company name and address she gave me.

I looked up at her and smiled. "Here's what we're going to do . . ."

Chapter 4

Ben Cameron heard the snickering long before he reached his office. Then he heard Gleason's belly laugh. Not that Gleason goofing off in the morning was anything out of the ordinary. He'd been the class clown at Ohio State, and he never grew out of it. But the hum of excited chatter was at a decibel level usually not heard until Friday afternoon's happy hour down at Gilligan's Pub.

He rounded the corner and stopped dead in the hallway, staring at the crowd gathered around his brand-new office. Five years of working his ass off in the bland, cloth-covered walls of his cubicle, and he'd finally earned a promotion and a coveted real office with a *real* door. The CAMERON on the brass plate on the door sternly reminded the cubicle dwellers that he had broken free.

Broken free to a real office that apparently was the center of the morning's attraction, from the looks of it. Puzzled, he threaded his way through the people clustered around his door. "Hey, Nancy, what's up?" he said to his secretary, who was leaning against the wall, looking like she'd either just run a half marathon or had some truly excellent sex in the copy room. Her face was flushed and red, and she was gasping for air.

She shook her head, still wheezing, and held up a hand to point to his office. Ben said, "Excuse me, pardon me, excuse me," a few more times, until he worked his way over to the building flower shop. No, wait. It only looked and *smelled* like a flower shop. It was actually his office.

Huh?

"What the hell is going on?" he asked, sort of generally but mostly directed at Gleason, who was seated in Ben's chair and pounding his fist on Ben's desk.

Laughing. Really loudly.

Gleason caught sight of Ben and pointed a shaky finger his way, then collapsed into another wave of hysterical laughter. "Hey, everybody! Darling Schmoopy Pie Benny Bunny is here!"

Ben was all for a good practical joke, and Gleason was the master, sort of the George Clooney of advertising, but this was going a little far. Gleason knew that today was the most important presentation of Ben's career—for the Jelly Jam candy company account. And Ben couldn't even see his display easels over the profusion of flowers and ribbon-tied balloons.

He stopped just inside the door and gaped in disbelief. "What the hell is going on? What did you do, and why would you do it today?"

Gleason, who'd finally managed to quit laughing, started howling again. "Wasn't me," he said, shaking his head. "R-r-read the c-c-card." He held out an enormous envelope—larger than a legal pad—to Ben, his entire body shaking with mirth. "It's from Lizzie."

Ben glared at his former best friend. "Could I have a little privacy, man?"

Nancy piped up from behind him. "Oh, no need. We've all already read it."

He whirled around and glared at her, too, then opened the unsealed envelope. Somebody was going to get his (or *her*) ass kicked over this. The entire executive staff of Jelly Jam was due in thirty, no, *twenty-seven* minutes. He didn't have time for this crap.

He pulled out the card and stared in disbelief at the giant pandas kissing each other on the garish red and pink cover. Then he opened the card. Under the printed drivel, there was a handwritten note:

To my Darling Schmoopy Pie Benny Bunny,
Huggie wuggies on your big presentation today. Bring some Jelly Jam home to your precious Jelly Belly.
XOXOXOXOXOXO, Lizzie

Ben's jaw dropped open about a foot and a half as he read and reread the card, trying his best to ignore the smacking kissy-face noises coming from everyone around him.

"*Mwah, mwah, mwah*, Benny Bunny. Jelly Belly is waiting for you," said Hank from the art department. Ben shot him a death glare, but it didn't slow Hank down in the least. Of course, the thirty other people saying "huggie wuggie" and "Schmoopy Pie" weren't helping, either.

Ben took a deep breath and used his best Little League coach voice. "GET OUT! NOW!"

It took a while, but he finally managed to kick them all out of his office. All but Gleason, who had a scary gleam in his eye. After Ben shoved the last person out of his office and shut the door, Gleason spoke up. "So, how long you been dating this chick? Anything I should know about? My tux fitting for the 'big day,' maybe?"

Ben's lip did an involuntary curl back over his teeth. "Are you nuts? I've been dating her for what, two months? She seemed normal before this. A lot of fun. This is just totally from the planet Jupiter or wherever the hell weird women are supposed to be from." He scanned the acres of flowers crammed into his office. "I'll have Nancy give these away to all the secretaries in the agency. It smells like a perfume factory exploded in here."

Ben shoved two vases and a potted plant out of the way, so he could get to his desk and put his briefcase down. "What are you doing in here, anyway? We have Jelly Jam in fifteen minutes. Shouldn't you be getting ready?"

Gleason grinned at him. "Oh, man. I couldn't leave before I saw your reaction to *this*." With that, he leaned over and reached for something hidden behind the desk.

As the top of an enormous orange furry head started to rise into view, Ben felt the groan coming up from deep in the vicinity of his intestines. "You have *got* to be kidding me," he said, staring at the largest stuffed bear he'd ever seen.

"Nope. Guess Jelly Belly thought Schmoopy Pie needed a little moral support," Gleason said, snickering.

"I've gotta call her."

"You've *gotta* call her."

"After Jelly Jam."

"I'm thinking *now* might be better. Who knows what she'll do to you in the space of the next hour? Singing telegrams to the conference room?" Gleason cringed, but he was still grinning. Ben wanted to smack him, but refrained. Instead, he stabbed the speaker phone button on his phone and dialed.

Lizzie answered on the first ring. "Schmoopy Pie? Did you get my little present? I can't wait to see you, my cuddle wuddle wubby bubby."

Ben gaped at Gleason, who'd clamped a hand over his mouth and was making loud snorting noises under his fingers. "Um, Lizzie? What the heck is going on? Is this some kind of joke?"

"Benny Bunny! How could you say that? Jelly Belly is so hurt by your mean widdle comments. Are you coming over for dinner tonight? I'm making your favorite dinner!"

Lizzie's voice sounded a little hurt at first, then hopeful. What it didn't sound like at *all* was the voice of somebody who was kidding.

So where is Lizzie, and what space alien took over her brain?

"Ah, Lizzie, I have to go to my meeting, but I'll definitely be over tonight. We need to talk," he said, frantically gesturing to Gleason to get out. Gleason ignored him completely, but stuffed a fist in his mouth to keep from laughing out loud.

"Benny? Don't you think 'Mrs. Lizzie Cameron' sounds just yummalicious? Ta ta, Schmoopy. See you tonight!" she trilled then hung up.

Gleason recovered enough to speak first. "Dude, you're toast. She's gone around the bend. Next thing you know, she'll be poking holes in your condoms."

Ben grabbed the giant orange bear and tossed it against the wall. "Oh, no. No way, man. There will be no condom poking or schmoopy woopy-ing or any other damn thing. This relationship is history."

Ben didn't mention the sick feeling in his gut. He and Gleason had never done the girly "talk about your feelings" thing, and he wasn't about to start now, even if the idea of hurting Lizzie was making him nauseous.

Especially in a room filled with flowers and a giant orange teddy bear.

As they navigated their way out of the office through the piles of flowers, Gleason shook his head and pulled his jacket closed over his rounded-from-too-many-beers belly. "It's estrogen, man. It's like brain poison. After they reach a certain age, they start going freakazoid. Then it's all downhill after that."

Ben stopped to stare at his office one last time. "The bizarre end of another promising relationship. Time to dust off the 'it's not you, it's me' speech."

Gleason headed down the hall. "Jupiter, man. I'm telling you. Estrogen poisoning and Jupiter."

Chapter 5

RULE 2: *A perfect strategy starts small and then—only if necessary—escalates. However, there CAN be emergency exceptions.*

"Men are from another planet, I'm telling you," Annie said, tossing her ancient, scuffed leather backpack on the couch as she stalked into the room. "Or maybe another freaking galaxy. Nick may not even be *human*."

I knew better than to ask any questions when she was on a "men are jerks" roll. I just waited, enjoying the warmth on my tummy from my new dog, who was snuggled under the blanket on my lap. (Yes, the New York apartment building's air-condition-until-people-turn-into-icicles thing is a whole 'nuther story.)

I didn't have to wait long.

"You would not *believe* Nick. He's—he's—he's so stinking *nice*," she said, scowling. "He did my inventory for me when I was at lunch."

"I thought you hated doing inventory?" I asked.

"I do. It was incredibly thoughtful of him to do it for me," she said, sighing. Then she flopped on the couch and punched a pillow. "Can you believe it?"

"That *bastard*," I said, clutching my chest and fluttering my eyelashes.

She turned her scowl on me. "You don't get it. I'm trying to find a way to break up with him without all the awkwardness of having to quit and find a different job, too, and he keeps doing nice crap for me. How can I dump somebody who just did my inventory for me?"

"It's a problem," I agreed. "Pizza or go out?"

"Pizza. I don't have the energy to go out."

I grabbed the phone and punched the speed-dial number for Gino's. "Right. I can see how *not* doing all that inventory would wear a person out."

Her lips quirked in an almost-smile. "Oh, shut up. I gave him the body oil, by the way. He said to tell you thanks. Then he turned about eight shades of red when he figured out what it was. Like, the man is twenty-six years old and has never used warming body oil?"

"He *must* be an alien," I said dryly, then ordered our pizza and hung up. "Meanwhile, I'm down to only sixty-three-and-a-half cases of the stuff to push on unsuspecting customers."

"Well, I'll buy some, if you give me your employee dis-count again," Annie said, pulling off her shoes. "A couple of my friends were in the store this afternoon, and they liked it."

"Sure. I'll bring some more home tomorrow, if I survive another day of Mrs. P. fluttering around, worrying about Lizzie," I said, stretching my legs out carefully. My boss had driven me half mad all day with her not-so-subtle reminders that I only had twenty-nine days left to convince Awful Ben to break up with Evil Lizard, er, Lizzie.

Trust me, I remembered.

"So, any news? Is Lizzie free of Awful Ben?"

I glanced down at the lump in my lap and grinned. "Well, I have some news, but it's not about Lizzie."

I flipped the blanket corner off of the puppy's head. "Ta da! I have a new dog. Her name is Lulu."

Annie jumped up and came over to take a closer look. "What do you mean, you have a dog? Is this it?"

Lulu looked up sleepily and cocked her head at Annie. Annie stared at her for a moment, then looked at me. "Is that really a dog? It looks like a rat that got a bad home perm."

"That's so mean," I said, patting Lulu's head. "Not all of us can have beautiful curls like you, Annie."

Lulu sneezed, which I took for agreement, then she stuck her head up and sniffed at Annie's hand.

Annie just stood there, shaking her head. "Why a dog? Why *this* dog? And why Lulu?"

Laughing, I held Lulu up for Annie to take and stood up,

brushing dog hair off my jeans. "She was in the hallway when I left for work this morning with a note that said 'free dog.' What could I do? Somebody abandoned her, and she was all alone in the world. Plus, she just looks like a Lulu. I don't know, I tried for trendy names, but somehow she looks like a Lulu."

Annie held Lulu up and stared at her face. Lulu promptly sneezed in her face, and Annie shoved her back at me.

"Oh, gross. I cannot believe you decided to adopt the ugliest dog in the world, who evidently has a respiratory problem. Do dogs get weird doggy strains of flu? Can humans catch flu from dogs?"

She ran for the kitchen and turned on the faucet, muttering something about pandemics, then scrubbed her face with water and antibacterial soap. She toweled her face dry, then tossed the towel on the counter. "You do realize that we have to pay a pet deposit and extra rent if we keep her, right?"

I snuggled Lulu closer to me. "I know. She's my dog, so I'll pay anything extra. But I really want to keep her, Annie. She's housebroken, even. I left her here while I was at work, and she never peed in the place or ate my shoes, or anything."

Annie sighed. "It's not like I'm going to say no, Shane. You never ask for anything for yourself. You gave me the big bedroom and won't let me pay more than half the rent. If you want the . . . *dog*, you should keep her. Our schedules are different enough that she'll never have to be alone in the apartment for too long a stretch."

She flopped back down on the couch, still staring skeptically at Lulu. "So, did you hear from Lizzie?"

"Not a word. And believe me, I heard about it from Mrs. P. all day long. Lizzie promised she'd pull the flower-dump-baby-talk special on him today, but I don't have any idea how it went."

Just then, my cell phone rang. The screen read Winstead-Smythe. Lulu growled a little, and I patted her silky curls to calm her down.

I flipped open my phone. "Lizzie?"

"Shane, is that you? I did it, and he's on his way over. He said, 'we have to talk.' That's good, right?" Her voice was high-pitched with excitement or anxiety or—just an educated guess—maybe annoyance that she'd had to call me.

Why did she have to call me?

"Um, Lizzie, *duh*. I mean, whenever a guy says 'we have to talk,' it's usually because he's getting ready to dump you, right?"

There was a *loooong* silence.

"How would I know? Nobody has ever broken up with *me* before," she finally said, in a "how could you imagine such a thing, you peasant" kind of voice.

Lulu's growl deepened, and her lips pulled back from her teeth a little. Evidently her keen canine ears caught the sound of condescension, too.

I tried not to grit my teeth. Bad for the orthodontia. "Right. Sorry. I forgot. Well, yes, it's a good sign that you pushed him over the edge with the flowers. Did you send at least five bouquets and your syrupiest note?"

She laughed a very cold and wicked laugh that sent icicles through the phone line to my hand. "Five bouquets? Darling, I never do things halfway. I sent a thousand dollars' worth of flowers, plus assorted balloons, and one gigantic and putridly-orange stuffed bear."

She laughed again. "The card was a thing of beauty, trust me. I even called and asked his secretary to open it and read it to me, in the guise of being worried that the florist hadn't gotten it right. That way I knew the entire *company* would hear about it."

I held out the phone and stared at it, wincing in sympathy for poor Ben's humiliation. *Maybe I should only take clients I actually like from now on.*

I put the phone back to my ear. "That ought to do it, Lizzie. Be sure and keep up the theme of the four Cs tonight when he comes over: cloying, clingy, and completely crazy. You should be dumped before midnight."

"I'd better be," she said darkly. "I've got better things to do than play around with this. Plus Aunt Estelle is counting on you, if you know what I mean."

I made a face at the phone. "Yeah, I got it. Let me know how it goes, okay?"

"I will, don't worry. If this all works out, maybe I'll be sure there's still a place for you at the store after Aunt Estelle retires and turns the store over to me. Of course, we'll have to update the look entirely, so Sensuality doesn't look like a thrift store reject anymore, but with my guidance, I'm sure it will work out. Ta."

"But—"

Click.

When Mrs. P. turns the store over to HER? Thrift store reject? Mrs. P. is retiring? Oh, please, no. I am so not ready for this.

Lulu, meanwhile, had started barking at my phone. Either modern technology freaked her out, or she didn't like Lizzie, either.

I quit staring into space and snapped my phone closed, then put it on the floor, under the chair. Lulu promptly jumped down out of my lap and stood, fur bristling, staring under the chair and growling.

"That evil witch. There's no way Awful Ben could ever have been awful enough to deserve *her*. The man ought to give me a medal. Can you believe she thinks she's going to take over Sensuality? Annie, what if . . ."

Annie walked in from the kitchen carrying a couple of Diet Cokes. "I want to hear all about it, but first we have to talk about a little BFB."

I held my hand out for the soda and looked up at her, confused. "BFB?"

"Best friend benefits. Since I happen to be roommates with the Breakup Artist, I want her help. For free."

"Oh, no." I could see where this was going.

"Oh, yes. I want you to get Nick to break up with me."

The doorbell rang, and she went to answer the door, grabbing a twenty out of our pizza-fund cookie jar on the way.

Saved by the extra cheese.

*   *   *

"I'll think about it, okay? I can't do better than that. I have to get to know him a little better," I said, popping open the top button on my jeans. *Probably shouldn't have had that fourth slice. Although Lulu did help with the extra cheese and pepperoni bits.*

I grinned at my new dog, who now lay belly-up across my lap, snoring, the picture of contented bliss.

Annie folded her arms across her chest, face settling into her "I want it and I want it now" expression. "Look, who got you through the Keith mess?"

I sighed. "You did."

"And? You were a puddle of melted self-esteem after you got that wedding invitation," she said, stating the obvious.

I closed my eyes, trying not to visualize the damn thing, so of course I did, in full living color. Cream paper with gold embossing inviting me to the wedding of Keith to his darling fiancée, Brittany the bimbo. Of course, the only problem had been that he'd still been dating *me* at the time, and I hadn't known anything about any fiancée.

While I was collecting the fragments of my shattered self-esteem and gluing the pieces of my heart back together, I'd thought about writing a book. I'd wavered between two titles: *Leave Them Before They Leave You*, or *How Bad Karma Ruined My Life: My Experiences as the Breakup Artist*.

That experience, as much as any other, had cemented my personal philosophy—total control, all the time.

Alesia Holliday

My eyes popped open, and I grinned. "You *were* spectac-
ular at his engagement party," I admitted.

She grinned back at me. "The part where I stomped right
up to him and called him a lying snake, then told his fiancée
all about you and dumped the ice sculpture in his lap?"

"Exactly." I'd refused to go, but Annie'd dragged her latest boyfriend along and made him videotape the whole thing.
I'd watched it about a hundred times while I got over the deceitful double-dater. The ice sculpture bit had probably hastened my recovery by a good three months and saved me
countless boxes of tissues.

I smiled, remembering, and Annie pounced. "Aha! So you
admit that you owe me," she said.

"Fine. I owe you. I'll come down and talk to him at the
store for a while. I need to know more about him to help
you," I said, secretly wishing Nick would quit his job and
move to the Yukon before I got a chance to go to SpinDisc
and talk to him. "Hey! Aren't you the one who told me never
to do this for friends again? I don't want to be the only one
not invited to your wedding to Nick!"

She rolled her eyes. "Get real. Like I'd ever marry Mr.
Bland Nice Boy. I need a little more excitement in my life."

"Annie, you can't build a life with somebody on drama.
You're going to realize this someday, right?" I stood up and
put my snoring puppy on the chair, then started picking up
napkins, cups, and the pizza box to toss out. Then I paused
to look at Annie. "Right?"

She laughed, but then her smile faded and she looked at

me, tiredness and something darker flickering behind her eyes. "Shane, drama is all I know. Just help me out, okay?"

As she wandered off down the hall, I realized I didn't know what to say to that, having seen her parents in action. It's not like I was much of a credible source on dating issues, either.

What genetic code is written into our species that makes the whole process so difficult? It's not like female . . . say . . . *raccoons* go through some whole agonizing dance—"he didn't call me; he called me too often; my friends don't like him; we have different *needs*."

They just say, "Hey, male raccoon, wanna have raccoon babies and wander around scrounging for fish together?"

Or, you know, so I think. It's not like I'm a raccoonologist or something. But you see my point.

Why is something we all crave so desperately so impossible to hold on to?

"Shane? Hello! Get the door already!" Annie yelled at me from down the hall, and I realized somebody was tapping on the door.

Sounded like Michel's tap. He had weekly door-knocking themes. This week it was the theme song from *SpongeBob SquarePants*.

I tossed the pizza trash I was still holding, crossed to the door and yanked it open. "I'm so over *SpongeBob*. Can't we go back to the retro month? *The Addams Family* or *Gilligan's Island*, maybe?"

Michel and Farren stood there holding a beautifully

wrapped box, and a frame. They were grinning like a couple of very well dressed hyenas. "Surprise! Happy birthday!"

I moved back to let them in. "Um, it's not my birthday."

Michel dropped a kiss on my cheek as he walked past me. "It is now, love. With presents, even!"

I shut the door, then they presented the box to me with a flourish and called out for Annie. "Annie, get your butt down here! We have presents and news!"

Annie walked down our tiny hallway toward us, putting her hair back in a ponytail. "What's up?"

"We've got it! Ta da!" said Farren, then he scrunched up his face. "What the heck is that noise?"

Michel looked around. "It's like a cross between a freight train and a tornado. Did you get some freaky new alternative CD?"

Annie laughed. "No, that's Lulu. Ask Shane about it."

I smiled and led everybody over to my chair, where Lulu was still sleeping like the dead. Well, if the dead have an advanced case of sleep apnea.

Michel rounded the corner of the chair, looked down, and recoiled back. "What in God's name is that?"

Farren leaned over the back of the chair and looked down. "Why do you have the scary hairy guy down the hall's dog? It doesn't have long to live, by the sound of that breathing. Advanced lung disease, I bet."

Lulu opened one eye and stared up at everybody, then opened the other eye and blinked up at us. Her funny little curly tail started wagging furiously.

I smacked Farren in the arm. "What do you mean, Hairy Scary Guy's dog? He moved out days ago. And she's not sick, she just snores."

Michel looked at me, eyebrows shooting clear up his forehead. "That's a dog? Are you kidding? What kind of dog is that? She looks like a . . . a goat?"

I reached down to pet Lulu, who was now making snuffling noises and wagging her entire bottom half. "Yeah, yeah. I thought she looked like a mutant sheep, myself. But doesn't she look better, now that she's all clean?"

"She looked *worse*?"

Farren reached down to pet her. "Hey, doggie, how are you? Did the mean Hairy Scary Guy abandon you? Are you going to live with Shaney Waney now?"

Michel rolled his eyes. "Of course it's not. You're not keeping that ugly thing, are you? Shane, if you wanted a dog, I have a friend who breeds champion Papillons, and they're beautiful. You don't even know if that thing has diseases."

Farren picked Lulu up off the chair. "She doesn't have diseases. Hairy Scary Guy's last girlfriend was a vet. Doggy has had all of her shots and is fine."

We all looked at him in shock.

"Hairy Scary Guy had a girlfriend?" Annie and I said simultaneously.

"It really is a dog?" Michel asked.

I glared at him, then reached out to take Lulu from Farren. "Of course she's a dog. Well, what's her name, then, Farren?"

"I told you, her name is Doggy. Hairy Scary Guy didn't have much imagination."

Michel stared at him. "When did you ever talk to Hairy Scary Guy?"

"I never did. But I helped his vet girlfriend carry some of her stuff out when she dumped him. She said he was a pig and kept asking her to do kinky stuff in bed, like put a leash on him and tell him he was a bad Rover."

We all paused for a collective "Euwwwww."

"Okay, enough about the dog, already. We have presents. Look!" Michel held up the frame and turned it around so I could see what was in it. "The Breakup Artist is in business!"

We all gathered around and stared at it. Inside the frame was a mockup of an ad for . . . me. *Oh, crap. Did I really agree to this?* I clutched Lulu a little tighter and read:

SEVEN WAYS TO LOSE YOUR LOVER
She's the Anti-Date Antidote.
She's a reverse Cyrano de Bergerac.
If you're dying to be dumped, call the Breakup Artist.

It listed a phone number, and that was all. I didn't recognize the number. I looked at the guys, dazed. "Is this really a good idea? Am I insane? Is that really enough information? Plus, whose phone number is that?"

Farren shrugged. "Hey, what can it hurt? There are so many nasty men out there, you'd really be performing a public service by helping women get out of relationships with them."

"And men," said Michel.

"Plus, think of all that lovely money," Annie pointed out.

Michel nodded. "Exactly. And for the good guys, just think how much better it will be for their self-esteem to think that breaking up was *their* idea, instead of having to go through the pain of getting dumped. The phone number is a voicemail service we hooked you up with."

Annie danced around us, beaming. "Plus, think of all that *lovely* money," she repeated.

(Did I mention that Annie can be a teensy bit materialistic?)

"Open the package, already," Michel said.

"What is it? I'm almost afraid to look." The last present they'd given me had been penis-shaped pasta. It was still stuffed in the back of the cabinet, somewhere, because it's not like we were going to actually *eat* it.

"It's for your new business, silly girl. Open it already," Farren said.

I handed Lulu back to him, ripped the paper open, and looked at the small box. "What?"

"Just open it, Shane," Annie said.

I opened the box and found a stack of business cards. They were pale gray with silver lettering, and they simply said:

The Breakup Artist
Thirty days to a breakup or your money back.

. . . and gave my new phone number.

"Nice. Minimalistic," I said, past the huge lump in my

throat. "I'm completely freaked out by the whole idea, but . . . thank you!" I threw my arms around Michel, then Farren and Lulu, and gave them both fierce hugs. "You're the best friends ever."

"Hey!" Annie said, hands on hips.

"Well, except for Annie," I said, grinning. "Do you think this will work? Will anybody call?"

"The ad starts running tomorrow, so we'll know soon enough," Michel said, wandering over to the kitchen to scrounge for food. "Are we watching *America's Next Top Model* tonight or what? I'd *kill* to get Tyra Banks into one of my designs. Meanwhile, what about Lizard Lizzie and Awful Ben? What's the scoop?"

"I wish I knew, Michel," I said, glancing at the bottom of the chair, underneath which my cell phone lurked in suspense. "I wish I knew."

Chapter 6

Ben looked around Lizzie's elegant living room, trying not to sweat while he waited for Lizzie's roommate to go get her. This was the part he hated the most about relationships. The *end* part. Even knowing how relieved he'd feel afterward wasn't enough to get him through the actual breakup stage stress-free.

Just once, he'd like to go out with somebody he liked enough to *not* spend most of his time dreading the end. And it's not like he was a commitment-phobe, either, no matter what his last girlfriend had screamed while she threw his shoes out of the window of her fourth-floor walkup.

These days, it kinda seemed like the *women* were the ones telling the guys, "Good-bye, see you, not ready to settle down." He'd always figured some day he'd find what his parents had. Love at first sight, couple of kids, happy ever after. He'd been complacent. Known it was coming down the road some day for him, like it had for his brother and two sisters. He was a freaking uncle six times over now, but still had never once gotten close to popping the question.

He'd never admit it to anybody—still could barely admit it to himself—but he was getting a skinch concerned. And when perfectly normal women went all psycho on him, it made him worry a little bit more.

He looked up and tried to shake off his brown funk when Lizzie stepped out of her room and posed for a moment in the hallway, wearing some little red dress that showed off legs that went on forever. He sighed. *Of course the ones who look totally hot have to be the ones who go psycho.*

"Benny Bunny!" Lizzie called, her face lit up in an enormous smile as she rushed down the hall toward him. He clenched his teeth together and tried not to grimace. *So much for the hope that she was on some kind of mind-altering pharmaceuticals this morning.*

She ran right up to him and jumped into his arms, almost knocking him on his ass. This was definitely a departure from her usual ice princess persona. He wormed his way out of the hug as quickly as he could, then grasped her arms and stepped back a little. "Lizzie? What's going on? You're acting a little . . . different."

She looked at him blankly, then muttered something that sounded like "four seas, four seas." "Oh, Schmoopy, I've just finally realized how much we belong together. Forever and ever and ever. Yours or mine?"

It was his turn for the blank look. "Yours or mine what?"

"Apartment, silly," she said, laughing. Then she pulled away and walked into the kitchen, returning with an ice bucket holding a bottle of . . . was that *champagne*? Oh, boy.

"There's no need for us to spend all this money living apart before the wedding. Plus, we really don't need a long engagement, do we?" She batted her eyelashes at him (when did she start doing that?) and poured the champagne into two crystal flutes.

He stared at her, stunned, while she rambled on about flowers and churches and dresses. ". . . Vera Wang is so overdone, really, but it will be expected. We may need to take out a loan against the next installment of my trust fund, but I'm sure you won't mind putting your little car up for collateral, will you?"

That last part broke through, loud and clear. His *little car*? "My little car? You want me to put the classic Aston Martin my grandfather gave me up as collateral for a *what*?"

She trilled a little laugh and patted his hand, then handed him one of the glasses. "Silly Schmoopy Pie! Let's toast to us. To our future!"

As she held her glass up in the air, he put his down on the table. "Lizzie, we have to talk."

"Of course, Bunny. Come sit here next to me," she said,

gracefully dropping onto one of her silk-covered couches and patting the seat next to her.

He warily circled her and sat in the chair across from her. "Look, Lizzie. I'm not really clear on how you got the idea that—I mean, if I did anything to make you think we were headed for marr—well, it's just that we've only been seeing each other for a couple of weeks, and . . ."

She rolled her eyes. "Oh, for God's sake, Ben. Get to the punch line."

Hmmmm. At least I'm Ben again, instead of Bunny. Or Schmoopy.

He shoved a hand through his hair, trying to find the words. "It's just . . . it's not you, it's—"

"You?" she broke in, blinking.

"Well, yeah. I'm just not ready for any kind of—"

"Commitment?"

"Right. Right. Not at this stage in my life. So I'm sure you can see that you'd be better off with—"

"Somebody else?"

"YES. Yes. Somebody else, who is more . . . ready to handle a—"

"Committed, adult relationship?"

"Exactly! Exactly," he repeated, wondering what was happening. Was she rushing him through his breakup speech? Just then, he caught her sneaking a peek at her watch.

She IS rushing me. What the hell is going on?

Lizzie blinked really hard several times, until a single tear rolled down from her eye. "Well, I can't believe how much you've devastated me with this, Ben."

He could never handle tears from a woman. Talk about your unfair weapons from God. "Oh, Lizzie, maybe I'm overreacting. Maybe—"

"No!" she said, almost shouting, then continued in a calmer tone. "No, no, you're completely right. We're at different stages, yada yada. I have to go . . . er, compose myself. I'm sure you can let yourself out. Good-bye, Ben. I wish you the very best in life," she said, sniffling a little. Then she stood up and rushed off down the hall toward the bedroom he'd only seen five times in two months.

She only liked sex if it didn't interfere with her social life, Ben reminded himself to keep from following after her.

That little sniffle really got to me, though. Shit. Plus, she looks totally hot in that dress.

He stood up and walked across the floor, still trying to figure out what had just happened. As he opened the apartment door, he remembered he'd left his briefcase on the couch. He closed the door again to go get it, and then he heard Lizzie's roommate in the hallway.

"I can't believe he went for it that fast! Man, he must be stupid, Liz!" she said.

He ducked back behind the wall so fast he almost smacked his head into Lizzie's bulletin board and listened.

Eavesdropping is bad. I'm a bad person. But what the hell, I'm in advertising. What's a little eavesdropping next to that?

"I can hardly believe it, but talk about completely right," Lizzie said, laughing. "How I managed to sit through the 'it's not you, it's me' speech without laughing in his face, I'll never know."

Ben felt his face get hot.

"The Breakup Artist scores!" Lizzie's roommate said, snickering. "Now you can go for that stockbroker you went out with last week."

The *what* artist? And *what* stockbroker? Ben took a deep breath, determined to confront Lizzie and find out what was going on. A man had to have *some* pride, after all.

As he turned around, he caught site of a note, right at eye level, pinned to the bulletin board behind him. "The Breakup Artist" was written in bold letters, and a phone number was listed underneath the words. Without thinking, he snatched the note and shoved it in his pocket. He took another step, then rolled his eyes at his own lameness.

What did he care why or how she did it? He was out of a relationship with yet another crazy woman, so maybe discretion was the way to go. Being laughed at made him feel like a chump, but it wasn't the end of the world. He quietly walked over to the couch and grabbed his briefcase, then let himself out of her apartment.

On the way down in the elevator, he shoved his hand in his pocket and felt the crumpled piece of paper. *The Breakup Artist, hmmm? I might just have to investigate this. . . .*

Because it sounded like the estrogen-poisoned Jupiterians were suddenly getting a little bit of help.

Chapter 7

My phone rang as I was brushing my teeth. Lulu jumped up from where she was curled up on the bathroom rug and started barking. I pulled my phone out of my pocket, glanced at the screen, then flicked a glance at my potentially psychic dog. "You have a thing against phones, or is it just calls from her?" I flipped the phone open, wiping my mouth. "Lizzie?"

"I've got to give you credit, Shawn. You did it!"

"It's *Shane*." *As you well know.* "And I did what?"

"It. You did *it*. Ben broke up with me! He gave me the 'it's not you, it's me' speech. Well, I had to help him along a bit, because he's so damn slow, but still. It's over! I'm free!"

"You're welcome," I said, making a face.

"Right. Well. Thanks, and all that. I'll tell Aunt Estelle you didn't screw it up," she said.

"Gee, how nice of—"

Click.

How can that woman be related to Mrs. P.? It boggles the mind. I closed my phone and padded down the hall to my room, then jumped on my bed and looked at my new box of business cards again. I pulled one out and stared at it, considering.

The Breakup Artist = 1
Awful Ben = 0

It was a *good* thing. I'd saved a human being from the clutches of Lizzie. One phone call had nothing to do with the feeling in my chest. I chewed on the corner of my lip, trying to analyze what I was feeling. Finally I came to the conclusion that the pepperoni on the pizza were the culprit.

Indigestion tastes a lot like regret.

Lulu was unimpressed with her new dog bed (special trip to Dogs R Us after work), so she wound up sleeping next to me, mostly under the blanket, with only her smushed-in face peeking out.

If you pretend hard enough, the snuffling reverberation of a snoring dog sounds exactly like the ocean.

Solstice smiled at me from under her new purple and pink bangs when I walked back into the shop from lunch the next day. "Hey, Shane, I sold another bottle of body oil! I had to break into the second case to restock the shelf!"

"Great. Only sixty-two cases to go," I said, trying for the half-full thing. It was a beautiful, crisp fall day in New York—my favorite kind—and I'd vanquished Awful Ben. Lizzie was happy. Mrs. P. was happy. (Solstice was always happy. She usually smelled a little funny-weed smoky, too, but we *so* won't go there.) And Annie was only working the afternoon shift, so Lulu had company all morning.

The only tiny glimmer of doom on my horizon was the part where I had to go down to SpinDisc at six and spend some time with Nick, so I could figure out how best to get rid of him for Annie.

In a *nice* way, as she'd worriedly reminded me for the thousandth time that morning, because he was so puppy-like. (She'd said "*cute* puppylike," flicking a glance at Lulu, which had lost her a few points with me. Lulu, however, either didn't understand pointed references to her lack of beauty, or the Cheerios Annie had been feeding her under the table made up for it, because her tail had been wagging like mad.)

"You're awfully concerned, for somebody who wants to get rid of him so badly," I'd observed, but she'd shot me one of her "this conversation is over" looks, and I'd backed down.

So I had five hours of relative peace in front of me before I had to go find a way to be mean to a human puppy. My grandmother would have been so proud. *Not.*

I sighed and wandered to the back room to put my purse away and unpack the shipment we'd received that morning. Another load of Body by Boris lingerie, probably even more ugly than the last shipment. Army camouflage bustiers, for the GI Jane hooker in all of us. I never would have stocked it, but I'd gotten ten prepaid orders since one of the latest hot crop of starlets wore it to an awards show last month. You could never underestimate the insidious Hollywood effect on the fashion marketing machine.

If only Michel would get his designs made, I'd shove this Boris stuff out in a heartbeat to make room for them. His pieces are unbelievable.

"Yeah, and if he'd make me an outfit or two, maybe I'd finally get a date," I muttered to myself.

"It's not that you can't get a date," Mrs. P. said from behind me, scaring at least five years off my life. "It's that you never want them once you get them. What happened to that nice Lawrence boy?"

When my breathing rate slowed back down to normal, I put my hands on my hips and gave her my stern look. "Didn't you promise to quit lurking? You just scared me to death."

She laughed, clearly tickled that she'd startled me. "Oh, pshaw," she said.

"*Pshaw?* Have you been inhaling Jane Austen at warp speed again? Or TiVoing some BBC mystery channel?" I asked, shaking my head and (rather cleverly, I thought) avoiding the question about old Larry Boy.

She crossed her arms over her chest. "You're avoiding my question, Shane Madison. What happened to Lawrence?"

"Lawrence who?" I said innocently.

"Lawrence you know very well who. He was a sweet man. He even made time to come down to the shop and organize the storeroom for you, as I recall," she said.

"Yes. Larry the sweet man who had time to come down to the store, because he was caught embezzling from his job and got fired," I said, enjoying the look of shock on her face. "He's probably doing ten to twenty in Sing Sing now."

I bit my lip, considering. "Is Sing Sing still a prison?"

"No! I mean, yes, it's still a prison, and no, I never would have thought it of Larry. He was a Virgo!" She fanned her face with her hand and then sat down. "You just never can tell about people," she said sadly, shaking her head. "Lawrence—a hardened criminal. He's probably organizing the canned goods in the prison kitchen in alphabetical order by now. You know what those Virgos are like."

"Well, I don't know about hardened, but he did steal my video rental card before he left, and he used it to rent a stupid martial arts movie that he never returned. I had to pay twenty-one ninety-nine for *Fists of Flying Dragon Butts* or whatever it was called," I said, scowling at the memory.

Then a random happy thought floated through my plans for vengeance upon the hapless Larry-call-me-Lawrence. "How's Lizzie, by the way? Is Awful Ben gone for good?"

"Oh, she's wonderful. She's dating some investment

banker with an *enormous* . . . portfolio," Mrs. P. said, snickering.

"Mrs. P!" I said, pretending to be shocked. "You're so bad!"

She chuckled. "I'm too old to be very bad. But I do want to talk to you about that adult pleasures display. Ever since I spoke to that darling Kirby Green at Whips and Lace, I've been thinking about—"

I held up my hand, not wanting to hear it. The last time we'd had this conversation, my brain cells had nearly imploded from hearing my darling, grandmotherly boss talk about a vibrator named the "Alexander the Great" model.

With details. And catalog *pictures*, even. She'd had a plan to test-drive a few, and I'd poke myself in my own eye with a display hanger before I'd listen to *that*.

"Shane, you're too repressed. I've told you over and over that you need—"

"No, thanks. Grandma taught me everything I needed to know about sex—namely, that we should learn about it from our friends in junior high, as God intended."

I shuddered at the thought. "Grandma would have been drummed out of the Steel Azaleas social club if any of her blue-haired friends even *suspected* she'd told me the first thing about the birds and the bees."

My phone rang, saving me from a lecture about healthy attitudes toward sex or whatever else she'd been about to share. I smiled in fake apology, grabbed my phone, and dashed out of the back room. It was Annie.

Again.

"You're still coming at six, right?"

"Yes, as I confirmed the last three times you called," I said, wondering what could be making my normally even-keeled roommate turn neurotic. "How's Lulu? Did you remember to take her out?"

"Yes, of course I did, and I gave her fresh water, too, which she probably needed after she peed a gallon or two. That little dog must have an enormous bladder," she said, laughing.

Then her voice turned serious and got all whispery. "Shane, it's just . . . he *kissed* me," she moaned.

"Was it terrible? Is he a drooler? And why did it take him six weeks to kiss you for the first time?" I asked, not really curious, but willing to listen to avoid facing Mrs. P. and her potential vibrator stories.

"No! He's shy. It was, well, it was . . . great," she said, sounding a little hysterical.

Okay, color me confused. "If he's such a nice guy, and he's a great kisser, tell me again why I'm encouraging him to break up with you? Isn't he the kind of guy that every single woman in the city wishes for? He's straight, right?"

I heard voices in the background on her end of the line. "Yes, I'll be right there, Nick," she said in a normal voice. Then she hissed at me again. "Shane! Just get down here and fix this! I can't take much more!"

"But—"

Click.

I hate the way everybody hangs up on me.

"Shane! Shane, darling, I need to talk to you!" Mrs. P.'s cheerful voice called out from the back room. I sighed. If she started talking about sex again, I was *so* out of there. I trudged back to face her.

She was seated at the desk, hands clasped in front of her, flashing an enormous smile.

Oh. God.

"Look, if this is about stocking the more . . . exotic products from W&L, you know I think we're too upscale for that. What if—"

"No. It's not about that. It's about me making you a partner in Sensuality. What do you think about that?"

"I . . . what did you say?" I asked.

She smiled and repeated herself. "It's about me making you a partner in Sensuality. What do you think? I know you love the business, and you've certainly improved the bottom line."

"I-I-I don't know what to say," I said weakly, sinking down into a chair.

She unclasped her hands and looked down, drumming her fingers on her desk. "Well, before you say anything, here's the tiny little catch. I'm having a bit of a cash flow problem. Not even a problem, really, but more like an issue."

She raised her head and looked at me. "I need a bit of a buy-in from you for the partnership."

"What kind of buy-in?" I asked, still dazed at the idea. It had never occurred to me that Mrs. P. might ask me to join her in the business. I mean, she knew I wanted to be a boutique owner one day, but . . .

"Fifty thousand," she said.

(That flushing noise was my partnership dream, in case you're wondering.)

"Fifty thousand *dollars*?" I asked, gulping. I had, oh, about five hundred dollars in the bank. Or I *would* have, as soon as I cashed the "get rid of Awful Ben" check Mrs. P. had written me.

"I know, I know," she said, looking distressed. "But my accountant says there are bills due and a little tax thingy, and this is the only way to do it. Then we can work out a structured buy-in based on your time here, or something like that, but he'll explain it all to you."

"I see," I said, head still spinning. *Where in the world would I get fifty thousand dollars? And, what's a tax "thingy"?*

"The thing is, I kind of need it sooner rather than later," she said. "So, think it over and get back to me."

She jumped up and smiled. "It will work out, dear. Things always do. There's nobody I'd rather have working with me than you."

As she rushed out of the store, I just sat there, speechless. *Fifty thousand dollars.* Somehow, *I needed to come up with fifty thousand dollars.*

I remembered the check in my purse. Okay, forty-nine, five. Laughing like an idiot, I reached for my phone to call Annie and fill her in. As I flipped my phone open, another random thought crossed my mind.

It might be time to put the Breakup Artist to work.

Slowly, I dialed the number to check for any voicemail messages that might have come in from my ad. Even if there were one or two, and I could do one breakup a week, I might be able to raise the money in a year or two. I punched in the numbers for my access code and waited, hoping for at least a single call.

"You have one hundred and thirty-two messages."

Holy breakup, Batman. What the heck do I do now?

Chapter 8

As I pushed open the grimy glass door to SpinDisc, I wondered if I could come up with an emergency root canal or something else more fun to do than work on breaking Nick's heart.

"Hey, Shane! It's so good to see you!" Nick came bounding across the floor to hug me, his face lit up with enthusiasm, or joy, or something like that. Some emotion that was decidedly not sneering, nasty, condescending, or in any way like the usual expressions of my best friend's typical dates. He was, to Annie's utter horror and dismay, a truly nice guy.

(You can see why he had to go, right? Yeah, me neither.)

He hugged me, snapping me out of my gloomy thoughts. "Hey, are you meeting Annie? She never mentioned it."

I just bet she didn't.

"Um, yeah, where is she?" I asked, hoping she hadn't gone home and left me to figure out a way to have an entire conversation with Nick without her. I'd met him a few times, when he dropped her off or picked her up, and had been to the store several times, but we'd never exchanged more than a few polite sentences before.

"She went to get coffee. She said she hates the new coffee I bought for the coffeemaker, but it's the kind she said last week was her favorite, so I don't know why she hates it now," he said, brows furrowed in apparent distress. "I really pay attention to what she likes and doesn't, but she seems to change her mind a lot."

His mind seemed to catch up with what he was saying, because he suddenly bit his lip. "I mean, not that she's capricious, or anything, it's just that . . . I mean, I'm not complaining. Of course, it's a woman's prerogative to change her mind and all, it's . . . er . . ."

The little bell attached to the door jingled as a couple of potential customers walked into the store. Nick stopped in the middle of his sentence and heaved a sigh of what was undoubtedly relief. "Whew! I mean, I have to go help them, Shane. You can wait in the office if you want or hang out here till Annie gets back," he said, sidling away from me.

It was a tough fight to keep from laughing, but I managed it and wandered around the store, checking out the new CDs and keeping an eye on Nick as discreetly as I could manage. He helped the two teenagers find Shakira's latest and even blushed a little when the bolder of the two girls tried out a couple of belly dancing moves on him.

My mouth fell open at that point. A grown man who blushes? And uses the word *capricious*? In New York? Maybe Annie was right, and Nick wasn't the guy for her. He was totally cute, especially with that flip of bangs that constantly needed to be brushed out of his face, but maybe he should be waiting for some nice midwestern girl who crocheted or something. Not to mention that any man sweet and attentive enough to remember what kind of coffee she liked would come across to Annie as a smotherer.

Nick didn't stand a chance. Better to let him down gently.

Or was I just making more excuses to myself for what I was about to do to him?

While I was pondering my moral quandary (and hating the idea of being a person who has moral quandaries), the girls giggled their way out the door. Not ten seconds later, Annie walked in with two tall cups of coffee, and I snuck a glance at Nick.

Oh, no. Oh, no, oh, no, oh, no.

You know that expression "he wore his heart on his sleeve"? Well, Nick's heart was all over his entire freaking shirt. When he caught sight of Annie, his face glowed like he'd won free iTunes downloads for the rest of his life.

Or like his entire reason for existence had just strolled in the door carrying ten bucks' worth of latte.

Annie saw him, and she scowled.

Oh, major and serious crap.

"Hey, Annie, it's about time you showed up," I said, pasting a perky smile on my face.

Annie peered at me. "Are you nauseous? You look kinda green," she said, walking across the floor toward me.

"Yeah, so I don't do perky all that well. Plus, the look on Nick's face is making me feel a little green," I mumbled to her. "You didn't tell me he was *that* far gone, Banana."

She rolled her eyes and whispered back at me, "I told you he did my inventory for me, didn't I? You think somebody does inventory over a casual crush? And stop calling me Anna Banana. We're not in high school anymore, for God's sake."

Nick hesitantly took a couple of steps toward us, watching Annie as if looking for a sign—any sign—that she wanted him to (select one): come over/kiss her passionately/ask her to marry him.

Yeah. It was that obvious. The poor guy had it *bad.*

"So, Nick," I said, taking pity on him. "How's school going?"

He smiled and took another few steps toward us, clearly being careful not to stand too close to Annie. "It's great, Shane. Thanks for asking. This is my last semester, and my ranking is okay, so I'm getting some pretty good results from the interviewing."

I laughed. "Nick, the false modesty has to go. Annie told me you were first in your class at Columbia and that's one of the toughest MBA programs in the country, isn't it? You must be flooded with offers."

He looked down at the floor, but I could see his cheeks redden. The man *had* to toughen up, or the corporate sharks in the business world were going to eat him alive.

"I do okay," he repeated. "And lots of the job offers involve way too much travel or even moving cross-country." He cast a quick glance at Annie. "I really don't want to be the kind of corporate grind who has no life. I watched my dad do that to my mom, and it's not the way I want to live."

Annie tossed her curls and sighed, clearly impatient with the whole topic. "You're only twenty-six, Nick. It's not like you want to get married and have kids right now, is it?"

His whole body seemed to slump in on itself at her words—the physical embodiment of deflated hopes. Suddenly, I felt like the lowest form of scum. I was the scum that other scum disenfranchised.

I was supposed to be thinking up ways to convince Nick he had to break up with Annie, not thinking up ways to adopt him. *Guilty consciences are for other people, right? Potential business owners don't have time for guilt.*

Or sympathy.

Or any warm and fuzzies.

Has anybody but me noticed how much time I spend justifying my evil ways?

I lifted my chin and took a deep breath. "Nick, we have to go. You don't mind if Annie leaves a few minutes early, do you?"

"Well, she was supposed to be on for another three hours, but, well, sure," he stammered. "If she needs to go."

Annie shrugged. "Okay, I'm outta here. See you tomorrow, Nick."

I tried not to look back; I really did. Biblical references to pillars of salt weighing heavily on my mind, and all. But I couldn't help myself, and I shot a quick glance back as we opened the door to leave.

There he stood, in the exact same place, staring after Annie with frustrated longing painted all over his face.

Or else he was seriously constipated.

Either way, it made me nauseous all over again.

"Shane? You coming?" Annie said impatiently, holding the door open.

"Yep. I'm coming. Straight down the path to hell," I mumbled.

"What?"

"Never mind."

Riding the subway is a great way to people watch, if you're so inclined. Unfortunately, direct eye contact of any kind in the city is tantamount to a sign that says PLEASE COME MUG ME. So, I'm more of an "avoid eye contact and think deep thoughts" kind of girl. (I also try not to breathe when at all possible, to avoid the smells.)

Here's the thing about me and guilt: I don't like it. (You were expecting something deep? Some dark secret from my childhood? A bona fide closet skeleton clattering in the dim recesses of my mind? Sorry, not so much.)

It's simple, really. Feeling guilty makes me cranky.

I don't like to be cranky.

Annie interrupted my foul mood by elbowing me in the ribs, which didn't help with the cranky. "What?" I snapped.

She held up her hands, which is harder than it sounds when you're clutching a pole and trying to keep from falling over into the unwashed body squeezed in behind you. "Whoa. It's our stop, that's all. Don't bite my head off."

"Sorry. Bad mood."

We shoved our way out and joined the crush of people heading for the stairs to the street level. When we finally hit daylight, I took a deep breath, then promptly started coughing.

Annie pounded me on the back. "It's smoggy and ninety-two degrees out here. What are you thinking to breathe like that?"

I caught my breath and moved away from her. "At least it's not urine-scented air. I hate the subway, have I ever mentioned that?"

"Only about every single day since we've moved here. And you can quit right now with the guilty conscience thing."

She strode down the sidewalk as if she owned it, while I threaded my way through the crowds and hurried after her, trying to keep sight of her hair shining in the distance. I caught up at the edge of the sidewalk, where she stood tapping her foot, waiting for the light to change.

"What guilty conscience thing?"

She rolled her eyes. "Oh, please. Every time you break somebody up, I have to live with the angst and the drama. You feel massive guilt about it, like you're somehow the great Grim Reaper of dating doom. You're repressing your issues."

Issues are repressed for a reason, I figure.

She shot me a look. "Listen to me. If one person in a relationship wants out badly enough to ask you for help, they're not really going to make it as a couple, are they?"

The light changed, and she stalked across the street, still berating me. "Plus, that's kind of egotistical, isn't it? Like it's all up to you?"

I narrowed my eyes and followed her across the street and toward home. "Okay, that was just ugly. Why am I suddenly egotistical when it's *you* who is all 'poor Nick must be let down easy or he'll suffer from the loss of my wonderfulness'?"

She glanced up at our building and stopped, pulling out her key. Then she turned to look at me, and the anger in her eyes faded into a weary sadness. "You saw him, right? You saw his face when I came in? Like I was his dream of love suddenly come to life?"

I nodded. I'd seen it. Anybody who'd walked into the store would have seen it.

She shook her head. "I can't live up to that, Shane. You saw up close and personal how the people in my family ruin anything that even resembles love. It's better to get out now."

*   *   *

Lulu went nuts when I opened my bedroom door, jumping up and barking her tiny mutant-sheep bark. I scooped her up and cuddled her as I wandered around the room, searching for evidence that she'd forgotten she was apartment-broken. Then I snapped on her new collar and leash and we went outside to take care of the essentials. After we got back, I set out her dog food and fresh water and watched as she snarfed up the food in what seemed to be her normal, "I haven't eaten in six weeks" style.

By the time she sat back and let loose with a giant doggy belch, I'd kind of lost my own appetite. The fact that Annie was sulking in her room didn't help any. I paced the living room for a while, then finally decided there was no time like, well, like now. But the oxygen level in the room had dropped at the mere thought of making the calls, so I put Lulu up on the chair for a nap, grabbed some fudge out of the fridge, and climbed out the window.

Thirty minutes or so later, I leaned over the railing on my postage-stamp-sized fire escape landing and tried not to hyperventilate. Out of one hundred and thirty-two messages, after I'd weeded out the cranks and the perverts (plus the extremists trying to save me from my evil ways), I was left with twenty-seven who might actually be legitimate.

With the help of a quarter-pound of dark chocolate almond fudge for moral support, I'd left voicemail messages for twenty-one people, actually made appointments to meet five women and one guy, and I was down to my very last call.

*This is really happening. I'm going to turn into the Grim
Reaper of dating. Welcome to Bad Karma City.*

I heard the window open behind me. "Slow breaths,
Shane. Slow breaths," Annie called, from her perch on the
windowsill. "Think of all that glorious money. You can do
it!"

I smiled, glad she was through with pouting. There was
nobody better to have in my corner when I was beginning
potentially disastrous ventures. Like the time I bought blue
eye shadow, the summer of the tube top, and—now—the
start of a new business.

She was right. I could do this. How hard could it be to
make the perpetually self-absorbed men of Manhattan think
that *they* were the ones doing the breaking up?

"I'm a professional, for God's sake. I have *business
cards*!" I muttered.

"Go, you!" Annie cheered. "Give me an S! Give me an H—"

"Enough, already. I have to make one more phone call."

She laughed, but stopped cheering and went back inside.
I took a deep breath and touched the amethyst pendant I always wore. Annie's mom had given it to me for good luck,
when she learned I was going to leave Florida for a job in
New York—the center of all evil and licentiousness. Annie's
dad, being more practical, had given me a can of pepper
spray and a gift certificate for self-defense classes. Then
they'd yelled at each other for half an hour about whose gift
was better.

Shaking my head, I dialed the phone, almost hoping

Melissa (probably not even her real name) was out. I wasn't sure I was up to another of the awkward phone calls. Naturally, she answered on the first ring.

"Hello?"

"Um, hi. Melissa? This is Shane—er, I mean, I'm returning your call? About the breaking up?" I hated it when my declaratory statements came out sounding like questions, but I felt like a big dorkwad saying, "This is the Breakup Artist."

"About what? Shane who?" She didn't sound unpleasant, just impatient. I couldn't blame her.

I sighed and tried again, dorkwad or no. "This is the Breakup Artist. You left a message?"

"Oh! Right! I didn't really expect—well, I kind of thought it was a joke. You really do help people get out of relationships?"

"I really do. For a fee. Would you like to meet and discuss your situation?" After all the calls, I had my sales pitch down pat. I wasn't going to agree to help anybody until I met them in person. One advantage of being a freelancer was that I didn't have to work with anybody who squicked me out on a personal level.

"Wow! This is so great! I have the worst problem. I mean, he's not a terrible guy, but he's like a barnacle. No, a leech. No, I don't even know what the word for him is. He wants to get *married*. Like I'm going to get married when I'm only twenty-five. Puh-*leeze*!"

"Well, I hope I can help. Can you meet . . . um . . ." I fumbled for my tiny calendar. "How about a week from Tuesday?"

"No, that doesn't work at all. I need to get rid of Tony now. How about we meet tonight?"

A tiny warning flag started waving. Maybe this girl was a freak. Maybe I shouldn't get involved.

"Well, I'm sorry, but I'm really booked up. We haven't discussed my fee yet, either." Several people had said no when they heard the five-hundred-dollar figure, which is why I brought it up on the phone. No need to waste time meeting in person if they couldn't afford me.

She cut me off. "Five thousand dollars, if you meet me tomorrow and promise to have him gone in thirty days."

"What?" I said, sounding a little squeaky. I cleared my throat. "Um, what? Five thousand dollars is much more than—"

"I don't care. I have the money, and if five grand assures me of success and your personal attention, it's yours. Believe me, I'm desperate."

"Well, I guess I can fit you in tomorrow," I said, thinking of how much five grand would help me on the path to entrepreneurial success.

"Of course, I need references," she said. "And you only get part as a down payment and the rest on successful conclusion of the breakup. Don't forget your money-back guarantee, either."

I blinked. "No problem. I'll have a list of references and my standard contract for you tomorrow. Now, where shall we meet?"

After we discussed logistics and hung up, I stood staring

into space for a while. Seriously. Five freaking thousand *dollars*? I shook my head, realizing I would have sucked as a con artist. Then I climbed back in through the fire escape, trying not to step on Lulu, who was dancing around my feet. "Annie! I need a standard contract!"

Okay, here's my secret that would probably cost me my membership in the trendy New York singleton club (if there were one), but I can actually cook. Not scary gourmet meals that normal people are afraid to eat, but yummy, healthy food that makes people happy. Comfort food, even.

(I get around the total lack of trendiness factor by claiming to be retro.)

Farren, who managed never to be far off when there was food to be eaten, wandered into our tiny kitchen, almost stepping on Lulu, who was lurking underfoot in hopes of catching food fragments. "Hey, Muttley, how's it going? Won't Shane give you any yummies?"

He walked over and leaned against the counter. "Chicken pasta salad? Did you put those tiny sliced peppers in there?" He started to stick a finger in the bowl, and I slapped his hand.

"Yes, I used a little banana pepper, just for you. And reassure Michel that it's free-range chicken, freshly off the . . . well . . . range. Homemade mayonnaise, even. If you guys will set the table, we can eat before the AC dies again and the heat spoils the mayo," I said, garnishing plates with apple slices and spinach leaves. Then I dropped a few tablespoons full of chicken shavings into Lulu's dish, sending her into paroxysms of doggy joy. Much snarfling commenced.

As Farren and I carried the plates and bowls to the table, I realized I might not be cooking for a while. "Dig in, everybody. All of my free time for the next few weeks is going to be used up for the new business, so you'll be on your own with cooking." I said.

Annie looked up from slicing a fresh loaf of pumpernickel bread from the corner bakery. "Oh, I didn't even think of that. The last time I tried to cook, I burned microwavable mac and cheese."

Farren groaned. "It wasn't pretty. On the bright side, we have lots of dog food now."

Just then, Michel flung open the door and rushed in, twirling around. "Ta da! My fortune is made." He swept us a deep bow.

Lulu came running in from the kitchen, barking, then skidded to a stop and started licking her foot, all nonchalant like she'd known it was Michel all along. He leaned down to pat her on her curly head, then bounced back up and grinned at us.

I started laughing. "Which fortune is it this time?"

"What happened to the disposable shoe idea?" Annie asked, lips quirking as she tried to hide a smile.

"Or the combination mustard and catsup? Mustup, did you call it? Or was it Catturd?" I asked, clutching my stomach to keep from howling. "I'll never forget how hideous that orangey-yellow stuff was, and you made us eat the whole batch!"

Michel folded his arms and stared down his patrician nose at us. For an instant, I could picture him as some ancient aristocrat, ordering the servants about. Then he laughed and threw a pillow at me, ruining the effect totally, especially when Lulu started barking wildly and chasing her own tail around and around.

I tossed the pillow back to him. "No more pillow throwing! If you knock the pasta salad off the table, Annie will be cooking, and it'll be on your head."

"Hey, that's a little harsh," Annie protested. "I can order a fine Chinese takeout."

Michel put his finger and thumb to his mouth and blew out a piercing whistle, and everybody froze, even Lulu. "Will you people just shut up! I'm trying to tell you my news."

Farren walked over and patted him on the shoulder. "I'm sorry they're such baboons. Tell us your news."

Michel gave Farren a quick hug and then flopped down on the couch. "I have the chance to take part in the next *Tomorrow's Designers Today* show! My design prof put my name in as someone with true artistic vision! If I could make it on the show, and maybe even get halfway to the finals, my future would be in the Louis Vuitton bag."

I sat down and started dishing out pasta salad. "That's wonderful news!" I said. "Isn't that where that clown Boris got started with his Body by Boris designs? If TV can do all that for someone with no talent, think what it could do for you!"

Annie jumped on the couch and hugged Michel. "Wow! Ralph Lauren better watch out!"

I noticed that Farren wasn't celebrating. He wasn't even smiling. Michel evidently noticed it, too, and his own smile faded. "Aren't you happy for me?"

Farren forced a smile. "I'm really happy for you, you know that. I'm just wondering . . . isn't there a huge cost for materials for the entry portfolio? We really demolished our savings with the new furniture, plus the consultant startup, and since I don't have a job right now . . ."

Michel stood up off the couch and crossed over to Farren. "It's okay. It's only five grand—that's the max they allow us to spend on portfolio materials. I can find that much, somehow."

He ran a hand through his hair. "This is the chance of a lifetime, Farren. If I miss out for the lack of something as simple as five thousand dollars, I know I'll regret if for the rest of my life."

I sat there saying nothing, while the number five thousand flashed in my brain. The exact number Melissa had offered to pay me to get Tony to dump her. Ten percent of the money I needed to buy in to my partnership.

Or one hundred percent of my friend's dream.

Who says there are no such thing as coincidences?

"How soon do you need it?" I heard myself asking. My words sounded far away, as if I were listening to syllables formed under the gentle swell of ocean waves. The receding tide of my own aspirations, if I gave Michel the money from my prospective new client.

But what kind of friend wouldn't try to help? Michel and Farren had kept us from being evicted in the early days, when Annie and I had gotten fired from a series of low-paying jobs. They'd always seemed to have a few extra dollars or some food for us when the cupboards were Old Mother Hubbarded.

Isn't it my turn?

"Well, I need the upfront money like now. But the finalists get ten grand to work with, and if I win, the grand prize is an apprenticeship with a top designer and a contract worth one hundred thousand dollars!" His face literally glowed, lit up from within by the fire of his own certainty.

Farren's face looked more like somebody who was afraid of getting burned.

Again.

Chapter 9

Ben turned off the speaker phone, grinning like a fool. Gleason jumped up and smacked one meaty hand down on the conference table. "You nailed it, man. You nailed that deal!"

Ben leaned back in his chair, pretending to be nonchalant about snagging the biggest account of his career. "Who's your Jelly Belly now?" he drawled. "That's a million-dollar account, thank you very much."

Gleason flapped his elbows in a crazed version of the Chicken Dance, then stopped mid-cluck. "Hey! And all the jelly beans you can eat, maybe?"

Ben laughed, then stood up and stretched. "I don't mind telling you they made me sweat when they mentioned Barclay's proposed campaign. That damn agency has cost me more than a few clients."

"Well, they didn't cost you this one. I bet you'll make senior A.E. over this one," Gleason said.

"Ben Cameron, senior account executive," Ben said, nearly in a whisper. "I admit I like the sound of that."

As they walked out of the conference room, Gleason elbowed Ben. "Speaking of jelly bellies, whatever happened with psycho Lizzie?"

Ben rolled his eyes. "Oh, that. Yeah, it's over. It was weird, though."

"Weird, how? Did she cry and beg you to stay? Happens to me all the time," Gleason said, nodding sagely.

Ben started to answer, but then had second thoughts. Did anybody really need to know he believed that Lizzie had been trying to get rid of him? Not great for the ego or the reputation. Besides, he had a certain new account to announce.

"I'll catch you later, man. I need to go spread the good news about Jelly Jam. Beers after work?"

Gleason nodded, then held up his hand for a high five. "You bet, man. You're buying, though, Mr. Got Rocks. We can celebrate both of your successes: the new account and freedom from Lizzie."

"The beers are definitely on me," Ben said. Then he headed down the hall to see just how close he was to adding "Senior Account Executive" to his business cards. Life was good. Life was *damn* good.

So why did he keep obsessing about the Breakup Artist?

Chapter 10

RULE 3: *Strategy, strategy, strategy. Study your opponents for signs of weakness you can exploit. Breaking up is serious business.*

After a crazily busy morning of taking Lulu to the vet (Hairy Scary Guy's ex—Farren had given me her card; clean bill of health, needed a shot, eighty-nine dollars I couldn't really afford) and waiting on a busload of romance novelists who were in town for a conference (they couldn't pass up a boutique named Sensuality; seventeen autographed bookmarks, three free books), I managed to escape only a few minutes after twelve to meet Melissa at Jorge's Bistro.

She'd called early that morning for references, and I know she'd later spoken with Mrs. P., who was the most respectable reference I could give, so I figured I had a good chance that she was really going to show. I dashed down the six blocks to the trendy restaurant and ducked inside, dodging the rail-thin hostess and looking for my new client. She'd said to look for dark hair, a black suit, and black high-heeled slingbacks.

As I looked around, I realized the description fit every woman in the place (plus the two men at the corner table). New York's basic uniform: black, black, and more black. Luckily, my jeans and buttercream yellow silk and lace chemise were a little more distinctive, and one of the black-sleeved arms in the back waved to me.

As I made my way through the crowded room to the table, the butterflies in my stomach started tap dancing. Now that I was actually going to meet a real, live prospective client, I was trying hard not to freak out.

Trying hard not to feel like a total fraud.

Trying hard not to think of my new business as a heartless plan to manipulate clueless men. Why did that old song about Karma chameleons keep running through my head?

Seriously, just once, I needed some good Karma. Where was a falling piano or a runaway train when I needed to rescue someone?

Just as I felt my stomach climbing up into the vicinity of my trachea, Melissa stood up and held out her hand. "Hi, I'm Melissa Frangelli. You must be Shane."

I admitted I was and held out my own hand, which was promptly power shaken. The power shake is the trademark of all up-and-coming baby executive types in the city. The suit she had on had to be worth three grand, so she was definitely an up-and-comer. Maybe a stockbroker.

Or—worse—maybe she was a *lawyer.*

Whichever she was, she was *hot.*

I sank down in the chair across from her, trying not to stare at her. First Lizzie, now this. Couldn't I get one single client who didn't make me feel like chopped liverwurst?

I shoved my hair out of my face and mustered up a weak smile. "So, I can see why this Tony doesn't get the hint. You're kind of gorgeous." I wasn't kidding, either. She looked like an Italian-American film star. Maybe a young Sophia Loren crossed with Jennifer Love Hewitt.

She blinked, then smiled back at me. "Wow. That's not what I usually get from women; more a sideways catty bitchiness. Unless . . ." She shot me a considering look. "I'm not gay, okay?"

"Yeah, me neither, unfortunately. I think it would be easier, sometimes," I said, shaking my head.

We both burst out laughing and startled the snooty-looking server, who sneered at us. This only made us laugh harder and, just like that, the tension between us dissipated into a casual camaraderie that lasted through our steak fajitas (no sour cream for me; extra guac for her).

As we pushed dishes to the side, I opened my mouth to ask about Melissa's situation, but she beat me to it.

"Here's the thing. Tony isn't a bad guy. In fact, he's kind of wonderful. He's a darling, really, and we've dated on and off for years. It's just that he's so . . . he's so . . ." She broke off and twisted her hands together.

I leaned forward, trying to help. "Annoying?"

She bit her lip. "Italian."

"Ah." I leaned back again, unsure how to respond. I mean, hel-*lo*, Melissa *Frangelli*.

She nodded. "I can tell what you're thinking. You're thinking, so what's the big deal, with a name like Frangelli what kind of bigoted person doesn't want to go out with a nice Italian boy?"

"Um, no. I—"

"You're thinking, who does she think she is, too good for Tony, too good for the neighborhood, too good for the people who loved her and raised her and fed her cannoli?"

"Well, actually—"

She smacked her hand down on the table, making the silverware jump. "I don't care what you're thinking. What right do you have to judge me? I'm the one hiring *you*, here."

I held up both hands. "Melissa? Sanity break here? You seem to be confusing me with your grandmother."

She blinked, then drew in a shaky breath and started laughing. "Oh. Oh, I'm such an idiot. I'm so used to arguing about this that I . . . oh, damn."

I grinned. "Nah, you're not an idiot. As the child of an overbearing parent, let me just say that I recognize the signs. You want to tell me a little bit about why you're so eager to get rid of this wonderful specimen of Italian manhood?"

She shot a sharp glance at me, then relaxed and returned

my smile. "It's a long story, but the headlines are that I'd like to live a little bit. My whole life has felt like part of a pattern set by somebody else. If not in stone, then at least in high solids, high performance, concrete curing and sealing compound."

I raised an eyebrow, and she saw me and laughed. "Sorry. I'm an investment manager, and one of my funds is in chemical sealants."

"Ah. You want to break out of the rut, I get that, but how do you feel about Tony?"

She gave me a long, considering stare. "You're not a shrink, so I'm not sure why you want to know this kind of thing. I mean, 'breakup artist.' Come on. It's the kind of New York-itis nonsense I usually make fun of. Like pet psychologist. Or aura healer."

"I don't blame you. I'm not much on pet auras, myself. But I found out that I have a kind of talent for helping people get out of relationships with the least possible stress and controversy. So, things can be amiable and amicable all around. To be completely candid, I've only recently taken it public, because I'm trying to save money for an investment of my own," I said, wondering why I was telling a total stranger my whole life story. Although, I was pretty much interrogating her about her own. All's fair, I figured.

She must have seen something she trusted in my face, because she nodded, almost to herself. "Okay. The truth? I love Tony. I can even see myself marrying him and having beautiful Italian babies and living happily ever after."

"Well, I can see why you want to get away from that," I said, lips quirking.

She laughed. "Sounds stupid, doesn't it? But I want to see what else there is in life. It seems too easy that I've found my Prince Charming right in my backyard. We were high school sweethearts, for God's sake. It's better to make a clean break now and move on."

She looked up as the server brought our check, and we each grabbed for it. Melissa shook her head. "No, I'll get this. I'm getting ready to pay you five grand, right? What's a lunch ticket on top of that?" She put some bills in the folder and set it on the table.

I caught my breath a little at the "five grand." Then I looked at her suit again. She could afford me.

She answered the question I hadn't asked. "No, the fee is fine. I want to be your top priority. I'm afraid that Tony is gearing up to ask me to marry him, on my birthday at the end of October. I have to get him to want to break up with me before that. Trust me, to avoid the specter of every mother and grandmother in my neighborhood hating me for all eternity, five grand is cheap."

She rummaged around in her slim bag and withdrew a check. "Here's the first half, second half to be paid upon success."

I stared at the check for nearly thirty seconds before I reached out to take it. As my fingers touched the paper, an almost electric shock went through me.

I'm really doing this. Oh, my God.

She held on to the check a moment longer. "Money-back guarantee if you can't make Tony break up with me in thirty days, right?"

I stared at her, almost in a daze. "Money-back guarantee. Thirty days. Yes, my word on it."

She laughed and shook her head. "Okay, I feel a little like a willing victim of some kind of pyramid scheme, but desperation breeds strange breakup buddies, and all that."

I jerked my head up from staring at the check, and stuffed it in my purse and tried to look professional. "All right, then. Do you have time to take a walk and tell me about him?"

She nodded, and we walked out together. I couldn't help but wonder, as I walked out the door, what kind of karmic-power whammy a neighborhood of Italian mothers and grandmothers would yield.

Just, you know, in a pet aura kind of way.

Chapter 11

Ben threaded his way through the after-work crowd at Gilligan's Pub, trying to force his face muscles out of the perma-grin they'd been stuck in all day. Then he saw Gleason bellied, literally, up to the bar and gave up the effort as a lost cause.

As soon as he got within back-pounding range, Gleason smacked him a good one. "Landing Jelly Jam was the foam on the top of your pint of ale, baby. Got rid of psycho Lizzie and promoted all in the same week. Hell, man, let me rub your elbow and see if some of that luck rubs off on me."

Ben dodged, but not quickly enough to get out of the way

of Gleason's meaty hand punching him in the arm. Luckily, Ben had picked up his beer with the other hand, so it didn't slosh all over the place.

A man hated to waste good beer.

Ben took a long pull on his beer, then put the mug down and turned to Gleason. "You know, there was something weird about the Lizzie thing."

Gleason snorted out a laugh. "You mean, weirder than that shit on the phone? And the flowers? No way, man. You'd have to be talking vampire Pomeranians for that."

Ben rolled his eyes at the reference to Gleason's latest cheesy horror flick fave. "No, no vampire dogs. But I think . . . okay, forget it. I'm probably imagining it."

Plus, did people really need to know his girlfriend had manipulated him into dumping her? That was kind of pathetic.

Gleason narrowed his eyes, suddenly all sharp focus like a terrier who smelled a rat.

"A rat named Lizzie," Ben mumbled.

"What? What's going on? This is your pal Gleason, Benny Bunny. You can tell me anything."

"Our friendship is history if you ever call me that again."

Ben raised his hand for another round and stared off down the bar, away from Gleason. "Are there any nuts?"

Gleason poked him in the shoulder. "You mean besides Lizzie? Spill it, Cameron."

Ben hesitated, then shrugged. "This is just between us, right?"

"What's just between us? And, yeah, you know it is."

Ben finished off his beer, then wiped his mouth with the back of his hand. "I think I've been hosed." Then he started to explain.

For a good five minutes after Ben filled him in on the so-called breakup, Gleason kept opening and closing his mouth, but nothing more coherent than "oh, shit" came out. Finally, after he'd drained his second beer, Gleason looked up at Ben. "You know what we gotta do. We gotta check it out."

"Check what out?"

"This Breakup Artist dude. We gotta find out more about him. Maybe bust his balls a little. What kind of guy does this to other guys? It's just wrong, man."

Ben nodded, then stopped. "How do we know it's a guy?"

Gleason's mouth fell back open, then he shook his head. "That'd be even worse. We gotta find out. What've we got to lose?"

"I don't know. Self-respect. Dignity, maybe. Do I really want to meet the jerk who coached Lizzie on how to get rid of me?" Ben felt a cold chill run down to the short and curlies just thinking about it.

Gleason's shoulders slumped, and he sighed. Then he jolted upright. "Hey! What if we go undercover? He—"

"Or she," Ben reminded him.

"Or she, okay, probably doesn't know what you look like. He sure as hell doesn't know me. You got the number, right? How about we call and say we want to hire the guy?"

Ben shook his head. "No way. No way, no way. I don't want to hear about the Breakup Artist ever again. Let's just let sleeping relationships lie, already."

He lifted his mug in a toast. "To the Breakup Artist. May he—or she—rot in his—or her—own personal hell, and may I never, ever hear his—or her—name again," he said, giving Gleason his "I'm totally serious, man" face.

Which is why he didn't understand how, three beers and one phone call later, they'd set up a date for Gleason to meet the Breakup Artist in person.

In her *female* person. So the ball-busting part of the plan was definitely out, but he was way too toasted to move on to Plan B.

"This has got to be the weirdest thing I've ever done," Ben mumbled, realizing he either needed to pound down some coffee or go home and hit the bed pretty quickly. He stood up and shoved his credit card receipt in his pocket.

Gleason laughed, standing up from his stool with only a touch of a wobble. "Nah, this is nothing. You know what I saw today that was really weird? An ad for pet psychologists." He belched and started walking. "You think they have little doggie couches?"

Chapter 12

Napping is such an important part of the day, don't you think? Especially when you really should be thinking up schemes to break up your new client.

I'd just punched the couch pillows into the perfect shape for a little pre-dinner relaxation, and Lulu was wrestling her stuffed toy rabbit into submission on the floor, when Farren came crashing in through the apartment door. The adrenaline spike that shot through me when the door banged against the wall put an end to my napping aspirations, so I opened one eye and glared at him. "What? You can't knock, suddenly? I knew we never should have given you a key."

"What? Key? *What?* I have news! News you need to hear now!" He bounded across the floor and jumped on the couch, practically landing on my lap. I yanked my knees up to my chest and stared at him, and Lulu jumped up and dropped her slobbery toy in his lap.

"Shane! I got it! I got it, I got it, I got it," he crowed in a sing-songy voice, bouncing up and down on the couch. "And, euww, that's disgusting, Lulu." He gingerly picked up her drool-laden toy with two fingers and tossed it across the room. We watched Lulu dash across the room after it. (Slobber and fetch was her favorite game.)

Then I looked back at Farren, who was wiping his hand on his pants. "You got what? A winning lotto ticket? Chicken pox?"

"The PART! I got the part on *As the Sun Sets*! I'm the snarky valet parking attendant with a mysterious past. It's only a temporary role, but I know it could lead to bigger and better things once they see me in action."

"That's fantastic, Farren!" I grabbed him in a huge hug. "Does Michel know yet?"

"No, I can't reach him; he must have his cell turned off."

He grabbed Lulu and jumped up and started doing a little dance with her. "Just listen to the best part: my agent got me a signing bonus! I asked for five thousand, but he only got twenty-five hundred. Still, that's halfway there for Michel's supplies for the design contest!"

I bit my lip, the check from Melissa burning a hole in my conscience, then I sucked in a big breath, considering.

True friends are really family without the bother of genetics, right?

Mind made up, I grinned at Farren. "Actually . . . we may have enough already."

Lulu and I headed out after dinner (leftovers for me, lamb and rice delight for her) for my first Breakup Artist intervention. Elinor worked at a knitting shop in the Village, and she'd told me during our phone call of a too persistent, wannabe boyfriend, Duane. Duane had taken up knitting to help himself stop smoking and, after a few classes, wanted to take up Elinor, too.

We met at the Coffee Beanery a couple of blocks off of Columbus Circle. Elinor was a surprise in person. Maybe in her late twenties, she was almost colorless, as if the bright hues of the fuchsia and orange knitted purse she carried had bled the radiance out of the woman who carried it. She had dishwater-blond hair, brownish eyes, and was sort of medium.

Medium height, medium weight, just medium all over. After Lizzie and Melissa, I was, frankly, surprised that *Elinor* needed help getting rid of guys.

Lulu growled a little, and I glanced down to find her sitting next to my leg, staring up at me, almost as if she were my conscience in a furry package. Almost as if she were chastising me for being judgmental.

Almost as if I'd had way, *way* too much caffeine.

Shaking off insane anthropomorphize-tastic dog thoughts, I tossed the rest of my latte in the wastebasket. We sat outside at a tiny metal latticework table, while Elinor fidgeted with her decaf soy chai latte and snuck appalled-looking glances at Lulu.

"I'm really more of a cat person," she said for the third time, twisting her napkin and biting her lip. "I didn't mean to be rude when I asked you what it was."

I got the feeling Elinor wasn't big on the assertive thing.

"It's okay, don't worry about it. I thought she was a mutant sheep," I reassured her, slipping a piece of croissant to Lulu under the table in a silent apology. "Lulu doesn't get her feelings hurt easily. Plus, she's my cover."

Elinor blinked at me, then bit her lip again. "Oh, right. Your cover. So you'll pretend to be an ordinary person walking your dog, but you'll keep me in sight the whole time, right?"

"Well, I am an ordinary person, and I will be walking my dog. Definitely, I will keep you in sight the whole time. There's nothing to worry about."

Her hands were shaking as hard as the stock market post-Enron. I needed to help her calm down, or we'd never pull this off.

"So, tell me more about Duane. I've never heard of a guy trying to pick women up at the knitting shop, but it makes sense, in a crazy kind of way. Knitting is hot and trendy now, right?"

Elinor gave me a real smile for the first time. "Oh, yes. It's simply wonderful that so many people are trying it out. Why, my new Purling for Pearls class has the maximum enrollment of twenty for the first time, ever! We're planning to do a scarf and hat combo, and—"

"Right. I don't mean to interrupt, but we only have about twenty minutes until you meet Duane over at the International festival, right? Maybe you could tell me more about him?" I hated to see her happy yarn-induced glow fade, but I needed to find out more about the nearly departed Duane.

The color washed back out of her face and she looked down. "He's very nice, but he's so old. I also get the idea that he's looking for a nice 'little woman' to clean and cook for him, from the things he's said. His ex-wife left him to start her own business and find someone less . . . fuddy-duddyish, I think."

I nodded. "I see. But you don't think you can politely say 'no, thank you'? I mean, I'm not trying to drum myself out of business, but five hundred dollars is a lot to pay on a retail salary. Trust me, I know all about retail salaries."

Gently retrieving her third napkin from her twitching fingers before it, too, joined the pile of shredded paper, I smiled. "If he's nice in an older-gentlemanly kind of way, a simple 'no, thank you' should be enough to discourage him."

She shook her head. "No, I tried that already. He doesn't seem to hear me. And he spends a lot of money in the shop, so my boss would be furious if I make him angry. It would be for the best all the way around if Duane thinks that it's his idea to stop pursuing me."

I nodded, trying to think of the best way to work this one. Staring off into the distance, I barely noticed the people power-marching by us on the sidewalk, until one of them stopped right in front of us, power suited, cell phone earpiece glued to her ear, BlackBerry in hand. I blinked and looked up at her, but she was staring down at Lulu with a sort of sneering distaste.

"What *is* that thing? It looks like a dust mop with ears." Lulu growled at her, but I was too speechless at the unprovoked rudeness to say a word.

The woman paused to type something in her BlackBerry, thumbs flying across the miniature keyboard, then shot one last look of disgust at Lulu and marched off toward wherever snotty bitches spend their days.

Lulu stopped growling, but gave me a look of such sadness from her enormous liquid-brown eyes that I thought I might have to rethink that anthropomorphize thing. I picked her up and cuddled her on my lap. "I'm sorry I didn't stand up for you, baby. I was kind of shocked speechless. Stupid woman with her stupid cell phone and her stupid BlackBerry, and . . ."

My eyes narrowed, and I glared after the nasty dog-hating moron, then turned to smile at Elinor. "I think the dog hater there just gave me an idea."

Her eyes widened. "Really? Is it about dogs? Because I don't know if Duane likes dogs or not. I think he said something about a cat one time, but—"

"No, no, no. Not dogs. About the business bitch, there.

So you said Duane is an old-fashioned guy who believes a woman's place is in the home, right?"

"Well, yes."

"Okay. You're a woman who works two jobs and plans to start her own business very soon."

"I am?"

"You are. And you spend most of your time on your cell phone, talking and text messaging potential investors."

"I do?"

"You do."

"Um, Shane? Nobody actually ever texts me. I don't know how to do it."

"Oh, honey. I can fix that," I said, smiling. Lulu licked my chin and hopped down off my lap.

Five minutes later, Elinor was a texting whiz, her cell number was programmed into my phone, and we were on our separate ways to Columbus Circle to meet Duane.

The poor man was doomed.

I lagged about forty feet behind Elinor, trying to keep sight of her in the crush of humanity swarming Columbus Circle. The jewelry, art, and craft vendors were doing a humming business, and Lulu and I had to dodge out of the way of three strollers, a wheelchair, and a grocery cart.

Finally, I picked her up and carried her under one arm, her odd little face peeking out at everyone. The jewelry was amazing, but I was strong and didn't dawdle at all in front of the hand-wired amber bracelet and necklace set with the matching earrings.

Which nearly killed me.

Okay, I dawdled a little, until Lulu barked and I caught sight of Elinor disappearing around the corner of the funnel cake booth. I hurried over, trying to look casual, and nearly bumped into her when I rounded the corner. She'd stopped to talk to a man I guessed must be Duane, although he didn't look more than forty-five, so I wasn't sure where "so old" had come from. I shushed Lulu, who growled at him as I walked by, but I never even glanced at Elinor once.

I rock at this undercover stuff.

As soon as I got out of their line of sight, I called her.

She picked up on the second ring. "Hello?"

"Elinor, it's me. Pretend I'm saying something about investing in your new start-up business."

"Um, yes, that would be good," she mumbled.

"No, speak up! You have to sound like a hard-charging businesswoman, right? Say . . . say 'we'll crunch those numbers.' "

"We'll crunch those numbers, that's right," she parroted back to me. I heard a deep voice rumbling something in the background, but couldn't make out the words.

"Oh, sorry, Duane. It's my, ah, my . . ."

"Potential investors," I hissed, then wondered why I was whispering.

"Potential inventors."

"Investors!"

"Investors. It's my potential investors, Duane. I really need to take this, thanks," she said.

"Are you okay? Ready for the text messaging?" I mumbled into the phone, putting Lulu back down on the ground since the crowd seemed to be thinning out a little. She snuffled her way over to a french fry that somebody had dropped, but I tugged the leash before she could eat it.

"—now?"

Oops.

"Sorry, Elinor, I missed that. What?"

"Ah, will you text those—um, figures now?"

"You bet. Figures on their way. Hang in there," I said, then shut off the call and started composing a text message. As I peered down at my cell screen, Lulu barked again, twice. She stood, bristling, the fur on the ruff of her neck standing straight up.

I glanced down the sidewalk to see what she was barking at, then looked up and right smack into Duane's eyes. We both did that double-take thing, then he looked down at Lulu. I could see the "what is THAT?" forming in his mind even as he opened his mouth, so I dragged Lulu along and scooted on out of there, trying not to look at Elinor.

"So much for rocking at undercover, you annoying dog. I'm not going to bring you on surveillance any more if you can't learn to be quieter," I muttered at my clearly unrepentant dog.

Rushing down the path, I turned left at the batik tent and stopped to catch my breath and send Elinor a text message. I tapped my fingers on the screen for a couple of seconds, then came up with this:

POSSIBLE SPACE FOR OUR BUSINESS. MUST MEET WITH LANDLORD TONIGHT. U AVAILABLE? OTHER INTERESTED PARTIES—CRUCIAL TO DO THIS NOW.

Hitting SEND, I peeked around the corner of the tent and saw Elinor and Duane walking down the path. She had her phone to her ear and was talking to someone who wasn't me. He looked totally ticked off.

She clicked her phone off and then glanced down at it. They were close enough for me to hear them by then, so I pretended an intense fascination with a purple wall-hanging adorned with a stylized poodle-head design.

"So, Lulu, is this one of your ancestors?" I picked her up and she cocked her head and stared. "Are poodles your peeps, my little Chihugapoo?"

She turned to look at me at the word Chihugapoo, so I took it as confirmation. Plus, Hairy Scary Guy's ex the vet had said my guess was as good as hers on Lulu's lineage. "Whatever jumped over the fence of the kennel" was how she'd put it, but I thought that was a little crude, personally.

Elinor's voice (which sounded shaky) broke into my poodle study. "I'm sorry, Duane, but I really need to go see this space."

"I can go with you. Then we can finish our date," he said.

Oh, crap. Didn't see that one coming.

Elinor's voice firmed up. "No, no you can't. This is my business, Duane. I'm sorry, but it's going to be like this while I get this start-up going. You're a very nice man, but of course I'd understand if you would rather date someone who will be more available to you . . ."

Their footsteps stopped, but I didn't look over at them, even though it was killing me. I tilted Lulu's head up and gave her a warning glare, too, sending her psychic "don't even think about barking" vibes.

Duane finally spoke up. "Well, I guess you may be right. I think you're a great girl, Elinor, but I really am looking for somebody a whole lot less like my 'all business, all the time' ex. I hope you understand."

"I do, really I do. You're such a nice man, Duane," she said.

"I hope you're not feeling hurt. I'd hate to quit coming to the shop, but if you think it will be difficult to see me with other girls, I can—"

"No! I mean, no, don't quit coming to the shop. I value our friendship, and I'll be happy for you when you find someone who's not all businessy all the time."

I clenched my teeth together to keep from smiling, in case he happened to notice me. Then I heard their footsteps start up again, walking away from me, and I used the chance to make my escape.

As planned, I waited for Elinor back at the coffee shop, realizing about fifteen minutes later that it might have been smarter to get paid in advance. Lulu, sitting on my lap, seemed to agree, if sneezing on my decaf latte means "yes, you're an idiot" in Dog.

As I tossed yet another perfectly good, if slightly damp,

latte cup in the trash basket, Elinor finally showed. She came rushing up, pink cheeked and a little sweaty.

"You are brilliant!"

I grinned. "Well, brilliant is a little strong. I just have my tried-and-true techniques, and—"

She laughed. "Not you, Lulu. Duane mentioned her and how ugly—sorry, Lulu—she was, and how much he hated dogs. He's totally a cat person. So I immediately thought 'what would the Breakup Artist do?' Then I told him all about my five dogs who were like my family, and how I could never, ever be parted from them."

She bent down and rubbed Lulu's ears. "You wonderful dog."

Lulu, of course, loved it and made some very odd snorfling noises that sounded like piglet crossed with purring kitten.

Elinor stood back up and brushed her hands off on her skirt. "The dog thing, plus the business thing, and he was so totally gone. But there are no hard feelings!"

"That's wonderful!" I said, mildly wondering what percentage Lulu was going to demand. (Then, you know, sanity.)

Jumping up out of my chair, I hugged Elinor, who seemed startled. "Well, um, yes," she said, cheeks turning even pinker. "I need to pay you. Is cash okay?"

I could feel my own cheeks turning pink. "Um, yeah, but really, five hundred dollars is way too much for, what, an hour and a half's work?"

She stopped with her hand in her purse, looking hopeful.

"Wow. Really? I mean, I'm not trying to back out or anything, but like you said, retail salaries and all."

I wavered. Like that old saying goes, nice don't buy the boutique. On the other hand, if *anybody* needed help . . .

"Look, how about this. You promise to spend some of the money on something fun for yourself, and only give me what you can afford," I said, sighing a little, then glancing down as I felt a nudge against my leg. Lulu was wagging her whole body enthusiastically, like she approved.

Great. I'd acquired a conscience shaped like a furry mutant sheep.

Elinor's face lit up like Fifth Avenue at Christmastime, and I couldn't help but return her smile. *Maybe there was a teensy bit of good Karma in this gig, after all?*

As Lulu and I walked home, tired but happy—and two hundred bucks richer—I spared a thought for Awful Ben. He'd probably forgotten all about Lizzie by now. Luckily, like Duane, Tony, and the rest of my clients' soon-to-be-parted significant others, at least Ben didn't know a thing about the Breakup Artist.

Lulu picked that exact moment to squat on the patch of grass next to the sidewalk, and I wondered if she knew something of the "don't pee on my parade" variety.

Nah.

Chapter 13

Long, long, long day. Did I mention *long* day? I managed to avoid Mrs. P. when she called, since I still don't have any idea how I can come up with fifty grand in any reasonable amount of time. We pushed some more of the body oil in a "buy a Body by Boris, get a bottle of body oil free" in-store special. Surprisingly, it did get more of the hideous Boris designs out of the store.

Lulu nudged my foot, which hung off the edge of the couch. I looked down at her, and she gave me the dog version of a Jedi mind trick: *I AM the dog you want to take for a walk.*

Or it may have been the leash in her mouth that clued me in.

Heaving a sigh, I dragged my exhausted self off of the couch. This dog-ownership thing was more of a responsibility than I'd imagined. It made me realize it would be a long, long time before I wanted a baby. You can't shut one of those up in your bedroom with fresh water and a chew toy while you go to work.

We wandered down the street while Lulu searched for the perfect spot (and is it just me, or isn't one spot pretty much as good as another for this kind of thing? I mean, do we really need to sniff and run frantically back and forth twenty-seven times before we squat exactly where we started?), and I searched for the energy to make it to my appointment that evening.

In a change of pace, I was meeting a guy this time. Gleason somebody. He'd sounded a little loopy on the phone, but it wouldn't be the first time somebody had needed liquid courage to call the Breakup Artist. Er, I mean call me. This whole gig was giving me a split-personality complex.

Relief achieved, Lulu looked up at me and wagged her entire curly body. We wandered a bit more, since she'd been cooped up in the apartment all afternoon. A couple with matching DEATH TO THE MAN tattoos came out of a teapot shop and started toward us, then lurched to a stop when they caught sight of Lulu.

The woman looked at me and opened her mouth, and I

cut her off. "Rare French *Se Scenter Mal* terrier," I said, still walking. "Hideously expensive. Nicole Richie has one, you know?"

They nodded sagely. "Oh, yeah," the guy said. "I saw something about that on *Access Hollywood*." They started walking again, probably sneaking looks back at Lulu, but I never gave them a second glance.

Lulu trotted along next to me, panting and grinning up at me. "I know, I know, the syntax is probably all wrong, but you *did* smell bad when I first got you, right? And poodles are French. I'll tell the next one you're a Chihugapoo. Maybe we'll create a new trend."

My cell phone rang, and Lulu started growling. I looked at the display. "Chill, it's not Lizzie. It's my client for the evening. You don't even know him yet, and—and I can't even believe I'm talking to a dog like she's psychic."

I flipped my phone open. "Hey, Gleason. What's up?" He probably wanted to cancel. He wouldn't be the first to get cold feet when it came right down to the actual first meeting.

"I'm calling to make sure we're still on. We can't wait to meet you, ow! I mean, I really need help to get rid of Sarah." He sounded a little out of breath.

"I thought it was Tina?"

"Right. Tina. Her, um, middle name is Sarah, and sometimes I call her that."

Lulu started growling again, staring up at the phone.

"Hush, Lulu. Okay, Gleason, yes, we're still on, and I'll

meet you at O'Malley's at eight. Is it very loud there? We'll be able to talk, right?"

"Definitely. Can't wait. See you then. Oh, and I'll be the devastatingly handsome man in the gray suit with the yellow tie."

Lulu barked, and I rolled my eyes at the same time. "Okay, whatever. I'm tall with long, wavy, reddish brown hair, and I'll have on jeans and a white shirt. See you then."

I hung up the phone before Gleason could tell me about any more of his wonderful attributes. He didn't come off exactly right on the phone, but it wasn't anything I could put my finger on. Although the Sarah/Tina thing was weird.

"Come on, Lulu. I need to get moving, baby. Annie should be home by now to play with you." I started walking, but Lulu braced her feet against the ground and wouldn't move. When I tugged on the leash, she barked at me.

"What? Do you need more, um, relief? Well, get to it, already."

She didn't move, just stared up at me and barked again, a single sharp yap.

"Okay, I don't have time for this, Lou. Come on, Shane has to get going," I said, scooping her up under my arm and heading back for the apartment. She made a snuffly noise but didn't bark again.

As we walked, a messenger dude on a bike coasted to a stop on the road next to us, staring at Lulu with a now-familiar expression on his face. I held up one hand to stop any stupid comment before he made it but never broke stride. "Chihugapoo. Possibly psychic."

Lulu growled at him.

I love that dog.

Chapter 14

RULE 4: Never, ever get personally involved with the client or—even worse—the client's nearly departed. Chaos inevitably ensues.

"This was a stupid idea, man," Ben said for the third or fourth time, sitting at a table in the dimly lit back of O'Malley's Pub. "Tell me why, again, I'm wasting a perfectly good evening meeting a woman who thinks it's okay to break up other people's relationships?"

Gleason grinned his evil grin. "So we can tell her in person that she's a scum-sucking low-life pig of a—and I use the term loosely—human being."

Ben stirred the peanuts in the bowl around again, futilely hoping for a pretzel that he might've missed on his first two go-rounds. Damn women and their damn low-carb diets.

Even the sacred bar pretzel had been sacrificed on the altar of Atkins.

Disgusted, he shoved the bowl away and raised his decidedly high-carb beer with a flourish. "Oh, what the hell. Here's to sticking the Breakup Artist's routine right up her ball-busting ass."

Gleason's forehead crinkled up for a minute. "Interesting metaphor mixing, but okay, I can go with it. Cheers!" He raised his own glass, and they each drained the rest of the beer in their mugs. "No time for another, though. She should be here any minute. I need to go get a table on my own, so she doesn't see you right away. Just in case Lizzie showed her a picture or something."

Ben nodded. The plan was for him to give them a few minutes together, then walk up to the table and blast her. He had to admit that the idea gave him a kind of evil glee, like watching Tom Cruise go couch-jumper. Some people just deserved to be brought down. "Okay," he said. "Let's get her."

Ben flagged down the waitress, who was kind of cute in a tall, skinny, Lizzie way, and ordered a Coke. He was heading to the gym for a workout after he torpedoed the Breakup Artist and more than one beer would make him suffer. He watched Gleason snag a table up near the door and settle in to wait for their victim.

Not that she was a victim. If anybody was the victim here, it was him. He ignored the niggle that said, "You weren't all that happy with Lizzie, anyway, and if she wanted out, you didn't have any future, right?" and stuck it way down in his brain where he shoved all unappreciated conscience twinges. Like the "didn't go home for Sunday dinner when you haven't seen Mom for six weeks" and the "still haven't sent your sister a baby gift and the baby is starting preschool in a couple of months."

The door opened, and one of the hottest women he'd ever seen in his life walked in. She had long silky hair and a "works out but still curvy in all the right places" body. He watched his dream woman as she walked right up to Gleason's table and glanced down at him.

Then she kept right on walking.

Damn.

He watched her as she strolled over to the bar, where a shorter woman with curly blond hair sat on a stool. Then his dream woman planted a major liplock on Blondie.

Double damn.

He shrugged. Can't win 'em all. Then he turned back to look at Gleason, who was suddenly not alone. From the side, she didn't look like much. Long wavy hair. That brown that isn't quite brown, but red in the sun, like a really fine glass of Amber Bock.

Jeans and a plain white shirt, an outfit so plain and boring Lizzie never would have been caught dead in it. No wonder she spent her time dreaming up ways to break up other people's relationships. She probably couldn't find one of her own.

Gleason's laugh suddenly rang out, and Ben's eyes narrowed. That wasn't G-Man's fake "you're a client so I need to suck up" laugh, but a real "somebody tried to tell me they bought *Playboy* for the articles" laugh.

What the hell?

Time for Phase Two of the plan. He stood up and tossed some cash on the table, then sauntered over to their table. As he walked up beside them, the evil breakup woman looked up, still smiling from something Gleason had said, and her gaze met Ben's.

Looking into her greeny gold eyes, Ben felt something in his gut twitch. Not "shouldn't have eaten that fifteenth hot wing" twitch, but "holy crap, here we go, are these roller coaster things really safe?" twitch.

For a fraction of an instant, he actually thought about running. Then Gleason looked up, and it was too late.

"Ben! What a surprise!" Gleason boomed. "This is Shane Madison. She's a—ah, consultant."

She smiled up at Ben, and there was a moment when he actually felt light-headed. Then he shook it off and held out his hand to her. "Ben C-Cooper. Ben Cooper, pleased to meet you."

She stood up to shake his hand, and her body made the hot lesbian at the bar suddenly yesterday's news. She was somewhere between skinny and plump, caught in the middle. In the world of curves rounded enough for a man to get his hands around them.

Or sink his teeth into, he silently amended, catching sight of her ass as she moved around the table.

Where did that come from? Too much time around Gleason, and suddenly I'm a horndog.

"This is a weird coincidence," she said, glancing at him over her shoulder and, luckily, not catching him staring at her backside. "I've never met a Ben, and now two in one week. Well, I didn't actually meet the other Ben, but—"

Gleason cut her off, braying out a nervous laugh. "Yeah, there's suddenly Bens all over the place. We've got three on our softball team this season. What's wrong with these parents? You'd think more of them would have thought of manly names, like Gleason."

She laughed. "Yeah, I guess Ben's a really common name."

Gleason waited until Shane and Ben dropped into chairs before he opened his mouth to speak. Grinning like an unholy demon spawn from planet Budweiser, he speared Shane with a glance. "As it turns out, Shane, we have some news for you."

Shane tilted her head, and the long line of the curve of her neck sent Ben scrambling into action. "Wait! I mean, Gleason, I have to tell you something important about the thing."

Gleason looked at him like he was nuts. Which he probably was. But, what the heck, he was going with his gut this time.

"Ah, you know. The thing about the place?" He looked at Shane. "It's a stupid work thing, but it's kind of confidential. Maybe . . ."

She smiled. "Trust me, I know all about confidential work stuff. I'll take a break for a minute, so you two can have your chat."

As she made her way to the back where the restrooms were, Ben watched her the whole way, only snapping out of his daze when Gleason smacked him in the arm.

"What was that all about? I was getting ready to give her the one-two punch."

"Ah, yeah. About that. Now that I've seen her, I kinda want to—um, change our plans."

Gleason folded his arms across his chest and gave Ben the evil eye. "She's hot, and you want to bang her."

"What? No, that's not—no, that's ridiculous."

"Bull. You had that same googly-eyed look on your face when we saw Heidi Klum at the Knicks game that one time."

"No! I mean, well, Heidi Klum, come on, you yourself said you wanted to have her babies. She's—I mean, shut up. We don't have much time. Look, I just want to try a different plan."

Gleason stared at him, clearly still skeptical. "Like what?"

"Like . . . like . . . just telling her off is too easy. She can get up and walk out before we even get to the scum-sucking part, right?"

Gleason nodded slowly. "So, what? You want to kidnap her and tie her up naked, then tell her how evil she is?"

"No! And let me say that your mind is a very scary place. No, I want her to really suffer. What if I convince her that I like her, we start going out, then once she gets involved, I pull a David Copperfield."

Gleason narrowed his eyes. "You bang a supermodel?"

"No, you idiot! No, I disappear. Dump her cold. *Then* we

tell her that we know all about her and the scum-sucking stuff."

Tapping his fingers on the table, Gleason slowly nodded. "I like it. It has depth. It has scope. It's a plan, man. Let's do it."

Ben heaved a sigh of relief. For some reason, he seriously did not want Gleason to tell Shane that they knew all about her just yet.

Sometime soon, definitely. Just not . . . yet.

"But why can't I be the one to date her and dump her? She's hot." Gleason waggled his eyebrows in a fake leer.

"No way. I mean, I'm the wronged party here. I should get to wreak the vengeance, right?"

"Oh, all right. But the next time this happens, I'm the wreaker."

Ben nodded. "Absolutely. Now shut up, here she comes."

Still ten feet or so away from the table, Shane caught Ben's eye and tilted her head, a question on her face. He nodded and smiled, and she returned to the table.

He stood up as she approached, then sat back down as she took her chair, thinking his mom would be proud of that long-dormant display of the manners she'd taught him in sixth grade.

Shane smiled, that little dimple on the side of her mouth appearing again. "Are you all done with work talk, guys? I can head out, if you need to have a long talk."

"No," Ben blurted out. "I mean, no, don't leave. We're done with boring work stuff."

"Yep. Done. All done," Gleason added.

"So, what do you do, Shane?" Ben asked, then mentally kicked himself in the butt. *Dolt! You know what she does. This is going to be awkward.*

But she never missed a beat. "I'm the manager of a boutique downtown. Sensuality—hedonistic pleasures for the senses." She laughed, her cheeks turning a little pink. "Wow, don't I sound like commercial girl? Next, I'll be trying to sell you passion fruit body oil."

"What? And, may I just say, you could sell me anything," Gleason said, leaning toward her.

For some reason, the sight of Shane laughing with Gleason made the gut-twitchy thing worse, but Ben refused to freak out about it.

Much.

Shane glanced at her watch. "Not to be a clock watcher, but I need to spend some quality time with my feet up tonight. Um, Gleason, do you want to reschedule talking about that—ah, issue of yours?"

Gleason stared at her. "What issue?"

"Um, the *breaking* issue?" she mumbled, sneaking a glance at Ben.

Ben could almost see the light bulb switch on in Gleason's mind. "Right. Oh, right. The issue. You know, I've decided not to go with the breaking issue right now. I'm gonna—see how it plays out. Seriously. But thanks," he said.

She grinned. "No problem. Good luck, and I hope it all works out for the best."

"Really?" Gleason asked, eyebrows raised. "Doesn't that cut into your profits?"

"Sadly enough, there seem to be plenty of potential clients for my—um, consulting services," she said, shoving her hair back away from her face.

The odd thing was, she *did* almost look sad when she said it. Not at all ball-bustery. Ben kicked Gleason under the table.

"Ow! I mean, *oh*. Oh, look at the time," Gleason said, shoving his chair back. "I gotta run. Nice meeting you, Shane."

She stood up. "I should be going, too. It was great to meet you, too, Gleason, Ben."

Ben reached out, almost involuntarily, and touched her arm with his fingertips. "Would you—do you have a few minutes to hang out? I'm kind of in the mood to get something to eat and talk. I mean, only if you have time."

When she hesitated, he held out his hands, palms up. "Hey, it's no big. I just thought, you're a friend of Gleason's, I'm a friend of Gleason's. It's practically like we know each other already, right?"

She bit her lip for a moment, then nodded. "Sure. I could eat something. Something with beef, so I can take some back to Lulu."

"Lulu?" *Oh, crud. I'm 0 for 2 on women who go for my gender.*

"My dog. Or mutant sheep, depending on where you're standing," she said, flashing a smile that nearly made his knees go weak.

As they sat back down, and he flagged the waitress over, the same thought kept stuttering through his brain.

Man, I am in some deep trouble this time. This is way worse than Heidi Klum.

"So, wow. I've spent thirty minutes boring you to death about advertising," he said, inwardly wincing. The woman would never want to see him again.

But her eyes were sparkling, not glazed over. That had to be a good sign. Her lips curved into a smile, and Ben realized he'd missed half of what she said because he was staring at her mouth like a crazed stalker.

He shook his head, disgusted with himself. "I'm sorry, Shane, I didn't catch that?"

She laughed. "Either I'm boring you, or we're both tired. I was just saying that your idea for the candy campaign sounds pretty fresh and original to me. That's the kind of advertising I'd like to do for my store. Well, if it ever *is* my store."

The good feeling that he shouldn't have been susceptible to—after all, this woman was the Breakup Artist—spread, in spite of his best efforts to marshal his common sense. As she waved to the waitress and made a writing signal to ask for the check, he realized he wanted to see her again.

He wanted to see Shane again.

He didn't care about what she did with her spare time all that much, he rationalized, realizing he was doing it. After all, he and Lizzie hadn't had much of a future, anyway.

Shane drew some cash out of her bag, shaking her head when he tried to protest. "How about we go halvsies, at least? Then we'll both have enough money to do this again sometime," she said, suddenly sounding tentative. "I mean, not that we have to do this again. I was just saying—"

He touched her hand. "I'd really like that. To 'go halvsies' with you again. Can I call you?"

She nodded, her cheeks suddenly a little pink. Shane was about as different from Lizzie as two women could get, which is what made it so weird. There's no way this woman was a player.

So how could she be the Breakup Artist? It was definitely a puzzle.

As they made their way out of the bar, Ben smiled. He'd always loved puzzles.

Chapter 15

I opened the door and barely caught Lulu in midlaunch as she made a barreling leap for my arms. Laughing, I pushed the door shut with my hip, then clicked the locks into place (tricky, when you have an armful of dog). "Yes, I'm glad to see you, too, and yes, I have food. Look, yummy cheeseburger."

Lulu spazzed out, wiggling her furry body and trying to lick my face and snorfle the white paper bag all at the same time.

Annie came ambling down the hall in an oversized Columbia T-shirt. "Hey, Shane, how'd it go? Did you spend all this time with your BUC?"

"BUC?"

"Breakup client. How was he?" She rescued the paper bag from my hands and put it on the table, while I gave Lulu some snuggles.

"Oh, he was fine. He changed his mind, though. Didn't want to hire me after all."

She put her hands on her hips and frowned. "What? It took him three hours to decide not to hire you? I hope you charged him for your time."

I grinned and put Lulu down on the floor, so I could wash my hands and give her some cheeseburger. "No, but thank you to the bottom of your mercenary little heart. It was fine. Better than fine, actually. I met a friend of his, and we kind of hit it off."

Annie followed me to the sink, peering up into my face. "You're all glowy. Stop with the glowy and dish all!"

"There's no glowy. I don't know what you're talking about," I muttered, trying not to smile like an idiot while I washed and dried my hands. For some inexplicable reason, I wanted to keep Ben to myself. Just for a little while.

"There's definite glowy. Deets, now," she demanded.

I scooted past her and grabbed the bag, then crumbled a little burger for Lulu's dish, trying to figure out how to respond.

I met the guy I want to end my celibacy streak with?

Nah, too dramatic. Possibly true, but dramatic.

Annie followed me back into the living room, almost panting. "Spill it, Madison." She put her hands on her hips and pursed her lips, and I knew I had to quit stalling.

"Well," I began, then my cell phone rang. I fumbled for it in relief. "Hello?"

"Shane, it's Melissa. We're on for tomorrow. I've worked it out with his brother that I'm going to show up at his job site with a romantic dinner," she said in a breathless voice.

"Are you okay? You sound out of breath."

"Yeah, I ran up the steps to the fourth floor. Need to keep my quads in shape, right?"

I contemplated my couch-potato quads and sighed. "Right. I run the stairs all the time. Anyway, Michael was okay with you interrupting the big business consultation?"

Tony, a building contractor, was meeting building inspectors at a job site. Not really the time for romance. It was eerily similar to the Ben/Lizzie situation, but—hey—if it works, it works.

She laughed, but she sounded uneasy. "He and Tony don't always get a chance to catch up during the week. He doesn't know about the inspectors. If only they don't talk before tomorrow night, I'll be okay. You'll be there, right?"

"I'm playing the caterer, right? Remember to go ballistic when he doesn't dump his inspectors for you," I said. "Plus, don't forget the four Cs—"

"Cloying, clingy, and completely crazy," she interrupted. "Yeah, I got it. Tony's really focused about his business. It's been in his family for three generations," she said. "I'm kind of nervous about this, to tell the truth."

"Okay. How does Mrs. Anthony DiRisio sound?" I asked.

Lulu barked at me, and I stuck my tongue out at her. Annie's eyebrows shot up under her curly bangs, and she started to open her mouth, but I shook my head and held up one finger.

There was silence on the phone, then a *whoosh*ing sound as she blew out a big sigh.

"You fight dirty, Shane," Melissa finally said.

I blinked. "That's not really fair. *You* called *me*. I don't have a stake in whether or not you raise beautiful babies with Tony. I'm just trying to do the job you hired me to do, right?"

"Yeah, no stake except for the five grand," she said.

It was my turn to be silent.

"I'm sorry, Shane," she said. "You're right, this was my idea. And it's not like he doesn't have his faults. He's way too possessive and too arrogant. His idea of a romantic evening is dinner at his mother's house. We could never work."

I shrugged, then realized she couldn't see it. "Your call."

"I'm going through with it," she said, voice sounding determined.

"Okay, don't forget your props," I said.

"A silk sheet and way too much perfume. Got it."

"I'll bring the body oil," I said. "I happen to have an extra bottle or two."

"Body oil? I'm not seducing him at a job site," she shrieked.

"No, and especially not with me there. Euww," I said, cringing. "But you'll look like you're ready to, and appearance is everything in a delicate operation like this."

"You're either really good or really bad, and I can't figure out which."

"Me, neither," I muttered. "Talk to you later."

I clicked my phone shut and glanced at Annie. She held up her hand this time. "Stop. I don't want to know. My brain hurts just from listening to your side of that conversation. Anyway, we need to talk about Nick, and then I want to hear about Glowy Man."

She plopped down on the couch and snuggled in, obviously getting ready for a long chat. I stared at her, feeling my shoulders slump. Ben, Tony, and now Nick. Why did I feel like I was helping a bunch of really nice guys get their hearts broken?

Where were all the sleazebags when you needed one?

By the time I brushed my teeth for bed, I felt like I'd been run over by a DreamGlow delivery truck. Not only had I failed miserably at talking Annie out of making me pull a Breakup Artist on Nick, but Farren had kept us up till midnight with every detail of his first day on the set.

Evidently, playing the obnoxious valet parking guy who leers at the cute girls (his character is a straight guy), isn't as dead-end as it sounds. He had high hopes of being written in as the town matriarch's long-lost illegitimate grandson by her fourth husband's brother. Or her third cousin's uncle.

Or something like that. The only time I'd paid any real attention after the first hour of his story was when he'd nonchalantly mentioned that one of the makeup guys had been really friendly.

Michel's eyes had narrowed. "How friendly?"

Farren had laughed, shrugging. "I don't know. Just friendly."

"Friendly like 'welcome, new guy, friendly,' or friendly like 'the guy down at the bakery who wants to get your hands on his strudel' friendly?" Michel had asked, tone flat and smile gone.

Lulu'd started whimpering in her sleep, and I'd used the diversion as an excuse to hustle everyone out of there before the tension flared up into anything that might keep me awake for even a minute longer.

Annie walked up and leaned against the bathroom door frame. "Good job on getting them out before we had another session of 'Michel's insecure jealousies, part fourteen.'"

I sighed, putting my toothbrush down. Then I scooped up Lulu, so I could brush her teeth with the little rubber toothbrush the vet had insisted I needed. The doggy toothpaste looked like some kind of liver Jell-O, but Lulu loved it. I stuck my rubber-covered finger in her mouth and scrubbed around, then glanced at Annie. "I wish he'd get over that, already. It's only going to be worse with Farren in show biz now."

Annie laughed. "I'm not exactly sure that getting the parking-dude role is show business, but it's closer than he's gotten before."

"I'm sure it will lead to bigger and better things," I said absently, concentrating on eradicating canine plaque.

"You are a dear and loyal friend, Shane. It's why we all love you," she said, turning to head for her room. Then she stopped and looked back at me. "But don't think you're off the hook for talking to me about glowy boy. We'll talk tomorrow, 'kay?"

I dropped a kiss on the silky curls on top of Lulu's head. "You know, dogs have a great advantage over humans," I told her. "They never ask naggy questions."

"I heard that!" Annie yelled from down the hall.

I smiled the smile I'd been holding in ever since I got home. *Ben Cooper. Ben Cooper, of the tousled, chestnut brown hair and the brilliantly hazel green eyes, has my telephone number. But I don't even have to wait for him to call, because we're going to a gallery opening tomorrow.*

Catching sight of myself in the mirror, I stumbled a teensy bit. Annie was right. Definitely glowy.

Which isn't necessarily a bad thing.

Sinking down in the office chair in the back room at Sensuality, gazing mournfully at a pile of paperwork a foot high, I fumbled with my cell phone earpiece. "Yeah, yeah, I heard you. Nick. Me. You. Tomorrow. Got it. Are you really sure about this?"

Annie's tone didn't sound nearly as definite as her words. "Yes. I mean, yes. He's so nice, too nice. I'd break his heart, and then I'd have to live with it on my conscience, right? Plus, Michel wants to fix me up with some guy from design school."

"Really?"

"Straight guys go to design school, too, Shane. Don't be so narrow-minded," she said. "Also, I asked him to make sure this time. No need for a repeat of that scene with Rupert."

"Did Rupert come out yet?" I scanned the stack of mail, shaking my head. Bills and junk mail, the paper version of spam.

"I don't think so. He wanted to 'borrow' me when his parents came to visit. But enough about that, let's talk about glowy guy."

I couldn't help it. I laughed a little bit.

"Was that a giggle?" Annie squealed.

"No, it was definitely not a giggle. But, he's—well, Annie, he's just so great. He's funny and interesting and—and interested in me, too. He didn't glaze over when I told him about my ideas for the boutique. It was so . . . interesting."

"I'm guessing it was interesting?" she said dryly.

I picked up a pencil and twirled it around in my fingers

compulsively. "Don't make fun of me, I'm feeling kind of sensitive right now. He's cute; did I mention that he's totally cute? A little scruffy in a Luke Wilson kind of way. I don't know. He's straight, he's single, and I'm going out with him tonight."

"Hmmm. There's got to be more to it. Does he have a terminal illness?"

"Annie!"

"I'm just saying, this is New York. You met a single, straight, hot guy last night, and you're going out with him tonight. Does he have eight bastard children, and he only wants you for a future source of cash for his child support?"

I almost dropped the pencil. "*Annie!* Could you put aside your suspicious nature for once and be happy for me?"

She sighed. "I did that with Keith, remember? But okay, okay. I'm trying. Happy. But don't forget you're with me and Nick tomorrow, so no dates with Mr. Wonderful. What's his name, anyway?"

"Ben."

"Ben? That's too funny, after Awful Ben. Did you tell him about that?"

The pencil snapped in my fingers. "Ouch! I mean, no. Of course not. Do you honestly think I'd mention my little sideline as the Breakup Artist to a cute guy I just met?"

She laughed. "Yeah, you're right. It can be an amusing story you tell your grandchildren. Lulu! Don't chew my Kate Spade purse, or I'll take you to the pound! Gotta run, Shane. Later."

I clicked the button on the offending earpiece and yanked it out of my ear, resolved to sit at the desk until every piece of mail was handled.

"Shane," Solstice called from the doorway to the shop. "You need to get out here. We have customers."

Or, you know, I can deal with the mail later.

Chapter 16

Seven hours later, clutching my tray of Indian curry to my chest, I huddled as far back in the elevator as I could get. "Um, Melissa, not to be a wimp or anything, but you could have mentioned that the job site was thirty floors up in an *unfinished building*," I said, hearing my voice get a little shrieky.

She laughed. I was surprised she could laugh in that red dress without bursting out of it, but she did. She'd apparently taken my "dress sexy" suggestion to heart. "Come on, Shane. You're not afraid of heights, are you?"

Watching the rapidly shrinking skyline through the open-to-the-air elevator door frame, I nodded dumbly. "Yep, afraid of heights. Definitely afraid of heights. Never knew it before, but there you go. I need to go home now. Walk my sheep. Write my will. Apologize to God for everything I've ever done wrong."

The elevator lurched to a halt, making a freakishly loud moaning noise. "That can't be good," I said. "No way are elevators supposed to *lurch*. Or *groan*, even. No way. If I were the one inspecting this site, I'd—"

"You'd what?" said one of the yummiest guys I've ever seen. Okay, not quite as cute as Ben, but if I weren't in imminent peril of gruesome death, I might have been into the guy. Dark and dangerous, construction worker muscle-y, tall, gorgeous, and with cheekbones you could cut glass with . . .

Yeah. *That* hot.

I stared at him, dazed with equal parts terror and lust, unable to speak. He casually put an arm around Melissa's shoulder and kissed her cheek, then gave her the raised-eyebrow look. "Hey, babe. What are you doing here? Not that I'm not always glad to see you, but I have a meeting in a few minutes. In fact, I thought that you were them, coming up in the—"

"Elevator car of doom?" I squeaked out.

He turned to look at me, this time giving me the raised eyebrow. I tried to force more words past my dust-dry throat and finally came up with one.

"Help."

Tony—because it had to be Tony, unless she had *two*

lovely Italian guys after her—grinned and walked into the elevator and took my arm. "It's okay. If you're not used to heights, the elevator can be spooky. Step out this way and onto the floor. See? Solid floor."

He tried to lead me out of the elevator, and I stared around wildly. "Yes, the floor is solid," I said, reluctantly stumbling forward. "But there aren't any *walls*. Walls are a vital part of any building that I'm going to be standing in—especially when I'm on the thirtieth freaking floor."

I grabbed at Melissa's arm, nearly dropping my curry. "Walls. Walls, please?"

I tried not to focus on the bare concrete floor, or the fact that assorted lumber and what looked like painters' tarps were lying all around the place. Or the drop cloths blowing in the breeze—the breeze that came from the place where the walls should have been.

Hyperventilation commenced.

Melissa smiled at me, but she looked a little tense.

Ha! A little tense. There are no freaking walls!

"Tony, this is the caterer," she said loudly, shooting a glare at me. "She'll be going as soon as she sets up our special dinner."

"What?" I said, dragging my feet as she propelled me away from Tony and toward the center of the room. The wall-free room.

"Suddenly, five grand seems reasonable. Cheap, even," I muttered.

"Listen, Shane, I'm sorry about the height problem, but

you need to snap out of it," she hissed. "I heard from my grandma's sister's niece that he's planning a trip to Falzone's Jewelry this weekend. Do you know what that means?"

I looked at her, dazed. "You have an incredibly gossipy family?"

She jerked my arm a little. "No, it means this needs to work. Or else."

Or else. Suddenly, my terrified brain quit scrambling around in my head and focused on the "else" part of "or else."

Or *else* I didn't earn my five grand.

Or *else* Michel wouldn't have enough to buy materials for the competition.

Or *else* my down payment on my share of the boutique was going bye-bye.

I grabbed my courage and my curry with both hands. "Where may I put this, Miss Frangelli?"

She closed her eyes briefly, then opened them and grinned at me. "Here would be fine. And call me Melissa."

Tony strode up behind us while I was arranging the food on the table and Melissa set out candlesticks. "Ah, honey, what's going on?"

She bit her lip, then pasted a huge smile on her face and turned to face him. "It's the anniversary of the first time you said hello to me, don't you remember, Punkin?"

He blinked, a boyfriend-in-the-headlights expression slowly crossing his face. "Punkin? Of course. That anniversary. Um, what does, I mean, are we having dinner? Now? Here?"

"Yes, darling. *Mi piaci, mi passione,*" she cooed. From the look on his face when I snuck a glance at him, it wasn't the kind of thing she normally did. Cooing.

But he didn't look like he was hating it.

Crap.

"That's great. But I have this meeting with the building inspectors. If only you'd called first," he said in a reasonable tone.

Melissa went ballistic. "What? Are you telling me that this stupid meeting with your stupid inspectors is more important to you than me? And I brought this *sheet*!" she said, whipping a red silk sheet out of her totebag.

I shuffled my feet and turned around, giving them some privacy and trying not to look like I was listening to every word.

Her voice rose. "I thought we could be wild and romantic. But you want to be all boring and blah-blah building inspector. Fine. I guess we have different needs."

Oh, oh. Overdoing it, Melissa. Don't go too far, too fast.

He put his hands up. "Whoa. Stop right there. If you want to be wild and romantic, I'll change my meeting. Hell, I'll take a loss on the entire building. I love you, Mel. You know that."

He stepped closer to her and put his fingers under her chin and raised it gently. "This whole surprise is like one of my fantasies come true. Don't leave, *mia tesorina.*"

Eavesdropping shamelessly, I watched as he bent down to kiss her. From the way her arms rose to circle his neck, she was a goner.

Hell, I was a goner. Why was she so determined to break up with a guy like Tony? And, if she succeeded, could I have him?

I said a quick good-bye and headed out of there. They were caught up in a major lip-lock, so it's not like they noticed. I was so discouraged at my utter failure to make the slightest progress in Melissa's case that I hardly registered the wind shrieking through the open cage of the elevator. It only took me two or three minutes to pry my fingers off the rail when we hit the ground level.

The prospect of my date with Ben was the only thing keeping me from rushing home to drown my sorrows in Cheetos. Plus, Michel and Farren had promised to "sheep-sit" for Lulu, so I knew she was in good hands. They'd said something about a collar with more bling.

I couldn't show up at the Heron Gallery in my fake waitress gear of black pants and white shirt, but I'd left an adorable outfit back at Sensuality. I kinda wanted to make a great impression on Ben.

He certainly had on me.

The lights were dimmed, the music was Yo-Yo Ma—very silken, very Asian, and the smell of the canapés was reminding me I hadn't had any dinner. The Heron Gallery would have been just about perfect if not for the woman in the orange vinyl and safety-pin mini. She stepped about ten inches closer to Ben than I wanted her to be. "Isn't it a wonderful piece?" she drawled. "Clearly representative of the artist's disenchantment with the commoditization of our modern satire-infused culture, don't you think?"

Safely on her other side, I rolled my eyes at the odd shape spotlighted on the acrylic platform. What*ever*. Then I glanced down at my rose silk cami and black cotton skirt. Outglammed by safety pins and vinyl. It was a new low.

Ben tilted his head and glanced down at Miss I'm Stuck in the Sixties, then back at the piece. "Not really. I was thinking more that it looks a lot like the carburetor float from my Aston Martin, with ostrich feathers glued to it."

Her eyes bulged nearly as far out as her fake eyelashes, then she stalked away from us, muttering something about "plebeians" as she went.

Ben grinned at me. "Sorry, I can't stand that fake *artiste* stuff. I hope I didn't offend you."

I smiled back at him. "Nope. Not a bit. Although if you'd played along, you might have gotten lucky. There was a lot of skin bursting out of that vinyl."

He shrugged, which did great things to his shoulders in his short-sleeved shirt. (Did I mention I have a thing for shoulders and arms? Yum). "Not what I call lucky. I'm pretty content right where I am," he said, distracting me from ogling his chest.

He put his hand lightly on my back and steered me through the crowd of other gallery hoppers in Heron. I slowed down in front of a large canvas hung on the gallery's center wall. "Would you call this another—what was it?— example of the artist's disenchantment?"

Ben studied it for a long moment. "Definitely. At least, somebody's disenchanted. It might be me, though. Are you up for something to eat?"

"Definitely. Can we check on my sheep first?"

"Your what?"

I sighed. "It's a long story. Do you like dogs?"

"I love dogs. But what about the sheep?"

"Well, there was a mutant sheep in the hallway one day . . ."

By the time I'd explained about Lulu and called to check up on her (she was in doggy heaven; something to do with sliced sirloin), we'd made it to the restaurant. I glanced up at the black and red sign over the door. "Sake Noir?"

He pushed the door open for me. "Trust me," he said. "It's a French-Asian Fusion, and it's terrific. Something about the music at the gallery put me in the mood."

"Mmm. Yo-Yo Ma. He's amazing," I agreed.

We followed the hostess to our table and sat down next to an ornate wall hanging of flying dragons. Ben thanked her for our menus and handed one to me.

"I saw him once," he said. "At Carnegie Hall. He's literally magical. I felt like I was hearing what it might sound like in heaven," he said, eyes faraway. Then he glanced up at me and laughed. "Sorry, that sounded a little woo-woo."

"No, not at all," I said, trying not to do something stupid like swoon at his feet. A man who could talk about something other than the Yankees, and he was having dinner with me. Life was *good*.

"I can only imagine how incredible he must sound in person. Anyway, I'm impressed you make time for cultural events. My last 'culture' was seeing *Avenue Q*. Puppets singing about Internet porn isn't exactly a highbrow experience," I said, suddenly feeling stupid.

He grinned. "But was it funny?"

"It was hysterical. There was this girl with a dream about a school for monsters . . ."

By the time we were sipping our post-prandial green tea (nothing so crass as fortune cookies at the Sake Noir), I felt like I'd known him for a long time. Our souls were surely meant to align in some cosmic way.

Plus, I wanted to jump him. *Bad*.

Okay, mostly the jumping part. It's not like you fall in love with somebody over dinner, no matter how delicious the Kobe Beef Poke Pines with sliced avocados, chile pepper aioli, and tobiko caviar was.

Ben signed the credit card slip and then looked up at me. "So, up for a hot fudge sundae?"

Oh, I'm so totally a goner.

Chapter 17

The next morning, Lulu snuggled on my lap, a shameless belly-rub hog. We'd made it through our morning walk with only three double takes, two "what is *that*s," and one astonishingly stinky poo deposit. "What did they feed you last night, Lulu? I need to have a talk with those boys about feeding spicy food to little dogs," I said.

She curled her head around so she could look up at me, tongue hanging out of the side of her mouth in pure bliss. I glanced up when I heard Annie coming down the hall. She was bleary eyed and dressed in an old Led Zeppelin T-shirt. "I evidently have great belly-rubbing talent," I announced.

"That's good, since you have no talent in the whole breakup business," she retorted, shoving her curls out of her face and heading for the kitchen. "Coffee?"

"Yeah, I *need* coffee after Melissa blasted me this morning. I take it you heard my side of that conversation?" I said, wincing.

"Yeah, I heard. So Tony wasn't turned off by the 'seduce him while he's working' idea?"

"Turned off? More like turned completely on. She said he canceled the inspection, and she didn't get out of there for two hours. Which was TMI, if you know what I mean."

Annie whistled. "Two hours? Can I have him?"

"I hear you. But he's all 'marry me, now,' and she wants her freedom. Plus, I guess he's fairly possessive, which annoys her."

Annie started laughing. "Yeah, but two hours. I could put up with a few faults."

Lulu jumped down off of my lap and trotted off to the kitchen. "Don't fall for the puppy eyes. She already had one breakfast," I said.

"That's okay, my sweetie. Isn't it, Lulu-pie? Don't listen to mean Shane," Annie cooed in a sickening baby-talk voice. "Have some of Annie's muffin."

"What happened between you two?" I said. "Before, you were all, 'euww, ugly dog,' and now you're talking baby talk and sharing your muffin with her?"

Lulu barked.

"Not that I mind," I said hastily. "But what gives?"

Annie stood up and glanced at me through the pass-through from the kitchen. "Okay, this is stupid," she mumbled. "But have you ever considered that dogs might have—well—like a sixth sense?"

"Maybe," I admitted cautiously. "What exactly are you talking about?"

"It's just that the phone rang last night—the land line—and I started to grab it without looking at the caller ID. But Lulu barked at the phone. Really barked, with her fur all standing up and everything. So, and this is totally ridiculous," she said, blushing. "Forget it."

"No, tell me," I said. "Was it . . . was it somebody you hate?"

"No! But it was Mom, and I've been avoiding her calls, because she wants me to take her friend's daughter out shopping while she's in New York this week." She poured coffee and walked into the kitchen carrying two mugs, face still a little pink. "If I'd answered, I'd be stuck. If I can hold out another two days, she'll have gone home to Florida."

I laughed. "That's so mean. How bad can she be?"

She rolled her eyes and handed me a mug. "She wants to know if there are any cheap souvenir shops, so we can 'spend the day' buying Big Apple keychains. In the shape of an apple. Because that's 'just the cleverest thing.' "

"Ouch," I said, feeling my face scrunch up. Annie hated touristy stuff. And actual tourists, too. She sometimes gave them the wrong directions, just for fun.

"So Lulu saved you from your mother and a day of kitschy souvenirs, you're saying?"

She blushed again. "I know, I know. It's totally lame. But, just in case, she deserves a bite of muffin."

Lulu sat down in front of me, crumbs stuck to her whiskers. "Fine, but no chocolate. Hairy Scary Guy's ex, the vet, says chocolate is poisonous to dogs," I said, then drank about half my coffee in one long gulp.

"What's her name? Doctor . . . ?"

I blinked. "You know, I don't have a clue. I was trying so hard not to imagine her and Hairy Scary Guy doing the nasty that I kind of didn't hear that part."

Annie shuddered and wandered back to the kitchen. "More coffee?"

"No, I need to get going. Big day today; the new line of velvet jackets is arriving. I need to redo the front window to look like sultry winter."

She laughed. "It's ninety degrees outside, Shane."

"Yeah, but this is retail. It's winter. Think cold all over."

Lulu barked once and rolled over.

"No, Lulu, not roll over, *cold* all over."

She barked and rolled over again, then looked at me with anticipation, tail wagging. Annie came running out of the kitchen. "Did you see that, Shane? She's a genius."

"Right. A genius with a slight hearing disorder," I said, standing up and brushing dog hair off of my lap. "I'll see you guys later."

"Six o'clock at the Flamingos and Bliss Reiki Institute, remember," she said.

"Why are we Reiki-ing, again?"

"Because Nick's all Mr. Business, and if he thinks I'm New Age-y, he'll lose interest."

Sighing, I opened the door. "Right. Reiki. I'll be there."

Sunk in gloom, I nearly missed my train stop. By the time I fought my way through the crowd to reach the platform, my foul mood had morphed into full-on misery. If I couldn't do a better job with the Melissa/Tony thing, I'd have to give back her check. Which would put me back at square one with my "buy into the boutique" fund.

Since I'd been avoiding Mrs. P. on that very issue, naturally she was the first person I saw when I walked in the door and took off my sunglasses.

"Hello, darling!" she crooned. "I'm so happy to see you! These velvets are gorgeous."

She wore a cherry red, velvet and lace jacket over a yellow and orange striped blouse. I skidded to a halt, mouth falling open, then put my sunglasses back on. "Mrs. P., is that you? It's awfully bright in here."

She grinned. "Don't be cheeky with me, young lady. You kids today don't know how to dress. All that black all the time."

I glanced down at my jeans and mint green tank. "Yep, I'm all about black," I drawled.

Solstice came out of the back room, arms full of a rainbow of velvet. "These colors are a bit much, don't you think? It's like the Lucky Charms leprechaun puked out a rainbow," she complained.

I scanned her black-on-black outfit, and Mrs. P. and I exchanged "what can you do" shrugs.

"Honey, we need to talk. Can you come in back and chat a bit?" Mrs. P. asked.

"Sure," I said, feeling my heart sink into my shoes. If she'd found somebody who had fifty grand on hand, I was dead. "Tax issues" didn't sound like something that would wait for me to break up a hundred unhappy couples.

I followed Mrs. P. to the back, wringing my hands. Then I realized what I was doing and smoothed my hands down my pants. *So* not gonna turn into the heroine of a Victorian novel. I straightened my spine and my attitude and leaned against the wall, waiting.

"I didn't know if you'd mentioned this to Solstice, so I thought we could talk back here," she said, rummaging in her enormous silver-sequined handbag. After a minute or two, she dumped the contents out on the desk and poked around in it.

"Aha!" She picked up a business card and waved it in the air. "I found it. This is my guy's number. You have an appointment with him next week. Don't be late. He's kind of funny about being late. Thinks it signifies fiscal irresponsibility or something."

I was stuck a step or two back on the conversational staircase. "Your guy? What guy?"

"My banker. Your appointment for a small-business loan. Get together your paperwork, collateral info, stuff like that." She handed me the card, then stuffed everything back in her purse. "Remember, don't be late! I have breakfast with Lizzie, so I have to run. She dumped that nice stockbroker fellow already, I think."

"Collateral?" I echoed weakly.

She patted my arm as she walked by. "Dear, don't mumble, it's unattractive. I think Lizzie is already regretting the loss of Ben, to be honest. See you later."

"Later," I said, sliding down the wall to sink into a huddle of boneless terror on the floor. Bankers and collateral.

I was doomed.

Chapter 18

Gleason threw his glove on the ground in disgust. "There's no way that was a strike! Get your eyes checked, Ump!"

Ben wiped sweat off his forehead with the bottom of his faded T-shirt. "Give it up, G. The man has noodles for brains. Anyway, we won by five runs, and I'm glad it's over. Let's go find a couple of gallons of Gatorade somewhere. This has got to be one of the hottest Septembers in history."

They headed out of the dugout to cross the field and shake hands with the losers. "Barclay's finest," Ben muttered with grim satisfaction. "They can eat our dust."

Gleason elbowed him in the gut. "Shut up and be gracious. First you take Jelly Jam, and now we kick their asses in softball."

They filed past the opposing side, "good game" and "way to go"-ing their way across the field, then trotted back to pick up their gear. Ben gave Gleason a raised eyebrow. "You kidding me? You're the one who wanted to leak rumors about Barclay embezzling from little kids and puppies."

Gleason held both arms out, the innocent expression on his face completely at odds with the evil glint in his eye. "Hey, I was kidding. Exaggerating for effect," he said. "Nobody would have believed the puppies part, anyway. Gotta be careful not to overdo these things."

They grabbed their stuff and headed for the parking lot and Gleason's tiny Civic Hybrid. "Speaking of overdoing stuff, aren't you getting a little carried away with this whole Breakup Artist thing? When are you going to tell her the truth and dump her ass?"

Ben stared straight ahead, and forced himself not to smile. "Soon. Definitely soon. I want to get her on the hook a little more before I crush her."

Gleason stopped at the car and opened the trunk, dumped his stuff in, then turned to stare at Ben. "Right. Except, you're not fooling anybody. You've got that shit-eating grin on your face, like when you first met Lizzie, before she went all frigid on you."

Ben shoved his bag on top of Gleason's and shut the trunk. "Lizzie never went all frigid. She was a great girl. We just weren't right for each other." He turned and leaned against the car. "And you know it ticks me off when you rag on my girlfriends. Cut it out."

"Yes, you are the last gentleman in this crude modern age, Sir Cameron," Gleason said, rolling his eyes. "And—hello? Your *girlfriends*? Is Shane a girlfriend now? Oh, man, you are so busted." Gleason folded his arms over his chest and gave Ben a pitying look. "Sure, she's hot, but she has the heart of a snake. A man-destroying, relationship-breaking snake."

"I've got her right where I want her. Don't worry about it," Ben replied, sounding a touch defensive. "I'm going to reel her in, then administer the patented Ben Cameron smack-down."

"Riiiight. Whatever you say, buddy. I'm gonna start writing this stuff down, so I'll have material for my best man's toast."

"Oh, shut up. Just because you haven't had a date in two months is no reason to go slice and dice on me," Ben said, wondering why the idea of a best man's toast didn't freak him out.

Much.

Chapter 19

Solstice promised to lock up for me, so I could head out of Sensuality early and find the Flamingos and Bliss Reiki Institute. As I headed for the train, I realized I'd left the instructions at home on the counter. When I pulled my cell phone out of my pocket to call Annie, it rang.

BIRDS OF PAIRADICE.

Okay, either a pet shop owner with poor spelling skills or a low-rent strip joint was calling me. Either way, I didn't have time. I flipped the phone open and answered with my "don't waste my time" voice.

"What?"

"Shane? This is Brenda. Brenda with the parrot?"

Oh. Right. One of my newest clients.

"Hey, Brenda. Do you work in a pet shop?"

"What?" she said, sounding distracted. "No, it's a bookstore that specializes in gambling and poker-related merchandise. Anyway, we need to go over this again. Are you sure it will work?"

I stopped next to the stairs to the train. "No, nothing is certain in life or breakups, but if you teach your parrot to say those exact words, I'm guessing it's going to get the result you want."

"He has to say 'Kiss me, Travis, kiss me hard'?"

"Yeah, but not like that. You sound angry, not romantic," I said. "Put some feeling into it."

"Look, you'd sound pissed off, too, if you were teaching your freaking bird to ask your scumbag boyfriend's scumbag best friend to kiss you."

I blinked. "Look, I advised against this. The whole purpose of my business is to avoid confrontation. But you're going to get big, ugly confrontation if you do it this way."

"My boyfriend is screwing my backstabbing sister. And his best buddy Travis lied and covered up for him so he could do it. This is the perfect plan. It gets back at both of them," she said bitterly. "He'll think I'm screwing his best friend, so I'll never have to see his ugly face again."

Note to self: no more Jerry Springer–style breakups. Euww.

"Anyway," she continued, "he's a big wimp. If he yells at me, I'll throw him out of the apartment."

I tried one more time. "Can't we go back to my original plan of teaching the bird something innocuous? I really, really liked 'the Yankees are big weenies.' That would drive him nuts, but not make him mad at you. Just willing to do anything to get away from you and your bird."

"Yeah, but that wouldn't hurt him as much. He's banging my sister. He deserves pain."

"But—"

"PAIN."

Another passerby brushed by so close he nearly knocked me down, and I gave up. "Okay. But call me and let me know how it's going, or if you change your mind. We can try a different way, all right?" I glanced at my watch and winced. Annie would kill me if I missed this Reiki thing.

"Look, I've gotta run. Can we talk later?"

"First, you have to tell my bird how to say it," she said.

"What?"

"Pepe is right here. Tell him how to say it, with feeling, like you said. I'll put the phone to his ear."

"What? Brenda, I'm standing out on the street, with a zillion people around. I can't teach your bird—"

"Three words, Shane. Five. Hundred. Dollars."

I sighed. "Fine, put him on the phone."

I waited a couple of seconds, glanced around at the crowded sidewalk in despair, then hunched over my phone. "Pepe? Say 'Kiss me, Travis. Kiss me hard.' "

Pepe made a weird squawking sound, then Brenda came back on the phone. "Louder. I don't think he heard it. Plus, you have to repeat things several times for him to get it. Okay, go ahead."

"But—oh, fine," I said, and closed my eyes and took a deep breath. "Kiss me, Travis. Kiss me hard. Kiss me, Travis. Kiss me hard. *Kiss me, Travis. Kiss me hard.*"

I opened my eyes when the applause started. A half-dozen commuters were circled around me, clapping and nodding their heads. One bald guy whistled approvingly.

A giant sinkhole never opens up in the ground when you need one.

Face blazing, I gritted my teeth and smiled, then did a half bow. "I'm done now," I mumbled into the phone, dashing for the stairs.

Five hundred dollars suddenly sounded really, really cheap.

I slipped into the back of the lecture a half second before the guy in the turban closed the door, then I scanned for Annie and Nick. They were in the second row from the back, squeezed into very small chairs next to an elderly woman wearing a red silk caftan. Mrs. P. would have loved it.

Annie caught sight of me and frantically waved me over. I dropped into the chair she'd saved for me, looking around. Shimmery hangings decorated much of the surface of the pristine white walls. Maybe thirty people filled the assortment of metal chairs, their clothes ranging from caftan chic to business suits.

"Where have you been? You promised to get here early," Annie hissed at me.

"I'm sorry. I had to teach a parrot how to talk dirty," I said.

The three people in front of me all turned around to stare at me.

"Oops. Guess that was a little loud. Sorry," I muttered, deciding on the spot never to say the word *parrot* again. Which, for some reason, made me think of Birds of Pairadice.

What kind of—*ah*. "Pairadice—pair of dice. Okay, I get it." I rolled my eyes.

"Hey, Shane," Nick said. "You're teaching parrots to play dice?"

"Hey, Nick. No, it's a long story. Sorry I'm late."

He grinned. "No big. As you can see, our guru is late, too."

The caftan woman leaned over toward Nick. "Excuse me, but a Reiki practitioner is not called a guru. You see—"

"Get your own boyfriend, Granny," Annie snapped, and Nick and I both stared at her, shocked.

"I'm sorry, okay. I've had a bad day," Annie said sheepishly. "I'm sorry, ma'am," she said to the offended woman, who merely sniffed and said something about certain redheads who clearly needed to have their homeostatic response amplified.

I slumped down in my seat. If we were amplifying home-ostatic responses, it was going to be a long, looong evening.

"You know, Annie, I really should go home and spend time with Lulu. I don't want her to feel like I'm abandoning her after what she's been through," I said hopefully.

Annie scorched a glare at me. "Nice try. She's not home, anyway. Michel and Farren took her to a puppies and guppies party."

"A what?"

"Shhh. Here's the speaker. You know I am *desperate* to learn about agropathic medicine," she said.

"Isn't that allopathic?" Nick asked.

"Whatever," she snapped. "I love it. Now be quiet and listen."

Nick looked a question over at me, and I shrugged. It would be a little hard to explain, "Yeah, she's in a bad mood because she wants me to get you to break up with her, even though I think she really, really likes you."

Plus, that would be breaking the best friend creed: "Never, ever betray your friend in any way, through thought or deed, to some guy." That was one rule I'd never broken, ever. I wasn't about to start now, even if I believed Annie was totally wrong this time.

I snuck a look at Nick and caught the half smile on his face when he looked at Annie. Then I slumped further down in my seat. Teaching the parrot to talk dirty might have been the highlight of my day.

*   *   *

Forty-five minutes later, all three of us were believers.

"Can you believe how nutritionally depleted and toxic our water and food supplies are in this country? We'd be better off starting an organic farm than living here in this cesspool of toxins," Annie exclaimed, as we shuffled down the stairs to the street.

"Yeah, except you don't even like picking up after Lulu. Can you imagine chicken poop? Or cow poop?" I shuddered. "That would be truly nasty."

"I don't know," Nick said, holding the door open for us. (Yeah, I know. He held the door open. Obviously Annie *had* to dump him.)

"I kind of like the idea," he continued. "We had horses when I was a kid, and it wasn't all that bad. Horses only eat healthy stuff like hay and oats, so when they—"

"Stop. It. Right. Now," Annie demanded, hands on hips. "We're talking about the wonders of Reiki, and the creation of optimum well-being. The laying of hands on our bodies, and—"

"I'll volunteer for that last part," Nick said, then his face immediately flushed bright red. "Um, sorry, Annie. Just kidding."

Annie bit her lip, the expression on her face wavering between intrigued and exasperated. "Right. Whatever. Oh, you know, Shane, I forgot I have that thing."

"That thing?" I didn't remember any thing.

She put a hand on my arm and, when Nick wasn't looking, pinched me. "The *thing*, remember?"

"Oh, right, the thing," I said, yanking my arm away from her. I was glad to help out, but it didn't need to involve physical injury, right?

"Nick, Annie has that thing. I haven't had any food since breakfast. Do you have time to get something to eat with me?" I said reluctantly. He was so cute in his ironed jeans and neatly pressed, white button-down shirt, and I was plotting to break his little Boy Scout heart.

He glanced at Annie. "Well, I kind of—"

She smiled at him. "Please go with Shane, Nick. She gets light-headed if she doesn't eat, and I'd be worried about her."

This was actually true, but the glowy smile she was flashing at him made me feel a little nauseous. Either she was a way better actress than I'd ever known, or she had feelings for Nick that *she* didn't even realize.

Hooo, boy.

"Okay, Annie, see you later. You'd better get going to your thing," I said, taking charge of moving things along. "Let's grab something at this deli, okay, Nick?"

Without waiting to see what he did, I headed for the deli. Now that we were talking about food, I realized I really was starving. Either Nick was going to follow along or not. There was only so much I could do in a situation like this.

Liar. You don't want to break them up, my pesky conscience sniped in my ear.

True, but irrelevant. If there were only another way to do it and still make Annie happy . . .

I pushed the door open and breathed in the delicious aroma of cold cuts and macaroni salad.

It's a New York thing.

Chapter 20

I'd already ordered my tuna on whole wheat, extra pickles, by the time Nick trudged into the deli and joined me. "Sandwich?" I asked.

"No, I'm not hungry," he said, spirits and shoulders slumped. "What was the thing?"

"What thing?" I stalled, trying to think of an excuse that would sound credible.

"She's dating somebody else, isn't she? You may as well tell me, Shane. I know Annie is too tenderhearted to hurt me."

I paid for my sandwich and soda, wishing that Nick could be one of the skanky rockers Annie usually brought home. It would have been easy to pull my Breakup Artist act on one of those. Especially that guy named Spiker. Now he was—

"Shane! Quit stalling." Nick gave me one of those "I can see right through you" looks that Gran had been so good at and took my tray out of my hands. "There's a table over there."

Since he was holding my sandwich hostage, I had no choice but to follow him. The three dollars left in my wallet wasn't going to buy me another one. We threaded our way through the narrow space between tables, and I sat down in the chair across from him.

He slid the tray across the table to me. "Well?"

I sighed. "I can't break the best friend creed."

"What's the best friend creed? Oh, God. She is sleeping with some other guy, isn't she?" He put his elbows on the table and dropped his head in his hands, mumbling something I didn't quite catch.

I unwrapped my sandwich and took a huge bite, then waited until my mouth was empty to interrupt. "Excuse me? What are you mumbling? And, no, Annie isn't sleeping with any other guy."

He looked up at me, face wan but hopeful. "No? That's— wait. Is she sleeping with some other girl?"

I blew out a huge sigh. "No, you dolt. She wants—she— I don't, oh, crap."

Nick's expression went from hopeful to filled with dread again. "She doesn't like me, does she? She wants to dump me."

Oh-kay. This is so not going well.

Taking another bite of sandwich, I chewed slowly, trying to think of a good lie. Then I took a long drink of soda.

Then I took another drink of soda.

Finally, I gave up. "Oh, hell. Who needs a best friend creed, anyway? *She* put me in this situation in the first place. Here's the deal: Annie likes you a lot."

"That's great!"

"No, that's bad."

"That's bad?"

"Yeah, that's bad. Because that's why she wants *me* to encourage *you* to break up with *her*," I said, sinking back in my chair. The Reiki thing had been less painful than this.

"Understand?"

He sat there, eyes widening, shaking his head. "Um, no. I don't understand this at all. Does she understand that I'm nuts about her?"

I nodded. "Yes, that's part of the problem. Annie has a history of bad relationships. So she thinks if she gets any more involved with you, she'll hurt you, and you're too nice, and she'll break your heart, and you'll give up your business dream and move back to the cornfields of Iowa."

He blinked. "Nebraska."

"Whatever. You're not tough enough, so she thinks you're too big of a risk," I said, then drained the rest of my soda.

He narrowed his eyes. "I'm not some kind of wimp."

"Nobody said you were, Nick. You're just that complete rarity—a truly nice guy."

"And nice guys finish last."

"So I've heard," I said, wondering about my own nice guy. Would it be rude to check my voicemail to see if Ben had called, when Nick was right here in front of me, suffering?

Probably.

"So, you understand how she feels, right?" I asked, starting to stand up.

"No," he said, folding his arms.

"Okay, well that's—um, no?" I sat back down. "What do you mean, no?"

"No. She likes me, I'm—I'm *damn* well in love with her. She can explain this craziness to me herself," he said, looking mulish.

I bit my lip. "Um, Nick? Don't say *damn* to try to look less nice. It's just too cute coming from you."

He put his head back in his hands. "I'm toast, right?"

Tapping my fingers on the table, I considered him, the beginning of a plan forming. The button-down shirts would have to go, and the ironed jeans (seriously, who irons their jeans?) were history, and he'd have to quit shaving, but . . .

I could do it. I was the Breakup Artist, right? Time for a little reverse engineering.

"Nick? I've got a plan. But you're going to have to become a very, very bad boy."

He looked up at me, puzzled. "What? Why? How?"

I could feel the smug grin sneaking across my face. "Annie will never know what hit her."

"I can't lie to Annie, Shane," he said.

"Fine. Say hello to the cows back in Montana for me," I said, standing back up.

"Nebraska."

"Whatever."

He stopped me with a hand on my arm. "On the other hand, a little white lie never hurt anybody," he said.

I sat back down.

He beamed a brilliant smile at me, and I could see the sweetness in his face that scared Annie so much. With any luck, it would be that same sweetness that would carry their relationship through the next ten or fifty years, or at least through the weeks when Annie was PMSy.

Now *that* was scary.

I leaned forward. "Here's the plan. How do you feel about tattoos?"

Finally home, snuggling with Lulu, whom I'd rescued from Michel's nefarious scheme that involved dressing her up in pink ribbons and painting her nails, I dialed Ben's number.

He answered on the second ring. "Shane, hey. You got my message."

I laughed. "Yes, and you need to quit being so chatty on voicemail. 'Shane. Ben. Call me.' "

"Yeah, I'm not much for voicemail. Sorry. What are you up to tonight?"

I thought about my bizarre evening. "Parrots, Reiki, and makeovers, oddly enough."

"What?"

"It's a long story. How about you?"

"Softball game. We kicked Barclay's butt," he said, sounding very happy about it.

"Who's Barclay?"

Ben laughed, and the rich tones flowed through the phone and tickled something down in my tummy, or maybe lower. "Barclay is the name of my biggest competition for advertising accounts."

I twirled a strand of hair around my finger, smiling. "So you're pretty competitive, are you?"

"Maybe. I try to get what I want," he said.

"Does that include dates?" I teased.

"Usually," he said, but his voice sounded funny, suddenly. Cold. "Except when I have third-party interference."

Lulu picked her head up from where it had been resting on my arm and made a little growling sound.

"It's okay, Lulu," I said, scratching behind her ears to soothe her.

"What's wrong with your dog?" Ben asked.

"Um, this is going to sound weird, but she picks up stress vibes over the phone, I think," I said hesitantly.

"Well, she must growl a lot around you, then," he said, his voice sounding even more stilted.

I sat up straight, wondering what the heck was going on. "Ben? Is there something going on here that I don't know about? Because you seem kinda cranky all of a sudden,"

There was silence for a beat, then he sighed. "No. No, I'm

sorry, Shane. I had a long day, and I guess I'm more tired than I figured. Sorry for sounding like a jerk."

"No problem," I said slowly. "We've all had long days, right?"

"Definitely. So, what are you doing tomorrow?"

It was my turn to sigh. "I have to work all day, then I have to help a friend with . . . unloading some old, unwanted stuff."

Like a hot Italian guy who wants to marry her.

"Oh. Okay. Well, call me if you get a chance. I'd, well, I'd kinda like to see you again," he said, voice warming up.

"Me, too," I said, hugging Lulu till she made a squeaky noise like her stuffed hedgehog makes.

"Soon," he replied. "Let's make it soon, okay?"

"Okay." I was ridiculously cheered up and strangely energized, like the Energizer Bunny on happy pills, as we said good-bye. I picked Lulu up and danced around the room with her. "He likes me, he likes me, he likes likes likes likes *likes* me!"

She sneezed in my face, which is Chihugapoo for "clearly the two of you have a bright future." (Or "my nose is smushed into my face due to some very strange interspecies breeding.") But I liked the first version better, so I was sticking to it.

"La, la, la, la, la, la, la," I sang, and did a little modified Chicken Dance across the floor.

Naturally, that's when Annie walked in the door. She took one glance at us and raised her eyebrows. "Whatever they put in puppy chow, I need to get me some of that."

Lulu's tail started wagging like crazy, and I put her down so she could run over to greet Annie. Annie dropped her backpack near the door and knelt down to hug and pet her for a long few minutes. When Annie finally looked up at me, her eyes were suspiciously red and swollen-looking.

"Are you okay?" I began to cross the room toward her, but she held up her hand to stop me.

"I'm fine. So what happened with Nick?"

I bent down to pick Lulu up. Annie could always tell if I was lying by looking in my eyes. "It was good, actually. I don't think you're going to have to worry about Nick anymore."

"Really?" her voice sharpened. "What did you say?"

"Nothing, really," I said, carrying Lulu back to the couch with me, and trying like crazy to improvise my not fully formed plan. "He mentioned this girl he'd met at grad school, and I may have said that you didn't expect exclusivity."

I snuck a glance back at her, and she was biting her lip and looking uncharacteristically waffly. "What? I mean, really? What girl?"

Shrugging, I petted Lulu some more. "I don't know what girl. Just some girl. Anyway, he seemed relieved about you, so . . . I just think we may have way overestimated the crush he had on you."

Lulu opened one eye and gave me what Gran would have called the hairy eyeball. "Shut up," I whispered.

Annie stood rooted to the same spot. "Oh. That's, well, that's great. Really. It's exactly what I wanted, right?"

Except she didn't sound at all like it was great, which confirmed my suspicions, which meant that I was totally justified in bending the best friend creed to help Nick win her over.

Right?

Lulu growled again, and I glared at her. "Why does the wooden boy get a cricket, and I'm stuck with a mutant sheep?"

"What?" Annie asked from just behind my shoulder.

Oh, crap.

"Nothing. Talking nonsense to my dog, that's all. I'm going to bed now," I said, jumping up off the couch and heading for my room.

I was subterfuged out.

Chapter 21

At Sensuality the next day, I made a vow not to deceive anybody about anything. This vow was tested almost immediately by a trio of college students who came in and asked me if I *adored* the new Body by Boris crop tops as much as they did.

Damn.

"Aren't they unique?" I said, smiling hugely, which was *so* not a lie. They were definitely unique. Uniquely hideous. But I got seven of them out the door with the girls, and another three bottles of the DreamGlow body oil, so I considered it worthwhile misdirection.

And *not* deceitful, I reminded the great karmic force of the universe. Then it occurred to me that I was looking for the karmic smack-down on every corner, like that redneck on the TV show. The warped, Americanized view of Hindu philosophy.

McHinduism. I didn't major in philosophy for nothing.

Rolling my eyes at my silliness, I straightened shelves and dusted until Solstice arrived, face buried in her latte cup. She usually wasn't coherent until at least eleven, but I needed her to handle the front while I unpacked and checked in the new lingerie shipment from W&L.

Plus, it was easier to daydream about Ben while I was alone in the back room, hands full of silks and satins. There was a green chemise that I'd had my eye on in the catalog, and now I might have somebody to wear it for . . .

Or I might be getting way, waaaay ahead of myself, I thought, remembering how he'd gotten a little weird on the phone the night before. What the heck had that bit about third-party intervention, er, interruption—*interference* been about?

I shook my head and started unpacking boxes. I was too busy to worry about it. He wanted me to call. He'd said "soon."

It was all good. "Aha!" I said, pulling out the green chemise and holding it up against my body. It would fit perfectly. And the color was—

"That's a great color on you," Ben said, suddenly standing in the doorway, as if I'd conjured him from silk and lustful thoughts.

I made a weird *urk* sound and stared at him. He leaned against the wall and grinned at me, and there was enough heat in the grin for me to wonder if the air conditioning had gone wonky. Then I realized I was still holding the chemise up against my chest, and I shoved it back in the box, my cheeks burning. "Um, Ben. Hi. Unpacking here. Busy. Very busy. How are you?"

He shrugged, still grinning. "I'm pretty good right now. I loved that green thing."

I blushed again. "It's good to see you, too."

"I thought I'd stop by and see if I could talk you into having me for lunch, since you said you'd be busy tonight," he said.

Um, what?

My brain processed what he'd actually said, rather than what my wishful thinking had translated, and it came out to the more mundane "have lunch with me."

"Shane?"

"Oh. Right. Sorry. I'd love to have you for—I mean, have lunch with you, but unfortunately I can't. I have to sort through all this new merchandise, and Solstice has a dentist appointment at lunchtime," I said, thinking evil thoughts about Solstice and her poor choice of timing for dental health.

Ben looked disappointed, which totally cheered me up. Then he started walking toward me, which freaked me out by an equal amount. For some reason, he made me nervous, in a "butterflies in my tummy" kind of way.

The butterflies were doing a polka by the time he reached me.

"So, Shane Madison," he murmured. "How about a kiss to sustain me on my long trek back to work?"

I smiled and nodded the teensiest bit. Then he leaned down and brushed his lips against mine, in the gentlest of kisses, and my eyes fluttered shut as I waited for more.

And waited.

I opened my eyes and looked up at him. "I wanted to make sure you were seeing me," he said, then he kissed me again. This time it wasn't as gentle, it wasn't as soft, and my body temperature soared up to about a thousand degrees. A minute or two (or an hour or two) later, Solstice's voice shattered the moment.

"Groovy, Shane, but, like, a root canal waits for no kissing. Later."

Feeling a little woozy, I pulled away from Ben and wondered if I had a fever. Surely one kiss wasn't enough to burn through me like that.

His hands dropped away from my arms, and he stepped back, giving me the same dazed expression that I was sure was reflected on my face. "Ah, well. Okay," he said. "Gotta go. I'll call you later," he said hurriedly.

By the time I could think of a reply, he was gone. I stood there, surrounded by boxes, wondering what the heck had just happened.

Wondering why it had felt so good.

Wondering when I could do it again.

I sang along with the radio the rest of the day, even to the stupid songs, which was a clear indicator of WARNING: TROUBLE AHEAD.

If only I'd been paying attention to the warning lights.

Melissa and I roamed around Uptown Babies, looking for exactly the right items. The problem was, I didn't know what that would be. Something that shouted "my eggs are anxious to meet your sperm and make little embryos," except, you know, in a tasteful way. Since the inside of the boutique looked like a nursery rhyme had exploded in it, that was going to present a challenge.

Melissa stopped next to a gorgeous, round baby crib, complete with lace and gingham canopy and bedding. "How about this? It's beautiful," she said, fingering the fabric with a wistful expression on her face.

"I may be nuts, but that looks like an 'oooh, wouldn't this be perfect in the nursery?' expression on your face, Melissa. What happened to super career woman who didn't want to be tied down?"

She dropped the fabric and wiped her hand on her red pencil skirt. "No, it was not. No way. I was just trying to find something to make the statement you talked about. I think the idea is brilliant, by the way. Tony may want to be married, but he certainly doesn't want to start a family this soon."

She wandered over to another crib. "He's told me many times how he wants to work on building the business for several more years before he even thinks about having kids."

I followed her over to an ultramodern, metal spaceship-looking crib. "This must be for those alien babies the tabloids are always talking about. Makes them feel right at home, right?"

She laughed and moved on. I followed her and tried again. "But what about you?"

"What about me, what?" she murmured absently.

"What about when do *you* want to have kids?" Catching sight of possibly the perfect bassinet for our purposes, I stopped walking and waited for her answer.

Her mouth fell open. "What? Me? Kids. No, no, no. I'm way too busy at work to even think about getting pregnant. No mommy track for me. Anyway, I'm paying you a lot of money to help me ensure that the issue doesn't even come up, right?"

I sighed. "Right. Let's head over there, in the corner. I think I see the perfect thing. And I already checked; the store has a thirty-day money-back guarantee."

"Just like you do," she said.

"Just like I do," I agreed, wincing. "Now let's go look at that pink, frilly bassinet. It's perfect."

"Perfect," she echoed, glancing back at the round crib one last time.

Suddenly, I had the feeling that Melissa's biological clock

wasn't quite synchronized with the rest of Melissa. We needed to get the heck out of that store, fast.

Bassinet or no bassinet.

I left the baby store, said good-bye to Melissa and gave her a few last-minute instructions, and headed straight for the leather shop. Nick had nixed the idea of a tattoo, but was willing to go for a little biker chic.

Which, I had to admit, cracked me up. The idea of Nick looking like a Harley-riding bad boy was about as likely as me ever being Lizzie-thin. But I had to start somewhere, right?

By the time I'd walked the eight blocks to Leather Zone, I'd almost quit obsessing over Ben's kiss, having relived it a couple dozen times. I wasn't any closer to figuring out why it had affected me so much, but it definitely made the hot, muggy walk a little steamier.

I hadn't minded one bit.

I walked into the wonderfully cool, air-conditioned store and glanced around for Nick. He wasn't there yet, so I figured I'd browse around for a few things that might help with his new bad-boy image. It's not like he was going to wear a full-on leather jacket in this heat. He was willing to suffer for love, not suffer heatstroke.

I smiled and murmured an "excuse me" as I moved past the tall, dark, and delicious guy standing in front of the biker tees, and wondered if Ben liked to ride motorcycles. Then I almost tripped over my own feet as I whirled around.

"Nick?"

He turned and flashed that sweet grin at me, and I almost fell over. Sweet, sincere, iron-his-blue-jeans Nick was wearing a faded T-shirt, very worn and slightly ripped jeans, and—*oh, holy cow, I'd created a monster*—he had stubble. Five o'clock shadow, or seven o'clock shadow, or whatever the heck time it was.

Standing there with my mouth hanging open, I realized a funny thing about my plotting and planning. "Sometimes it works in *spite* of me," I mumbled.

"What? Surprised?" he said, still grinning.

"Surprised? Nick, you're a hottie!" I shrieked, bringing the clerk lumbering around the corner.

"Is there a problem here?" he asked, flexing tattooed muscles that looked like they could bench press a Jeep.

"No problem, no problem," I hastened to say. "My friend is hot!"

Nick looked pleased and a little hurt all at the same time. "Gee, thanks, Shane. You don't have to look so surprised." He turned to the clerk. "We're fine, sir. Just surprising an old friend," he said.

The clerk nodded and wandered off, and I stared at Nick in total shock. "You might want to lose the 'sir,' if you want your attitude to match that outfit," I said, walking around him and checking out the whole picture.

Annie was toast.

"How'd you do it? Did you just happen to have a whole separate bad-boy wardrobe hanging around the closet? Lose your razor?" I completed my three-sixty, still shaking my head. "You didn't need my help at all."

Nick rolled his eyes. "Yeah, I can borrow my musician roommate's clothes and lay off on the shaving, but I'm still calling store clerks 'sir.' I'm thinking I need your help, Shane."

Choosing one of the less "I was arrested on *COPS* last week" versions of the wallet-and-chain combo, I headed for the counter. "Are you really sure about this, Nick? I can't even believe I'm saying this, but if you have to change who you are for Annie, is she really the girl for you?"

He raised his chin, looking grim. "I'm not changing who I am. I'm opening her eyes, so she can see past the Mr. Nice Guy label she pasted on me to the man inside."

I gave him the head-to-toe once-over. "Oh, she's going to see you now, Nick. No worries there."

A couple of girls wearing Harley-Davidson tank tops and cutoffs walked past us, staring so hard at Nick they almost walked into the leather cell phone cover display.

Nick, being Nick, never even noticed.

Annie was in so much trouble.

Chapter 22

It took two days for Melissa to call me and let me know how the evening had gone with Tony and their new baby bassinet. The plan had been for her to move a large suitcase of her most blatantly female and girly objects into his apartment while he was at work one day. The bassinet would go front and center in the middle of the living room.

Any normal man would have run screaming.

I scooted Lulu over on my bed, so I could retrieve my cell out from under her belly when it rang. "Hello?"

"He didn't run screaming."

"Melissa?"

"He. Didn't. Run. Screaming," she ground out. "You know, like you promised? Like why we put out a hundred bucks for that stupid pink bassinet with the three-hundred-thread-count sheets and the adorable little 'Princess is Sleeping' pillow?" Her voice warmed up during that part about the pillow, strangely enough.

"The bassinet is returnable," I offered, weakly.

Lulu rolled over for a belly rub, and I complied, wondering what could possibly have gone wrong.

"I don't care about the bassinet," she shrieked. "He freaking asked me to freaking move in with him!"

"Oh, this is bad," I said, throwing myself backward on the bed into my pillows. "This is bad. The bassinet didn't weird him out?"

"No! He thought it was *adorable*. That babies with me would be *beautiful*. Why should we wait, anyway? The sooner we get started, the sooner we can have a huge family of bambinos."

She was practically hyperventilating by then, and I wasn't far behind. "This man does not react like any normal guy I've ever known," I said.

"That's because he's *not* normal! He's Italian, you idiot. He's all about love, and integrity, and family," she shouted.

I opened my mouth, then closed it again. Finally, I summoned up the courage to ask, "And this is a problem, *why*?"

"Fine, then *you* marry him," she said, sounding like she was near tears. "I'm too young—my career—I don't want to turn into my mother."

Oh. Wow. Psychiatry R so not Us, but I'm sensing a problem here.

"Does Tony want to marry your mother, or does he want to marry you?" I ventured. "Did he ever say that he expects you to become like your mother?"

"No, it's not—Look. I don't have to explain any of this to you. I hired you to do a job, right? That's what you do, right? Ruin people's lives? So ruin mine, already," she said bitterly.

"But—"

"Either you come up with another idea in the next two days, or give me my money back. Tony wants to take me out to a *special* dinner this weekend, and you know what that means."

"Melissa, I'm sorry. I—"

She cut me off again. "Don't apologize. Just fix it."

Then she hung up, leaving me alone with the sour smell of my regret. Or maybe it was the sour smell of my dog. Either way, life wasn't any bed of roses.

An hour or so later, after I'd bathed Lulu with her new puppy shampoo and conditioner and taken a shower myself, we both smelled better, but my spirits were still in the sewer. Being accused of ruining people's lives put a spin on the Breakup Artist that hit uncomfortably close to what I'd been feeling deep, deep down under the parts of me that (a) needed the money, and, (b) were so proud of myself for my brilliant scheming.

By the time Annie got home from SpinDisc, I'd sunken into a black abyss of a mood. From the way she stomped into the apartment and slammed the door, I was guessing she wasn't much better.

Of course, it was quite possible that *her* bad mood was my fault, too. I closed my eyes and tried to recapture the warm and fuzzy—okay, warm and steamy—feelings from Ben's kiss, but it seemed like it had been days, instead of hours, ago.

Lulu hopped down off my bed and trotted down the hall for Annie, probably hoping for a little attention from somebody more fun than me.

"Not now, Lulu," Annie said, then I heard her steps striding down the hall. She walked into my room and sat on the bed in the spot that Lulu had just vacated.

"My day sucked," we both said at exactly the same moment.

Annie grinned weakly. "Jinx. You owe me a soda."

I waved an arm in the air. "Why not? A soda, a demolished engagement, a parrot to talk smutty. I'll just pull it all out of my butt."

Annie grimaced. "That's a visual I could live without. And what's up with the parrot talking smutty?"

I sighed and flung an arm over my eyes. "It's a long story. What happened with you?"

As if I didn't know. But maybe she got mugged or something, and this wasn't about Nick.

"Nick happened to me," she snapped.

Great.

I didn't say a word, and I certainly wasn't going to move my arm. When Annie can see my eyes, she knows if I'm lying. No way was I going to be telling the truth, so this was safer.

Much safer.

"You would not believe what he wore to work today," she said grimly.

"Go-go boots and a top hat?"

"Very funny. Jeans and a T-shirt," she said, smacking me on the leg.

"Oh, no, not jeans and a T-shirt! To work in a record store! How shocking," I said, trying to sound sarcastic.

"This is serious, Shane. He had on faded Levis and an old T-shirt that fit him like a second skin. Did you know he has serious muscles? He says he works out to burn off the stress from his MBA program. I bet it's all her fault."

I peeked out at her. "All whose fault?"

"That Nicole McDermott. His so-called study group friend from school. She's called for him at the shop a few times," she said glumly.

I moved over so she could lie down on the bed next to me. Lulu hopped up and snuggled in between us, hoping for more belly rubs. We all three stared at the beige paint chipping off my ceiling.

"I need to paint this room," I pointed out.

"He didn't even shave, Shane," Annie moaned. "He was so hot. Why does he have to be Mr. Über Nice and suddenly this amazing hottie? I can't take it. I have to quit my job."

Resisting the urge to roll over and look at her, I tapped my teeth together, thinking. She couldn't quit. That would ruin everything.

"Well, if you can't take it, by all means, quit," I said quietly.

"What do you mean, if I can't take it?"

Lulu lifted her head and looked at us. I avoided her gaze, too.

"I only mean, if your feelings for him are so strong that you can't even bear to be around him, you should quit. Weren't you the one who said he was better off without you?"

Tread lightly here, Shane.

"I didn't necessarily mean that. If he's over me this quick, it wasn't any big deal, right? So why should I quit?"

I held my hands up. "Don't get all huffy with me. I was just saying—"

"Well, *don't* just say. Who asked you?" she snapped. Then she swung her legs off the bed and sat up. "I'm going to bed. I need to quit thinking about Nick and the way his butt looked in those jeans."

I grinned at her back as she headed for the door, then wiped the grin off my face in a hurry when she turned around. "Nice, sweet, corn-fed Nick has a hot butt, does he?"

She sighed. "You have no idea."

I waited till I heard her bedroom door close, then I looked at Lulu. "Oh, believe me. I have an idea."

She wagged her tail and climbed up on my pillow, then promptly fell over sideways and started snoring. I stared at her in disgust. "Sure, it's easy for you. You're fixed."

Although, really, was the world ready for Chihugapoo puppies? Probably not.

Chapter 23

After a fairly quiet day at work and a lunch date with a prospective client (I told her to talk about her ex-boyfriend in lengthy and graphic detail; that always worked, unless the guy she was trying to break up with was a total perv), I stopped on the way home for fresh ingredients for my famous chicken alfredo. Somehow, my brain had misfired enough that I'd invited Ben over for dinner. It had seemed like a good idea four hours ago, when he'd called.

Now I was completely freaking out.

Making dinner for a guy should only occur way later in the relationship time frame. Like *after* you know if he has any food allergies. Or if he hates alfredo sauce. Or if his mother is a world-class cook, and he's going to spend the entire dinner talking about her, until you want to stab him with the shish kabob skewers and send his bloody remains to her house.

Hypothetically speaking.

Yet, here I was, two and a half dates into what I hoped might be a promising relationship, preparing to cook for the man. Thinking back to the night before, I had the sudden feeling that Karma was screwing with me again.

Firmly repressing all paranoidal tendencies, I paid for my purchases and headed for home. Ben would be over in about two hours, and I still had to take a shower, figure out what to wear, and decide how to break the news to Annie, Michel, and Farren that yes, I was cooking, and no, they weren't invited.

Oh, and they had to take Lulu with them. I needed a little time and space; some privacy to get to know Ben. My friends loved me. They would understand.

"So, Ben, why would anybody want to work in advertising?" Michel asked, leaning over the edge of the couch to snarf his fifth baby quiche. I watched the scene through the window from the kitchen, my fingers clenching on the edge of the counter, and vowed to cause each of my so-called friends intense pain and anguish in the very near future. I unclenched my fingers and picked up my veggie-chopping knife.

Annie elbowed me. "He's a hottie, Shane. If Lizzie's Awful Ben had looked anything like *your* Ben, she wouldn't have wanted your help."

"Shut up. Do you want him to hear you?" I whispered, but I didn't stop looking at Ben. In his khaki pants and white shirt, he looked good enough to eat. My panties turned all tingly at the thought.

Focus, Shane, or you'll chop your fingers off.

Annie's eyes widened. "You haven't mentioned your little sideline?"

"No, it hasn't come up. We haven't been seeing each other that long, you know," I said defensively.

She shrugged. "That's a good point. Anyway, it's not like it matters. Even if you two have dozens of dates, you'll end up sad and alone, with nobody but Lulu for company, while Ben screws his way through MBA school."

I dropped my cutting knife and almost amputated my left big toe. "Damn! Annie, what the heck are you talking about? And why do I have the feeling we're not talking about Ben anymore?"

She picked up one of my tomato roses and stuffed half of it in her mouth. After I bent down to retrieve my knife and dumped it in the sink, I smacked her hand. "Back away from the vegetables, and nobody gets hurt."

She bared her teeth at me, but backed away a step. "Nick's bimbo girlfriend stopped by. Nick and Nicole. Isn't that so cute you want to die?"

I kept chopping veggies for the salad. "What do you

mean, Nick's bimbo girlfriend? I thought she was his friend from study group. Really, do you think a lot of bimbos go to the Columbia MBA program?"

"Bimbo, business genius, what do I care? She was really pretty, Shane," Annie said, and I heard the anguish in her voice. "Nice, too. I hate her."

"Okay, I hate her, too, on your behalf, but can I point out that you wanted to break up with Nick?"

She shoved her hands through her curls, until they were sticking straight out from her head in a dozen different directions. "I know. I *know*. I think I may be nuts."

"Hey, speaking of nuts, do you have any?" Farren said, popping his head in the kitchen. "Except none of those pistachios. Who ever thought green nuts were a good idea?"

I whirled on him. "Don't talk to me about nuts, you traitor. I thought I could count on you, at least, to help me have a quiet evening with Ben."

He made kissy noises at me. "Shane, how can you say that? You know how I feel about you, my lovely girl."

"I know how you feel about my chicken alfredo, you Hoover. Get out of the kitchen and rescue Ben from Michel."

Farren glanced out toward the living room, where Ben and Michel were chatting. Lulu was happily ensconced in Ben's lap, blissed out on belly rubs.

"Oddly enough, he's holding his own, even though Michel is being particularly nasty for some reason," Farren said.

Warning bells went off in my mind. "Nasty how?"

"I don't know. He's been bitchy ever since I got home and told him about my day. I think my acting success might be getting to him."

Ben looked over and caught my gaze, and we smiled at each other. For a single second, it was almost as if nobody else were in the room.

Oooh, boy, do I have it bad.

Annie snorted. "What acting success? I love you, Farren, but you've had that job for like five minutes. I think there's more to it than that. Your friendly makeup guy's name didn't happen to come up, did it?"

Farren made a silent O with his lips, realization dawning, and Annie smacked him in the forehead. "You moron. You know how he is."

I picked up my veggie tray and shouldered them both out of the way. "Can we please have a nice evening? You've bullied your way into my dinner date. The least you can do is help me convince Ben that I'm totally hot and the answer to his every fantasy."

Annie snorted out a laugh. "Oh, oh. Shane shaved her legs for this guy. Cute capris, by the way."

I stopped and cast a sultry smile over my shoulder at them. "There was waxing, even."

Farren whistled. "Not-so-awful Ben doesn't stand a chance."

The table looked like a swarm of locusts had hit it, which is a fairly good indicator of a successful dinner party. Ben had eaten two helpings of my chicken alfredo and an enormous piece of pie. The blissful expression on his face when he'd tasted the chocolate mousse pie had reminded me of Lulu in the throes of a good belly rub.

I wondered what Ben would look like if I rubbed *his* belly. *Whoa. Sizzle alert.*

"Why don't we all have coffee?" said Michel.

"Why don't you all go home?" I countered, smiling sweetly.

"I have a better idea," said Annie. "Plus, I *am* home. Why don't you and Ben take Lulu for a walk, and the boys and I will clean up the kitchen."

Michel groaned. "But—"

"That sounds great," Ben cut in smoothly. "Thanks, Annie, guys. I'm sure Lulu needs a walk after eating three times her body weight."

"What? The vet said no table scraps," I said, casting accusatory stares at Annie and Farren.

Farren shot a guilty look at me. "I can't help it, she looks so pitiful."

"She's going to be pitifully fat if you and Annie don't shape up," I warned, standing up from the table. "Come on, chunky girl. Let's go work off some of those noodles."

Ben stood up, too, and carried his dishes to the kitchen. *He's totally hot, and he even has good manners. He must have an insane wife in his basement or something.*

He smiled at me when he came back. "That was amazing, Shane. I don't think I know anybody who can cook like that. Really great."

I snapped Lulu's leash on her collar and stood up, blushing a little. "Thanks. It wasn't a big deal. Homemade alfredo sauce makes all the difference."

As we headed out the door for our walk, I glanced back at my friends and gave them a big thumbs-up sign behind Ben's back. Annie and Farren were making "way to go" gestures, and Michel even smiled. It was huge on the approval scale.

We took the stairs, to get a little extra exercise, in spite of Lulu snorting her displeasure. Two flights down, Ben gave in and picked her up and carried her the rest of the way. From the expression on her face as she snuggled her furry face on his shoulder, he was her new best friend.

My dog, the hedonist: rub her belly, and she was yours for life. Not a bad philosophy, really.

Amazingly, the evening air had cooled off quite a bit from the blast-furnace heat of the day, so it was actually pleasant to stroll down the sidewalk. Also, the stores hadn't put their trash out on the sidewalk yet; bonus points for lack of stinkiness.

We walked and talked about everything and nothing. He was funny and yet—somehow—sane. *Talk about your unusual combination.*

"What's an unusual combination?" Ben asked.

Oops, was that out loud?

"Um, just thinking about the Chihuahua, pug, poodle thing," I said, silently apologizing to Lulu. She was sniffing a discarded sandwich wrapper on the ground, though, and didn't seem to notice me using her for a conversational distraction.

Ben looked at Lulu and shook his head. "She's definitely unique."

So are you.

Before all the blood rushed out of my head, I cast about for something interesting to talk about. "Speaking of unique, have I told you my famous frozen lobster story?" I began, but that's when Ben reached over, took my hand in his, and kept walking.

After the first tingle of shock, I tried to be casual about it; very "hot guys hold my hand all the time." Except for the part where my tongue was stuck to the roof of my mouth, I pulled it off splendidly.

"So what are you thinking about right now?" he asked.

"Trust me, you don't want to know," I said. "I mean, it's kind of a jumble up there right now. I have a lot on my mind."

"Like what? It has to be more interesting than the exciting world of advertising," he said, stopping for a red light.

"Well, I do have this side business, more of a hobby, really, but I'm trying it on as a kind of moonlighting thing," I ventured. Maybe he could give me the guy's perspective on breakups.

Ben stumbled a half step or so and let go of my hand. I looked down, but didn't see any broken sidewalk or tree roots that might have caused it. I reached for his hand again, but he'd pulled a little in front of me and didn't seem to see me.

Lulu stopped to do her business, so we quit walking, both looking anywhere but at her or at each other. (There's just nothing romantic about watching a dog poop when you're on a date.)

Then I did the scooping thing, and we started walking again, but the silence between us had an awkward vibe to it. "Um, Ben? Did you hear me about the side business?"

"Yeah, I mean, no. Side business? Oh, hey, wouldn't that be great for Lulu?" He walked over to a window front that featured a pug merchandise display. "Look at the matching food and water bowls. I think I'll run in and buy them for her."

He rushed into the store, leaving me and Lulu staring at each other. "That was weird, Lulu. He doesn't seem like the 'buy cutesy stuff' type."

She barked one time, which I'd come to translate as agreement.

We watched him through the door as he paid for the bowls, then walked back out to rejoin us on the sidewalk.

"Here you go. It's cheesy, but Lulu might like it."

I took the package from him, filing the incident under "I'll never understand men in a thousand years."

"Thanks. She'll, um, she'll be the envy of all the other Chihugapoos."

His lips quirked up in a half smile. "I bet she will." Then he looked at his watch. "Oh, wow. I didn't realize it was so late. I have a big presentation in the morning, Shane. I really need to get going."

Disappointment hit hard; suddenly my chocolate mousse pie felt sour in my stomach. "I, oh, well, okay. I was hoping we could have coffee or a glass of wine back at my place, since Annie threw out the guys."

For a moment—a tiny moment—the heat I'd seen in his eyes at Sensuality was back, and my insides went all sizzly.

The man plays havoc with my internal organs.

Then he looked away, and when he turned his head back to me, any heat I'd seen had vanished. "Thanks. That sounds great, but I really need to go. I'll catch the train at the end of your block, okay?"

"Sure. Of course. You have to be rested for work, right?" I realized I was babbling and shut up, and we walked the three short blocks back to my place in silence. This time it was definitely an uncomfortable silence. I searched my brain to figure out what had happened to make him go all cold and distant, but drew a blank.

Maybe I hadn't been enthusiastic enough about his gift? "Ben, I really, really appreciate the bowls for Lulu. They're great," I said, trying to put lots of "perky" in my voice.

"Yeah, you're welcome," he said, shoving his hands into his pockets. "Look, Shane, I need to tell you something. I know—"

My cell phone rang, but I ignored it.

Ben stopped talking. "Aren't you going to get that?"

"No, I can call them back, whoever it is," I said.

His mouth twisted a little. "Yeah, it's probably nothing important, right?"

"Ben, what is this about? You said you needed to tell me something?"

But he shook his head, then glanced down at my phone where it was clipped to my pocket. "Go ahead and answer it. I didn't have anything important to say, anyway. See you later, Shane."

Then he turned and strode off toward the train station, not stopping to kiss me. Or even to say good-bye. Lulu and I watched him walk away, at least one of us really confused, as my phone finally quit ringing.

Three seconds later, it rang again. I yanked it off my pocket and flipped it open. *"What?"*

"Shane? This is Brenda. Brenda with the parrot? And you owe me my money back. Not only didn't he want to break up with me, now he's begging me for a three-way with his slimeball friend Travis!"

Another brilliant success for the Breakup Artist. At this rate, I'll be able to buy into Sensuality with my Social Security checks.

Chapter 24

Ben waited for his train, hands stuffed in his pockets, and fought a fierce battle with his own common sense.

I should go back there and talk to her about this stupid Breakup Artist thing. We can have a good laugh about it. Then I can find out if that kiss was a fluke or not.

An ancient man wearing a ragged bathrobe, with a wrinkled face nearly as droopy as Lulu's, shuffled past him, then stopped and held out his hand. "Got a dollar, buddy?"

Ben pulled a few crumpled-up bills out of his loose-change pocket and handed them over, barely looking up. You didn't ride the subway more than twice without encountering at least one or two panhandlers.

The man snatched the money away and hurried off toward the other end of the platform, leaving Ben shaking his head. "Sure. Nobody even says 'thank you' anymore. Or 'please,' or 'you're welcome,' or 'I'm sorry I helped your girlfriend manipulate you into dumping her, because I'm sneaky and underhanded,' " he muttered.

Right. And there he stood, mumbling to himself on a subway platform over this woman. Next thing he knew, he'd be the one wearing his bathrobe out in public and begging for handouts.

Gleason was right. Shane was a heartless deceiver who messed with other people's lives, and the fact . . .

The fact that she had a gorgeous smile, made great dinners and kick-ass pie, and even the fact that her entire face lit up when she laughed at something he said, or something that weird little dog did . . .

Although, he did like the dog. Lulu couldn't help it that she was freaky looking. At least dogs were honest.

Right, dude. Honest. Because the whole "scam her into liking you and then crush her" is so honest on your part. You're Mr. Sincerity.

His train finally arrived and, as he stepped through the open doors, he realized something huge. Honest or not, he still wanted to kiss Shane again. He wanted to see if all her skin was as silky as her arms and legs had looked in that sexy little outfit she'd had on at dinner. He wanted to see her smile, hear her laugh, and feel her tremble against him, while his hands were buried in all that gorgeous hair.

He grabbed a strap to hang on to and took a deep breath, trying to focus on the campaign for Jelly Jam's new line of chocolate cordials.

Focus on how good those chocolates taste.

NOT on how good Shane might taste.

I've got it bad. How's that for honesty?

Chapter 25

RULE 5: *Men don't always react as expected; sometimes you have to throw out the rules and go with your gut.*

Lulu and I walked a little more, but our hearts weren't in it, so we took the elevator back up to the apartment. Neither of us were in the mood for more stairs, without Ben. She stood up on her back legs and put her front paws on my legs—her version of a hug. I petted her head, then thrust the bag with the pug dishes under my arm and picked her up and cuddled her. "I don't understand men, Lulu. I never have, apparently. What business do I have being the Breakup Artist, when I'm totally clueless about what makes them tick?"

She licked the corner of my chin, which was kind of gross,

since she had a bad case of dog breath going on. "We need to get you one of those dog mints, Lou. That's just scary."

The elevator shuddered to a stop, and I trudged down to our apartment, Lulu trotting behind me. We were still ten feet away from the door when shouts of laughter floated down the hall. At least *somebody* was having a good evening.

I pushed the door open, and the sight of Farren, Annie, and Michel dancing around the couch assailed my eyes. "What's going on, guys? The chocolate pie wasn't *that* good," I said, smiling in spite of my teensy bout of self-pity.

Michel jumped over the ottoman and made a dash for me. "I got it, Shane!" he shouted, then grabbed me in a huge hug and swung me around. "I got it, I got it, I got it!"

When he finally put me down, I was dizzy but still unenlightened. "That's wonderful! Got what?"

Farren rounded the edge of the couch and grabbed me in a hug, too. "The audition, Shane. He got the spot in the audition!"

Michel cut in, swinging me around again. "The finalists selected from the audition go on live TV on the *Tomorrow's Designers Today* show! Something like a thousand design students put in portfolios for the chance to be in the audition, but they only selected twenty-five of us."

"That's wonderful, Michel! I'm so happy for you! Wait, did you say *audition*?"

He finally put me down, and we were both out of breath. "Yes, they'll select ten of us from the audition to go on the show. But I'll surely be picked when my odds are one in two and a half, right?"

"Absolutely," Annie said firmly. "Champagne all around."

Michel's smile faded. "We can't exactly afford champagne, remember? There's one little hitch. I need about five thousand dollars to put together my portfolio for the audition. I may have to break down and call Dad. Maybe he finally yanked the board out of his ass."

Annie's mouth dropped open. "You need five thousand dollars? And no way should you call your Dad, you almost needed therapy the last time you two talked."

"Everybody needs five thousand dollars," I muttered. "It's the new nine ninety-nine."

She snapped her head around to pin me with a measuring stare. "What are you talking about?"

"Nothing. Don't worry, Michel. Farren and I have a little surprise for you," I said, heading for the kitchen to see if we had a bottle of champagne in the fridge. "Didn't we have a bottle left over from our celebration when Farren got the soap job?"

"Daytime drama," he called, still dancing with Michel.

"Sorry, daytime drama." I found the bottle and popped the cork with minimal spillage and poured champagne into our plastic glasses emblazoned with HAPPY ST. PATRICK'S DAY for everybody and then handed them around.

"To Michel! May he be bigger than Ralph Lauren!" I said, lifting my glass.

"Bigger than Vera Wang!" Annie added.

"Bigger than Armani!" Farren chimed in.

Lulu barked, dancing around between us.

Michel stood there, beaming, tears rolling down his face, and we clicked our plastic glasses together and drained them. I put an arm around Michel. "Honey, you might want to sit down. Farren and I are going to tell you the story of how we happen to have exactly the amount of money you need for materials, with maybe a few hundred left over to actually, you know, *eat* with."

As Farren blurted out the story of his signing bonus and my advance from Melissa, Michel's eyes got wider and wider, but Annie's eyes got narrower and narrower. Finally, Farren wrapped up the story. Michel sat there, speechless.

Annie, on the other hand, wasn't. Speechless.

"Are you nuts?" she said, jumping out of her chair and stalking over to point a long, bony finger of doom at me. "You can't spend that money. Every single thing you try with Tony and Melissa fails. You're going to have to give her that twenty-five hundred back."

I shrugged. "I'm going to try again," I mumbled.

"Try again? Try what? Everything you try with this man works out exactly the opposite of what you intend!" she yelled.

"Don't yell at me," I yelled back. "Can't you tell I'm trying to help a friend here?"

Michel finally found his voice. "Ah, excuse me. Since I'm the friend you're trying to help, do I get a say in this?"

Annie and I both turned to look at him. "No!"

Farren started laughing, and Lulu ran over to hide behind his legs.

Michel leaned forward. "I know this may sound self-interested, given that I could really use a loan, but have you considered working backward with this guy?"

I glared at him. "I don't need any help with—what do you mean, backward?"

He held both hands out, palms up. "If everything is working out exactly opposite, try a little reverse engineering."

I bit my lip. "What exactly would that involve?"

"Tell me what you've done so far, and let's go from there."

As I outlined my miserable failures at the job site and with the baby bassinet, I realized Annie was right. I had to give Melissa's money back.

"Annie's wrong," Farren said, jumping up and pacing around the room. "You can totally do this, Shane. We know what he wants, so it only follows that we know what he *doesn't* want."

"We do?" I said, feeling stupid.

"Of course we do," Michel said. "He wants a traditional Italian wife and mother for his bambinos, right?"

"It looks like it," I agreed glumly.

Farren plopped down on the couch next to me. "Then we give him a party girl."

"But—wait. Hold the phone," I said, synapses finally firing. "We turn Melissa into a sexy single party girl, and Tony doesn't want her anymore?"

Michel leaned back in the chair and folded his arms, looking smug. "Exactly. He wants *Little House on the Prairie*, we give him *Sex and the City*."

"I almost got cast as one of Carrie's boyfriends, but they said I was too pretty," Farren pointed out, for maybe the hundredth time.

"We know," we all groaned.

Annie nodded. "It could work, Shane. It really could. Why don't you call Melissa and find out if she'd do it?"

I grabbed my phone. "No time like the present, right? This has got to work out better than the parrot." Leaving them all staring after me, I headed out to the fire escape to make the call.

No way was I explaining the parrot.

Chapter 26

The next morning, at Sensuality, I fervently prayed for a peaceful morning. No phone calls, no crises, definitely no new Breakup Artist clients. I'd put a few new appointments on hold until I could resolve the Tony/Melissa issue.

Issue. Nice euphemism for "ruining the poor man's life," a little voice in my brain said.

"Oh, shut up, already," I muttered, then realized that speaking out loud to the voice in my head was a bad sign, on so many levels.

Meandering around the shop, neatening shelves and sipping my latte, my thoughts wandered to Ben and his bizarre departure the night before. It didn't make sense in any way, shape, or form.

But then, this was a man who bought pug dishes.

Too weird.

The chimes on the door rang as it opened, and I summoned up a smile and turned to face my first customer of the day. "Hello, welcome to—Lizzie?"

"Hello, Shawn," she drawled, pulling off her oversized glamour shades. "Is Aunt Estelle here yet?"

"It's Shane," I gritted out.

"Whatever. Is she here or not?" She wandered toward the DreamGlow display, somehow seeming to glide on her four-inch-heeled sandals. It was impressive, even if I did dislike her on an enormous and visceral level. The simple shorts and tank she wore probably had cost twice my monthly salary, I realized with just a tiny twinge of envy.

Must be nice to be built like a fashion model.

Closing my eyes, I sent up a silent prayer for patience. "No, she's not here. She's not due in today at all. I think she has her spa day."

"You do, do you?" She sneered at me as she said it.

"Um, yeah?" I didn't know where her nasty tone was coming from, but I wasn't in the mood for it. "What's wrong, Lizzie?"

She rolled her perfectly made-up eyes. "As if you don't know. I heard all about your sweet little partnership deal, and don't think for one minute you're going to get away with it."

I blinked. "Get away with what?"

Stalking toward me, she tossed her hair away from her face and sneered. "If you have designs on my inheritance, you can forget it, you—you—*clerk.*"

"Designs on your inheritance?" I said, laughing. "Somebody been reading too many gothic novels lately?"

She skidded to a stop in front of the Body by Boris beaded camo minis and pulled the top one off the pile. "Ooh, do you have this in a double zero?"

"I think so, but I'll have to look in the—wait a minute." I'd actually taken a step toward the back, like an idiot. "What? *What?* I'm designing on your inheritance one minute and you want me to look for clothes for you the next? Are you insane?"

She dropped the skirt on the floor and kicked it. "What did you say to me? How dare you!"

"I said, 'Are you insane,' you nutcase. And pick that skirt up off the floor right now." I was shouting by the time I got to "right now," which was, naturally, the exact moment that Mrs. P. chose to walk in the door.

Note to self: never yell at your boss's niece in front of her.

She looked from Lizzie to me, her sharp gaze missing nothing. Then she walked in, bent down, and picked the skirt up off of the floor. As she slowly straightened up, the fluorescent light glinting on her silver curls, Lizzie broke the silence first.

"Did you hear what she said to me, Aunt Estelle? Is this rude woman really the kind of person you trust with our shop, our money, and our customers?"

Lizzie did offended indignation really, really well.

But I was pretty indignant, myself. "*Our* shop? *Our* money? I've never seen you unpack a single box at Sensuality, Lizzie. And if you're implying for one second that Mrs. P. can't trust me with her money, I—"

"Well, if the shoe fits—"

"Stop it. Both of you." Mrs. P.'s voice was quiet, but it sliced through to silence us both.

She turned to her niece and handed Lizzie the skirt. "Please return this to the shelf, and I'd appreciate it if you'd show *our* merchandise a little more respect. That's a five-hundred-dollar skirt you were so cavalierly trampling all over."

Before I could do something childishly stupid, like stick my tongue out at Lizzie, Mrs. P. turned her attention to me. "I must confess that I'm a little shocked at you, Shane. I never expected to hear you speak to my niece this way. You must know that any partnership offer would be contingent on your being able to get along with Lizzie."

Oh, crap.

"Now, why don't we all go to lunch today and work out this personality clash?" she continued, and Lizzie and I shot identical grimaces of utter horror at each other.

Hey, there's something we have in common, just like those two witches in *Wicked*.

Loathing.

"Aunt Estelle, I have a hair appointment at lunch. I can't possibly cancel it; it takes simply months for Vashini to fit you in—especially if you cancel. Then he can get in a snit and refuse to see you again; I'd have to go to someone second-rate; it would be dreadful," she rattled on, breathlessly enumerating the reasons she couldn't *possibly* do lunch with a lowly clerk like me.

The hierarchy of class struggles, alive and well on Madison Avenue.

I stalked out of the room, unwilling to hear any more of her whining. Maybe also unwilling to do any whining of my own. In any event, I had boxes to unpack.

A little quality time with a box cutter was just what I needed.

Chapter 27

"Dude, you're freaking me out," Gleason said, propping his feet on Ben's desk. "You like her, you think she's hot, yada, yada, blah, blah, blah. But then you remember she's a lying snake, and you bolt. Does that about sum it up?"

Ben shook his head and tossed his pen across the desk at his so-called friend. "I don't really need you to go all Dear Abby on me. I had a meltdown. I admit it, let's move on."

Gleason rearranged his nuclear waste yellow tie, eyebrows furrowed. "I don't see the big dilemma. You want to sleep with her, sleep with her. Have a little fun, then dump her," he said, shrugging.

"You know, you surprise me sometimes with your complete and utter lack of moral character," Ben said. "I've known you for five years, but you still manage to surprise me. What does that say about me?"

"You're not very bright?" Gleason offered, smirking. "Seriously, who cares about moral fiber? This chick is the Breakup Artist, correct?"

"Well—"

"She hasn't bothered to tell you about her sneaky little sideline, has she?"

Ben squirmed in his seat. "We haven't actually—"

"Exactly," Gleason interrupted, swinging his legs down and leaning forward to smack the desk. "She doesn't have an honest bone in her body. And said body, as we both know, is hot. So bang her and be done with her."

He stood up. "Now that I've solved your problems for the day, let's get some lunch."

Ben's phone rang, and he waved Gleason out of the office. "Yeah, yeah. I'll meet you in the lobby in ten."

Maybe he's right. Not the bang/dump theory, but that I shouldn't get in any deeper with somebody who clearly lies at the drop of a hat.

Grabbing the phone, he pushed the button for LINE 1. "Good morning, Ben Cameron."

"Hello, Ben Cameron. How are you, Brat?" His sister's voice, full of laughter, came through the line. "You sound all professional and grown-up, Benjy."

"Hey, Fern. How are you? How's my beautiful niece?"

"Ivy is great. She's the smartest one in her class," she said, the pride evident in her tone.

"Naturally, she takes after her mother," Ben said.

"She takes after her uncle, too."

"Oh, so she's the best-looking girl, too?" He teased her, laughing.

"She misses you, Ben. We all do. When are you going to come spend the weekend with us? Boston is not that far of a trip."

He blew out a breath and grinned. "Ah, the nagging portion of the phone call begins. Soon, baby sis. Soon."

"Well, since 'soon' usually means 'at least six months from now,' I have some news. You're going to be an uncle again!"

Ben leaned back in his chair. "Wow! That's . . . wow. Congratulations. I'm so happy for you."

"I'm so happy for me, too. We've been trying for a year, now. I was starting to be afraid it would never happen."

"Oh. So I guess that means you actually have sex with the dork?" he said, squeezing his eyes shut. "Can we stop here? I don't want to hear another word about my baby sister doing the wild thing with the dork monster."

She laughed. "You two graduated high school long enough ago that I'd think you'd have gotten over calling him the dork monster."

"You should hear what he calls me," he protested. "Did you tell Mom and Dad?"

"Of course. They're over the moon. Mom wants to drag me

out baby shopping already. I told her I have enough left over from Ivy to outfit seven babies, but you know how she is."

He nodded. "Yeah, I know how she is. Maybe this will take the pressure off me now. Hey, are you going for another flower name? Maybe Daisy?"

"Always glad to reproduce in order to relieve parental pressure on you, Benjy. And it's a boy," she said. "I need to run and pick up Ivy from dance class, so call me later, okay? Promise?"

"I promise. Since it's a boy, how about Petunia?" He waited till she quit laughing. "And, seriously, I'm so happy for you. For all of you," he said.

After they hung up the phone, he sat and stared at nothing. Another baby. His sister had been married to his best friend from high school for nearly five years, and now they would have two children. His parents had been married for nearly thirty years.

I don't even have a dog.

Thinking of dogs brought Lulu to mind and, before he could waver, he dialed Shane's cell phone. "I miss . . . Lulu," he said when she answered.

She laughed. "She misses you, too. Is there any room for me in this relationship you two are building?"

"Maybe. What are you doing this weekend?"

"I've got a thing Friday, but how about Saturday?"

He smiled, inexplicably feeling happier than he had since the day he got killer seats to the Yankees and they kicked some Red Sox ass. "Saturday would be great. Call me?"

"I will. And, Ben? What happened last night?"

"I'm sorry about that. I'll explain it all this weekend, okay? We need to talk about some stuff," he said, deciding on the spot to get the Breakup Artist issue out on the table, so they could move past it.

"I knew it. You do have an insane wife in your basement, don't you?" she mumbled nearly inaudibly.

"What?" Ben took half a second to wonder if all women were borderline nutcases. "What basement?"

"Never mind. Saturday. Talk to you then, okay?"

"It's a date," he said. Grinning like a fool, he hung up the phone, then looked up to see Gleason standing in the doorway.

"You're going to bang her and dump her?"

"Definitely not. And I don't want to talk about Shane any more, G," Ben said, standing up.

"Dude, you're going down for the third time. Just don't say I didn't warn you."

"Fine. I won't say it. Let's grab some lunch and talk about something else."

"Excellent. Did you see the game last night?"

As they headed toward the elevator, Gleason rambled on about the game, but Ben only listened with half an ear. He was kind of shocked to realize that he'd been thinking about introducing Shane to his sister and the dork monster.

First dog dishes, then family introductions. He was toast.

Chapter 28

RULE 6: Never answer the phone when you're in the middle of a delicate negotiation.

Looking back, my day was a tribute to the soul-deadening power of voicemail.

From Annie:

"Shane, Annie. I asked Nick to get coffee with me after work, and he said no. It's not even a school night! He has never, ever turned me down for anything before. Who does he think he is? Did you know he has biceps to go along with that brilliant brain?" [Sighing voice, possible drool.]

From Michel:

"Michel from *Tomorrow's WORST Designers Today* calling. Shane, I have no chance against these people. The three top students from my class (including me, of course) made it in. I may as well have flushed your money right down the bidet." [Moaning voice, hint of a whine.]

From Melissa:

"We're on, Shane. A dinner party at his aunt's restaurant. But you have to come along as my new best friend. This is your last chance, got it?" [Demanding voice, firm on the "last chance."]

From Farren:

"They're killing me off! They're killing me off! One of the assistants to the head writer told me that the secret twin of the town's doctor's brother's grown child he fathered when he had amnesia is going to run me down with his car after I valet it out of the parking garage!" [Breathless voice, definite shriekage.]

From Nick:

"Shane, um, this is Nick. I said no to Annie, Shane. This playing-hard-to-get thing sucks. I think I hurt her feelings.

Do you think I hurt her feelings? I can't keep this up. You have to call me." [Anxious voice, hint of desperation.]

From the bank guy:

"Ms. Madison, I need to cancel our appointment for Monday. Important executive committee meeting. Please call to reschedule. We need to talk about your credit history, especially." [Stern voice, touch of pomposity.]

With one tiny ray of light thrown in:

From Brenda:

"This is Brenda. Brenda with the parrot? My ex's friend Travis found out about the three-way thing, and he punched my slimeball ex right in the head. There was a black eye and everything! I'm happy, my parrot is happy, and you definitely earned your money. I'm referring you to all my friends!"

Ah, I spoke too soon about the ray of light. If Brenda-with-the-parrot's friends are anything like her, I'm staying far, far away from them. And, seriously, what is up with that parrot?

Chapter 29

"Are you sure you need me for this?" I asked Melissa for the third time, as we took the cab to Tony's aunt's restaurant Friday night. "I mean, Tony knows me as the caterer from the dinner at the job site episode, right? Won't he be suspicious?"

She finished checking her lipstick in her tiny mirror, then snapped the silver-filigreed case shut and turned to me, exasperation evident. "Look, we've been over this. I told him you were a friend who'd agreed to play caterer for me. He's looking forward to meeting you."

"He won't be, after he sees you," I muttered darkly. She was almost wearing a dress the size of a hand towel. The silky teal fabric draped all of Melissa's curves in a way that suggested even more than it revealed. "You look like a trust-fund baby turned stripper."

She flashed a radiant smile at me. "Really? Thanks! That's just the look I was going for. You don't look so bad yourself," she added.

I glanced down at the simple rust-colored sheath dress I'd picked up at a consignment shop, moving a corner of the fabric away from the jagged tear in the cab's vinyl upholstery. The last thing I needed was a snag.

Well, okay, so the way the cabbie was driving, a snag was minor compared to a bloody, bone-crushing death, but I still didn't want the snag.

It *was* a great dress, and it fit me perfectly. "Thanks! So I'll be the best-dressed witness to your drunken spectacle," I said. "This had better work, Melissa. To be perfectly honest, I'm running out of ideas."

She stared at me for a long moment. "You are, aren't you?"

"I am what?"

"You are perfectly honest," she replied. "You tell me when you're out of ideas. You ask me why I want to get rid of a great guy like Tony, even when you desperately need the fee for helping me."

(I'd told her about the boutique and Michel's audition, in a moment of weakness. After all, I knew a great deal about her personal life. It only seemed fair.)

"Nobody's perfectly honest, Melissa. Everybody lies, even

the people who almost never talk to you. They say they love you, and then they leave," I said, staring out the window. "Everybody lies."

"You are very depressing woman," the cabbie said, handing a business card over the top of his seat to me. "Need acupuncture. Go this place, they fix."

I stared at the card, mouth hanging open. Now even cabdrivers were fixing me?

Melissa plucked the card out of his hand. "Thank you very much, that's very nice of you," she said to him. "If you take a left here, then pull in that little nook, we'll be good to go."

He nodded, then yanked the wheel into a screeching left turn that cut off two lanes of traffic. By the time my heart started beating again, he'd slammed to a stop in front of La Cucina.

"I think I'm going to throw up," I said weakly.

"You get needles. Help with vomit problems, too," he said.

I handed him some cash and even remembered to ask for a receipt. Then I followed Melissa out of the cab and up to the door of the restaurant.

I put my hand on her arm when she moved to open the door. "Are you sure about this? Do you really want to get drunk in front of your family?"

She grimaced. "No, I don't. But neither do I want to be forever known as the evil woman who broke Tony's heart. I can live down the party-girl label, especially after I work the sympathy angle when he dumps me."

I shook my head, still unsure. It had seemed like such a good idea when we were drinking champagne, and I was dealing in abstraction instead of the reality of Melissa's life.

Now? Not so much.

She took matters—and the door handle—into her own hands. "We're here, we're doing it, and that's it. It'll be great."

As I followed her into the restaurant, I wondered who she was trying to convince. Me—or herself?

Three hours later, I was a little glassy-eyed from one too many glasses of vino and convinced I wouldn't be able to eat again for days. When I'd mentioned my love of Italian cooking, Tony's aunt had ushered me back to the kitchen to meet everyone. The chef, who happened to be Tony's uncle, gave me a bit of a crash course in northern Italian entrees, and I'd loved every minute of it. I'd even received a standing invitation to come back anytime and eat with the family.

These were quite possibly the nicest people in the entire world. Or at least in Little Italy. It was pretty clear, too, that they loved Melissa like a daughter. Or a daughter-in-law-to-be. Either way, they adored her.

But I understood her reluctance to rush into marriage. I wasn't even the one dating Tony, and I was feeling a tad claustrophobic. Every second sentence out of anybody's mouth seemed to begin with, "When Tony and Melissa get married . . ."

Or, even worse, "When Tony and Melissa have babies . . ."

The shuddering cringe that ran through Melissa every time she heard the words was contagious—now we were cringing in unison. I mean, come *on*. They weren't even engaged yet, and people were discussing which kindergarten teachers would be best for their children.

As I watched, Melissa tossed back the rest of another glass of Merlot, her cheeks sunburn bright. Her smile grew bigger and sharper, until she seemed almost manic.

I figured the meltdown was due any minute.

That's when Tony's grandmother decided to get into the act. Grandma wasn't like any Italian grandmother stereotype I'd ever read about. In her Nikes and spandex running shorts, she was maybe seventy-going-on-fifty, and she wasn't what I'd call maternal.

Grandma dodged around the cluster of admiring men surrounding Melissa and stopped in front of her. "So, this is what you girls wear these days? You think you do my boy proud looking like a five-dollar streetwalker?"

Everybody gasped in unison, and crimson stained Melissa's already flushed cheeks. A slow, sultry smile spread across her face. "Your boy seems to like me just fine," she said, snuggling further under Tony's arm across her shoulder. "Ask him about the other night at his job site, why don't you?"

Gesturing at her dress, Melissa continued. "And I'd have to be at least a five-hundred-dollar streetwalker to afford Nicole Miller, no?"

Tony and Grandma both made weird gurgling noises, and I sat up, wishing I'd had coffee instead of that third glass of wine. Everyone else backed away, like kids in a schoolyard drawing a circle for a brawl.

Grandma may have only been four feet tall, but my money was on her.

Melissa proved me wrong. "I'm not anywhere near ready for marriage, and I wish everyone would get used to that fact," she said, standing up. "Tony is wonderful, and he and I have agreed to enjoy our single years while we still can."

She curled one finger at one of Tony's cousins in a delicate come-hither gesture.

He come-hithered in a hurry.

"So, let's dance, Vittorio," she said, taking his hand and slinking off toward the tiny dance floor near the front of the room, and leaving us all staring after her in varying degrees of shock. I covered my face with one hand, peeking out through my fingers as Melissa started dirty dancing with Vittorio right there in front of Tony's entire family. Grandma let loose with a string of Italian that turned the air smoky.

Tony sat there, speechless, for a long minute. Then he jumped up and headed for the dance floor. You know that expression "fire in his eyes"?

Yeah. Somebody needed to call 911.

The mood was pretty glum in La Cucina by the time, about twenty minutes later, Melissa and Tony quit shouting and making very intriguing hand gestures at each other. Vittorio sat next to me, holding ice to his jaw, trying to talk me into going out with him while keeping a cautious eye on Tony.

After one particularly heated exchange, Melissa stomped off the dance floor and down the aisle toward me. Midway, she stopped and turned around to face Tony. "Fine!" she shouted. "If you can't accept me for who I am, maybe you should rethink what you want."

"Maybe you're not what I want," he shouted back at her. "Maybe we should break it off right now."

It was like stop-action photography. Everyone and everything in the room froze into total stillness, seeming to wait for her response.

I held my breath, our plans and schemes nearly forgotten, somehow wishing she would apologize and they could make it all work out okay.

She turned to look at me, and there was so much sadness mixed in with the relief on her face that I didn't know whether to cry or pump my fist in the air in triumph. Ultimately, I wound up doing neither, merely watching as she took a deep breath, let it out, and responded in a very quiet voice.

"If that's what you want, Tony."

Then she walked in calm and measured steps toward me, took my arm, and—still calm, still silent—we left the restaurant and climbed in the first cab in the queue. On the ride, she didn't say anything for the longest time. Then she finally looked at me, eyes bright and suspiciously damp.

"He's a great guy, but he was suffocating me. The entire family was suffocating me," she said quietly. "We did it, Shane. We did it."

Yeah, but now maybe we both need the needles.

Chapter 30

My alarm clock shrilled at me, and I smacked it hard enough to send it crashing to the floor. Lulu, usually skittish about noises, barely opened one eye before she rolled over and shoved her head under the edge of my pillow.

She and I had spent an hour in Annie's room the night before, trying to help Annie figure out what she wanted to do about Nick.

"I'm so shallow, Shane," Annie kept repeating. "Why do I want him now that he's all hot and dangerous-looking?"

After being ignored for a good fifty minutes while I tried encouraging consolation, I'd finally snapped. "You don't only want him now. You wanted him then. You were just too stupid to go after him, because of your dumb idea that he was too nice for you. Well, guess what? Nice guys can be tough, too."

Lulu had jumped off of my lap and started barking at me, but I hadn't lowered my voice. "Just give him a chance, already. You're going to lose any hope you had with Nick if you don't quit waffling around."

She'd thrown me out of her room, muttering something about having already lost her chance, but I'd been too tired to argue about it anymore. There are only so many hours in the day that I can spend working on other people's love lives, or lack thereof.

I'd like to have at least a few minutes to work on my own.

After a shower, Lulu and I headed out for a quick walk, then back to the apartment for puppy chow (her) and coffee (me). While the coffee brewed, I threw on a denim skirt and peach and cream-colored top, ran a brush through my hair, and contemplated whether or not to bother with makeup that would only melt off before I ever got to the store.

Annie had the day off, so she was sleeping in, and then she planned to take Lulu to the park. For a "free dog," Lulu was living in the lap of luxury these days. I poured my coffee, sat on the couch, and patted my leg so she'd jump up onto my lap. We were both happier if we got in some good cuddle time to start the day.

I planned to work in the morning, then take the afternoon

off to rest, relax, maybe call a few prospective clients, and get ready for my date.

"Finally, Lou," I said to my sheep, "a peaceful day." Lulu barked at me. Not once, not twice, but *seven* times, which means that I should have known better.

I wonder if they ever do segments about psychic dogs on *The View*?

I'd only been at Sensuality an hour or so and was wandering around sketching a new floor layout on a pad of paper when Lizzie showed up. I immediately went into flight or fight response—I could literally feel the adrenaline shooting through my veins. (Or whatever adrenaline shoots through.)

She walked in carrying two large Starbucks cups and held one up as she came through the door.

"Peace offering," she said, smiling, and the expression "Beware of freaks bearing gifts" came to mind.

"Hi, Lizzie," I said cautiously. "You didn't have to do that."

"I know, Shane," she said, putting a slight emphasis on my name, as if she wanted bonus points for finally getting it right. "But I wanted to apologize for how we started off on the wrong foot the other day."

"Mrs. P. making you do it?" I asked, my lips twitching in spite of myself.

She looked sheepish. "Yeah, well. She can be quite convincing when she's on a tear."

I rolled my eyes. "Don't I know it. The whole Awful Ben situation comes to mind."

"What?"

"Never mind," I said hastily. *Ixnay on the Awful enBay.*

"I don't want to fight with you, Lizzie. If we're maybe going to work together, which I won't know until I can reschedule with the bank guy, but . . . we should try to work *together*. If you know what I mean."

She smiled such a beautifully sincere smile that I was instantly suspicious. Call me cynical, but this was quite a turnaround.

"Exactly," she cooed. "Exactly what I was thinking. We should work together. And I have the perfect project."

Uh-oh.

I glanced around the store, wondering what she would want to destroy, er, *change*, first.

"It's Ben," she said.

I stared at her blankly. "It's been what?"

"No, no, it's *Ben*. My Ben. Ben Cameron."

"Ah," I said, understanding dawning. "You know, it's the funniest thing, but I recently met a guy named Ben Cooper. He works—"

"That's nice," she said, waving a hand airily. "But back to my problem, here's the deal. I want Ben back. Since you helped him break up with me, you have to get him back."

I nearly snorted coffee up my nose. "I—er, excuse me? How do you figure that?"

"Well, the money-back guarantee, for one thing. It's satisfaction guaranteed, right? But I'm not satisfied at all. I want Ben back. So you need to fix it or give my money back," she concluded, clearly pleased with her astonishingly faulty logic.

"What? How do you come up with that?" I put the "bribe Shane" latte down on the counter. "The guarantee was that I could get him to break up with you, which I did. Anything beyond that is your problem."

She put her own cup next to mine and then looked at me, smug smile in place. "I don't think so, Shane. Anyway, don't you want me to report back to Aunt Estelle that we're getting along now?"

Evil witch.

I blew out a huge sigh. "Lizzie, even if I wanted to help you, I don't know how. You really did a job on this guy, so why would he want to go out with you again? He probably thinks you're insane, after the giant teddy bear and the flowers."

"I don't care how you do it. Just do it," she said, smirking. Then she pulled a business card out of her pocket. "Here's his phone number. You call him and fix it."

She slapped the card down on the counter. "I'll be sure to tell Aunt Estelle how well we're getting along now. We're practically sisters."

Before I could blurt out even one of the blistering remarks pounding through my brain, she flounced out of the store, leaving me with a pounding headache, *her* coffee cup to throw away, and Awful Ben's business card.

I stood there, clenching and unclenching my fists for at

least a minute and a half, before I finally calmed down enough to throw out the coffee cups and clean up the drops she'd spilled. Then I picked up Awful Ben's card, planning to throw it in the trash on top of the cups. I glanced at it as I strode back over to the trash can, and my steps slowed until I came to a complete standstill in front of the DreamGlow display.

Hyperventilating.

'Cause guess what? Awful Ben Cameron and my Ben Cooper had the exact same phone number.

I should have stayed in bed.

Chapter 31

"What do you mean, Awful Ben is your Ben?" Annie stood in the middle of my bedroom, wearing nothing but T-shirt and panties, waving her hairbrush around like a lethal weapon. "That's not possible. There are, like, a kajillion people in New York. How the heck can Lizzie's Ben be your Ben?"

I moaned and pulled the pillow off of my head. "I don't understand, I don't understand, I don't understand. Why did he say his name was Cooper?"

She flopped down on the end of the bed, narrowly missing Lulu. "Are you sure he said Cooper? I mean, that was the first night you met, right, and you were focused on that Gleason guy."

I stopped moaning and sat up. "Hey! Maybe you're right. I could have heard Cooper when he said Cameron. The bar was really loud that night."

Then I thought about it and threw myself back on my pillows. "No, no, no. Anyway, it doesn't matter. Cooper, Cameron, whatever. How can my Ben be Awful Ben? It's horrible, Annie. It's horrible. It's like suddenly discovering you've been dating Hairy Scary Guy."

She shuddered. "No, nothing could be that bad. What did that vet ever see in him?"

I threw the pillow at her. "I don't care! We're talking about my problems here, not Hairy Scary Guy!"

"You brought him up," she pointed out.

Lulu barked, as if in agreement. I glared at her. "Traitor. Who gave you your stuffed hedgehog, you rotten little sheep?"

She barked again, then licked my hand.

"Too late. You're in the doghouse. Literally," I said, wiping the dog drool onto my blanket. "Annie, what the heck is going on? Can this be some evil scheme cooked up by Lizzie?"

Annie thought about it for a minute, tapping her fingers on her chin. "I'd say yes, but it's too elaborate. Plus, I can't imagine Mrs. P. going along with it."

"It's got to be some hideous coincidence," she added.

"Right. Right. And I'm Miss America," I said. "Look,

there's no way it's a coincidence. I've got to talk to him about it and find out what the truth is."

"Which means you have to admit that, first, you're the Breakup Artist and, second, you made him break up with Lizzie," she said, reaching over and smacking my leg with the hair brush. "That should go over well. You'll be having hot, steamy sex any minute once he knows that."

I moaned again and dragged the pillow back over my head. "I'm never going to have sex again. Karma is delivering the mighty smack-down, and I am destined for a life of icy and barren celibacy."

"Well, as long as you don't overreact," she said dryly. "Are you still going out with him tonight? The fashion show?"

I jumped out of bed. "God, I forgot all about the fashion show. Michel will kill me if I miss his friend's debut. I don't have anything to wear."

As I frantically rummaged in my closet for anything that might be even halfway stylish enough to wear to a fashion show, trying desperately to push the Ben/Awful Ben nightmare out of my mind, Annie laughed at me. "Um, Shane? You know Michel expects us to wear his designs tonight, right?"

Saved by the fashion designer.

Slumping back against my closet door, I stared at Annie, nausea churning through me. "I can't do this. I can't. This is the insane wife in his basement, isn't it?"

Annie, being Annie, never even blinked. "Maybe it is. But if you like him as much as you say you do, burn the damn house down, basement and all. Sometimes you have to go out on a limb."

I raised an eyebrow. "Really? Not to change the subject from my own misery, but is that what you've decided about Nick?"

Annie shifted on the bed and looked down at Lulu. "Did I mention my dad called this week? He and Mom are getting a divorce."

"Again?"

"Yeah," she said, voice bitter. "He's filing the papers, he said. Guess how many times they've filed the papers, Shane?"

I was silent, guessing the question was rhetorical.

"Seventeen times. Seventeen fucking times, Shane. Probably fairly even odds on whether it's Mom or him in the lead on number of filings. They each keep a fucking divorce lawyer on *retainer*."

I knew better than to try to hug or comfort her. We'd been down this road together before. Sixteen times before, I guess. Plus all the bitter battles that never quite came to the paper-filing stage.

"This is going to sound like the worst thing in the world, but I actually envied you when we were little," she said, tears streaming down her face and so much anguish in her voice. "I wished that I were the one whose mom had died, so people would feel sorry for me. I used to think that being a Navy orphan was way better than being the loser kid of a couple of assholes."

I opened my mouth, then closed it again. I'd kind of suspected as much, but she'd never put it into words before. As the long seconds ticked by, I finally had to say something, if only to keep from standing there staring helplessly as my best friend imploded in front of me.

"They're not assholes, Annie," I ventured. "They both love you so much. They loved me, too, or I never would have survived and grown up to be halfway sane."

She clutched Lulu to her chest, and my little Chihugapoo licked the tears off Annie's cheeks. The sight of it earned Lulu steak dinners for the rest of her life.

Annie smiled shakily at Lulu, then scrubbed at her face. "Yeah, they love me. They love you. But they despise each other. So why didn't they just get the damn divorce sixteen filings ago?"

I shook my head, unable to answer with anything that made any kind of sense. Annie gently nudged Lulu off her lap and stood up. "I'm just saying, don't ask me about Nick this week, Shane. Not this week."

She walked out of my room, avoiding my outstretched hand, and by the time I heard her bedroom door close, the tears were streaming down my face, too. Lulu tucked her tail between her legs and whimpered, clearly picking up on the emotion in the room. "It's all right, Lulu," I said, picking her up to pet and cuddle. "Your humans are a little messed up, but somehow it's going to be okay."

She trembled and tried to bury her face under my arm. I thought about Annie and Nick, and then about Lizzie and Awful Ben, and I started to tremble, too.

Chapter 32

Several hours later, I was trembling again, but for entirely different reasons. Annie had begged off going to the fashion show, so Ben and I had gone without her. I'd tried to find a way to bring up Lizzie, or the Ben/Ben issue, or even make a laughing reference to the Breakup Artist. Like, "Hey, this will crack you up. You know your ex-girlfriend?"

But the techno-beat music pounding through the converted warehouse for the fashion show had made conversation impossible. The cab ride hadn't seemed right, either, especially after needles-cabbie guy on my last trip.

So here we were, back at my apartment, and Ben was acting almost as tense and uncomfortable as I felt.

I put my purse on the table, took a deep, steadying breath, and turned to face him. "We have to talk."

He shoved a hand through his hair. "Yeah, I was just about to say the same thing."

Okay, it's not wimping out to let him go first, right?

"You first," we both said at the same time. Then we did the nervous laugh thing.

Ben looked around. "Where's Lulu?"

"She's probably sleeping in with Annie. She likes to have her 'pack' around her when she sleeps," I said, fidgeting with my dress.

Ben scanned my outfit, so slowly and intently that my nipples hardened under the flimsy bra. "I know I said this before, but that is one terrific dress," he said, his voice suddenly husky.

"This old thing?" I grinned and perched on the arm of the couch. "Yes, it's fantastic. It's one of Michel's designs, you know."

The emerald green silk chiffon wrap dress fit me like a dream (which had only taken Michel twenty minutes of alteration, seeing as how I didn't have the figure of a ten-year-old boy, like the fashion models he was designing for). Between the dress and the makeup Annie'd applied for me, my eyes looked greener than they ever had, smoky and mysterious, and I even had cheekbones.

"Really?" Ben asked. "That dress is way better than any of the stuff we saw at that show tonight."

"I think so, too, which is why we're so excited for Michel's chances on the design show." I twisted my hands together and bit my lip, wanting but dreading what I needed to say.

"Ben, I have to . . . there's something I have to tell you about," I began.

"Yeah, me, too," he said, stepping closer to me and taking my hands in both of his. I looked up at him and tried to memorize every feature of his face, in case it was the last time I'd ever be close to him.

Large-scale deception tends to put a damper on many relationships. Or so I've heard.

He looked into my eyes and groaned. "You can't look at me like that and expect me to do this with any kind of rational thought," he said.

"Look at you like what?" I asked, almost whispering.

"Like you're devouring me with your eyes," he said, then dropped a gentle kiss on my forehead. "Like you want to be close to me," he added, then lifted a hand to stroke my hair.

I trembled, yet again, and he couldn't help but feel it. He smiled at me—a smile mixed with equal parts triumph and trepidation—and then he bent his head to mine. "Shane?" he whispered against my lips.

"Mmm hmmm?"

"Can we talk later? I have a major need to be kissing you right now."

I stood up and slid my arms around his neck. "I think that's a wonderful idea," I said.

If you sleep with him, you'll regret it in the morning, my conscience niggled.

If I don't sleep with him, I may regret it for the next ten years.

Ben threaded his fingers through my hair and seared me clear through to my toes with a sizzler of a kiss. By the time he lifted his head, I was leaning against him, knees weak.

"My bedroom is this way," I whispered.

My conscience never said another word all night.

It was still dark when a buzzing noise woke me up. I looked around, bleary-eyed, and realized I was sleeping horizontally across the bed, Ben's legs draped over mine and his arm around my shoulder. Peering at the clock, I blinked a couple of times. Four-fifteen? In the *morning*?

So we'd had, what? An hour's sleep?

What felt like a serious version of perma-grin spread across my face. The man had stamina.

But the buzzing continued. It wasn't one of my gadgets. I nudged Ben. "Hey."

He grunted and pulled me closer, which was a wonderful reaction but didn't solve the immediate problem. "Ben, wake up. Is that buzzing something of yours?"

He opened one eye, then the other, and an amazingly satisfied-looking smile spread across his face. "Hey, you. Kiss me."

"But—"

His lips cut off what I'd been about to say (not that I minded). But a minute or two later, I came up for air and the buzz was still buzzing. "Ben?"

"What? Oh, yeah. It must be my phone." He pulled away from me, trailing a hand across my back, which gave me a delicious case of the shivers. He stood and walked over to pick up his pants, giving me a magnificent view of a seriously fine butt. "Who would be calling in the middle of the night?"

Glancing at the screen display, the smile faded from his face, and he flipped the phone open. "What's wrong?"

I watched as he clenched his other hand into a fist. "Oh, damn. Oh, man. I'm so sorry. How is she?"

I sat up, pulling the sheet around me. From the tone of his voice, something was very wrong.

He nodded, then shoved his hand through his hair. "Yeah, of course. Is Mom there? She won't? All right. Yeah, I'm on my way right now. Hang in there, man. I'm just so damn sorry."

"Yeah, see you soon."

He hung up, then stood there, eyes squeezed shut, clutching the phone as if it were a lifeline.

"What is it? I'm guessing it's your family?" I asked hesitantly.

He looked at me, eyes widening almost as if he'd forgotten I was there. "Yeah, yeah. It's bad."

Putting the phone down, he grabbed his pants and pulled them on, then yanked his shirt over his head, but didn't say anything else.

He doesn't want to talk about his family with you, or it's just personal stuff. Either way, I should leave it alone.

"Is—is there anything I can do?" I asked.

"No. No, but thanks. It's my sister. She lost the baby," he said roughly, his eyes tortured. "She won't talk to anyone. Not the doctors, not Mom, not even her husband. He said she's bad. They're really worried about her."

I climbed out of bed and looked for some shorts to throw on. "I'll go with you to the airport, if you want."

He shook his head, shoving his feet into his shoes. "No, I'll take the train. It's actually faster. Somebody will pick me up at the station and take me to the hospital."

"Sure. Of course. If you need anything, let me know, okay?" I bit my lip, feeling helpless but not knowing what to do.

He stopped frantically throwing his clothes on and looked at me. "Hey, I'm sorry. This is not how I'd planned to spend our first morning together, Shane."

I held up my hands. "No, don't be silly. Go. Be with your sister. I know they don't know me, but please extend my condolences. I'll keep your sister and the baby in my prayers."

He hugged me tightly. Then he took my face in his hands and looked at me. "This was wonderful. Last night, you . . . you were wonderful."

I reached up to hold his hands. "You were pretty terrific yourself, buddy. Now go. Call me if you get a chance and let me know how she is, but don't worry if you don't have time. Just take care of your sister."

Nodding, he pressed an all-too-brief kiss on my lips and walked away. But he paused at my bedroom doorway and turned to look back at me. "Shane, there's still something I need to talk to you about. When I get back, okay?"

"Sure. Me, too. But go. We can talk about it all later," I said, making shooing motions with my hands.

For several minutes after he left, I stood rooted in place, hating myself pretty hard because deep down, mixed in with my genuine sorrow and sympathy for his sister and her family, was the tiniest glimmer of relief.

Chapter 33

By Tuesday morning, I was pretty worried because I still hadn't heard from Ben, but I had bigger loan officers to fry. Or, you know, sort of.

The fish in question stared down his nose at me across about an acre of gleaming desk top. A single sheet of paper, precisely centered, lay between us.

One damning sheet of paper.

"You understand that it's a question of your credit score," he said, his condescension frosting his voice and my butt.

Shoving my hair back from my face, I frowned. I really *didn't* understand. "No, I don't understand. How can I have a bad credit report when I've never used credit cards or any kind of credit?"

He nodded. "That's exactly it. You haven't built up any credit history that tells us you would be a responsible borrower. Your rent is always on time to your apartment, and that's commendable, but no student loans, no consumer loans, no credit cards."

He paused and frowned at me. "It's just not *natural*."

"I like to pay my bills, and I don't earn enough money to go into debt," I said, quite reasonably, I felt.

He pounced. "So how will you pay back this loan?"

"Well, I'll be a partner in the business. So I'll make more money. Didn't Mrs. P. explain this part to you?" I was confused. I thought the whole point of me going to her banker was that he would understand the situation.

Unfortunately, his understanding seemed to be working against me.

I tried again. "I have the new business, too," I said, rummaging around in my purse. "Here is one of my business cards."

See, business cards and everything. Serious businesswoman alert! Must give loan.

"Ah, yes," he said, taking the card between the tips of two fingers as if avian flu spores dusted the edges. "I'm sorry, but as I've said at least twice now, a start-up business breaking up relationships is not what we consider collateral, young lady," he said, mouth flattening and voice taking on a grim edge.

"But—"

"Really, I've spent far too much time on this already. I suggest you discuss another form of financing with Estelle if you really want to do this, although I must admit that I believe it is not in her best interest to enter into any kind of partnership with you."

Before I could say another word, he stood up and held out his hand. Almost dazed at the speed with which he'd crushed all of my hopes, I stood up and automatically shook his hand.

I might've felt better if I'd punched him.

As I walked down the street, battered and bruised, it occurred to me to check my cell for messages. Maybe at least Ben was back and could console me.

The screen flashed that I had four messages. I dialed into voicemail.

From Annie:

"Shane, Annie. I think Lulu might be sick. She yarked up her breakfast all over your new Nine West sandals."
She better be sick. I loved those shoes.

From Michel:

"It's Michel. I can't believe it! I caught him! I went to the set to surprise Farren, before his character gets killed, and I caught him with that makeup person." There was a sobbing sound, and then: "I cannot create when my heart is crushed beneath the very shoes that I bought him. I'm pulling out of the competition. I know you loaned me the money. I'll find some way to pay you back."

From Nick:

"Shane, I can't keep lying to Annie. I hate it. I can't hurt her. I have to tell her about this stupid scheme to make her notice me. If she doesn't like me for who I am, well, too bad for her. Plus, this stubble itches."

From Farren:

"I can't believe it! After all we've been through, Michel didn't even give me a chance to explain. The makeup guy was only hugging me because I just found out that my character isn't going to be killed off at all. I'm secretly the long-lost grandson of the town matriarch. Shane, I've finally got a real job!"

From Farren (again):

"Anyway, I still can't believe Michel. It's a question of trust, and if he doesn't trust me, he doesn't deserve me. I can't be his enabler for this stupid jealousy any longer."

I snapped my phone shut and kept walking, wondering

why the world was suddenly self-destructing around me. Then I called Hairy Scary Guy's ex, the vet, and arranged to bring Lulu in right away.

At least I could take care of my dog.

Chapter 34

"I can't believe Barclay kicked our butts in the play-offs," Gleason said glumly, staring into his beer mug.

Ben nodded, not even pretending to care, barely hearing the raucous noise of the sports bar all around him. He'd played the game in a half-assed way, only waking up when he was at bat. Then he'd slammed the hell out of the ball.

Channeling aggression, much?

Gleason looked over at him and slid the bowl of bar peanuts his way. "Hey, man. I wanted to tell you again how sorry I am about Fern and the baby. That's rough."

"Yeah, thanks. She's doing a little better. She finally let me coax her into eating something and started talking to the family again," he said, shaking his head. "She had this crazy idea that it was her fault."

"What? The miscarriage? I thought those were pretty much nature's way of saying something wasn't quite right?"

Ben nodded to the bartender, holding up two fingers. "Yeah, that's what her doctor says. But Fern went for her usual two-mile run, so she's blaming herself, even though the doctors all told her it was perfectly safe to run clear up until the third trimester."

Ben drained his third beer and wiped his mouth with his hand. "They tried so hard for that baby, and found out they were giving Ivy a little brother, and—well," he stopped, voice cracking.

Gleason clapped him on the back, then sat in silence. The opening bars of the Rolling Stones not getting any satisfaction pounded through the speakers overhead, and Ben barked out a laugh. *Yeah? Well, nobody gets any satisfaction these days. Babies die, men fall for lying women, we even lose at softball. Join the freaking crowd, Jagger.*

Ben got himself under control, then pulled some cash out of his wallet. "I feel like getting a sloppy drunk on, G. You up for shoveling me in a cab in a few hours?"

Gleason laughed, then his eyes narrowed, and he pointed across the bar toward the door. "I'm not. But she might be."

Ben swiveled on his stool in time to see Lizzie, dressed to kill in a minidress and high heels, heading straight for him. He groaned. "Man, I'm screwed."

"Not yet, but you might be." Gleason snickered. "Play your cards right, and you just might be."

Chapter 35

Lulu and I sat on the brandy-colored divan (Michel wouldn't have anything as mundane as a *couch* in his apartment) and tried to talk sense into him. So far, we weren't having much luck.

"Don't let your dog shed on my furniture, Shane. My life is utterly ruined; the only thing I have left is my good taste in classical furnishings," he said, handing me a coaster for my glass of water.

"Hey, be nice to my dog. She just got back from the vet, who poked and prodded her in very unpleasant places," I said, hugging Lulu protectively. "She had a tummy ache."

Michel quit stomping around and looked at Lulu. "Is she okay?"

"Yeah, she's fine, but all the rich, people food has got to stop. The vet said it can really make her sick. This time we were lucky, it was just a little constipation," I said, trying not to think about what was going to happen when that medicine took effect. *Euwww.*

I leaned back on the pillows. "Anyway, speaking of your classical furnishings, it's good that you have at least one virtue to fall back on," I said dryly. "What's this fabric on the pillows, anyway? It's gorgeous. Are these new?"

He yanked it out of my hand. "Definitely do not get that near the dog. Those are handmade Jacquard loomed brocade," he said, glaring at me as though I were about to use them for a chew toy or something.

"Oooh, fancy. Is that sort of like polyester?" I asked, giving him wide eyes and my innocent face.

"No, it is not like polyester," he moaned. "But of course you knew that, and this is your lame attempt to jolly me out of my fury with Farren."

I turned serious, fast. "Look, you idiot. You know Farren loves you. He called and explained everything. The makeup guy was only congratulating him on landing a permanent part. They're going to make his role into the grandson of somebody important on the show."

Lulu wagged her tail, sending thousands of dog hairs floating across the divan. I hastily brushed them off, hoping Michel hadn't noticed.

From the grim set of his mouth, he had. But he didn't say anything. Just clamped his mouth shut like a mutinous child.

Frankly, it ticked me off. "Wait a minute. Don't you have something to say? Like, 'I'm sorry I overreacted, Farren'? Or 'I was a buffoon; congratulations on your dream coming true, Farren'?"

Giving me a truly evil look, he snorted. "Yes, how about 'I'm sorry you're such an ass you told the freaking MAKEUP GUY about your role before you told ME'?" He was shouting by the end of the sentence, face red.

It wasn't pretty, and "not pretty" is awfully hard for Michel to do, so I knew how serious it was. I decided to work the *sane* side of the equation.

"You want me to what?" Farren yelled, pacing back and forth in my tiny living room, still wearing his cheesy parking valet costume from work. It was totally unfair that he looked so adorable in it. No wonder the makeup dude was hot for him.

"You want *me* to apologize to *him*, when he's the one whose unreasonable jealousy embarrassed me at work and showed a complete lack of trust and faith in me?"

Lulu and I looked at each other, then back at Farren. "Well, sure, if you put it that way, it sounds bad."

"What other way is there to put it? And I bet he was mean to Lulu about dog hair, wasn't he? I want to get a dog just

like her. How can I ever get a dog, if he's so anal about a little dog hair? Huh? Answer me that," he demanded.

"You want a dog just like Lulu? I'm not sure they *make*
dogs just like Lulu," I said, tilting my head and staring at my
mutant sheep.

"That's not the point, Shane, and you know it. Quit trying to oh-so-cleverly distract me."

"He called me clever," I whispered to Lulu.

Farren glared at me. "Hello? We're talking about me,
here?"

I sighed. "I know, and I'm sorry. I'm a little worn out
from trying to reason with the two of you. Is there anything
I can say that will help?"

"Yes. You can invite me to stay here with you until he
apologizes."

"Fine," I said, standing up to find Lulu's leash. "But I can
tell we're going to need more wine. Since you're my new
houseguest, you can come along and I'll tell you all about
how I don't have a chance in hell of getting a bank loan. And
how you are never, ever to feed Lulu people food again."

I stopped, mentally counting off disasters. "Oh, I almost
forgot—and about how Awful Ben is really my Ben."

"WHAT?"

I winced. "You don't need to shout. And, yeah, no business, no future, doggie constipation, and Lizzie's Awful Ben
is somehow now my Awful Ben."

Clipping Lulu's leash to her collar, I shook my head. "You

and Michel think *you* have problems. Welcome to my world."

Farren just stood there, mouth hanging open. "But, but, but . . ."

"Let's go. Wine first, whine with an *H* later." I opened the door, sneaking a glance at my cell phone. No messages.

"Lots of whine with an *H*, I'm guessing."

A couple of hours and a bottle of wine later, Farren had talked me into calling Ben. "Look, he's going through a tough time. He'd probably appreciate the call. A little support never comes amiss, right?"

"First, I don't want to bother him," I said, scooting Lulu off my lap. "Second, who says 'amiss'?"

"Oh, for heaven's sake, Shane, dial the damn phone."

Shocked into compliance by Farren's use of the *D* word, I dialed my damn phone. But I wasn't calling his cell; if he didn't answer his home phone, I'd wait till he called me. The last thing I wanted to do was interrupt a family crisis. Ben's number rang three times, then he finally picked up. "Hello?"

I stared at my phone, speechless. Because that wasn't Ben's voice. It was some woman's.

Wait. Family crisis, remember? Maybe it's his sister.

"Um, is Ben there?" I asked, twisting my fingers into Lulu's curly fur. She looked up and growled, which startled me so much I jerked my hand away.

The woman laughed, and it didn't sound like a very sisterly laugh. "Ben isn't available right now. He's taking a shower, and then I plan to help him get very dirty again, if you know what I mean."

Definitely not his sister.

Slowly, without saying another word, I closed my phone and tossed it on the couch. Lulu kept growling, but it wasn't me she was growling at. It was the phone.

Farren looked at my face, then at Lulu, and handed the bottle of wine to me. "You know, there's something curious about that dog."

I poured the rest of the bottle in my glass. "You have no idea."

Chapter 36

I think the whole "cry yourself to sleep" concept is an urban legend or an old wives' tale or something. Because I cried until I didn't have any tears left, and it didn't put me anywhere close to sleep. It did, however, give me a pounding headache. I tiptoed into the kitchen to find the pain relievers, trying not to wake up Farren.

When I opened the fridge just a skinch to snag a bottle of water, the apartment door crashed open. I jumped about a foot, the open bottle of Tylenol flew in the air, raining pills everywhere, and Farren yelled something incoherent, all at the same time.

Annie stood in the doorway, framed in the light from the hallway, and from the looks of it she was steaming mad. I bent down to pick up the medicine, before Lulu could decide it was doggie candy and eat it. "Have a bad night?" I called. "Did Nick tick you off again?"

She stormed into the kitchen. "Funny you should ask, Shane. Or should I call you Your Worship?"

Tossing the last of the pills in the trash, I stood up staring stupidly at her out of my swollen, bleary eyes. "What are you talking about?"

"You know, Your Worship. Or Your Holiness. Or whatever people are calling the Supreme Being these days," she snapped, leaning against the kitchen wall.

Farren sat up on the couch and peered at us through the window. "Um, what's going on?"

"Shut up and stay out of this, Farren," she said bitterly, tossing her purse on the kitchen counter. "Shane was just getting ready to explain how the hell she thinks she can play God with her friends' lives."

The light dawned in my fuzzy brain. "Nick told you."

"Yes, Nick told me. *Nick* told me. You didn't tell me. Not that there should have been anything for you to tell," she shouted, slamming her hand on the counter for emphasis.

My shoulders slumped and my heart sank down to about my toes. "Oh, Annie, I'm sorry. I only wanted to help—"

"By going behind my back to play me like one of your clients?" Her eyes glittered with anger, and hurt, and unshed tears. "I feel like such a fool, and you did it to me. You and

Nick. Well, guess what? I dumped him. And now I'm dumping you."

Farren had walked over to the kitchen doorway by then, and he put a hand on her shoulder. "Annie, listen—"

"No," she said, whirling around and yanking his hand off her shoulder. "I don't have to listen to anything. Since you seem to be camping on our couch, feel free to sleep in my room. I'm moving in with Michel until I can find another apartment."

I held my arms out at my sides, pleading. "Annie, that's ridiculous. This is a simple misunderstanding. I only wanted—"

She cut me off. "You only wanted? *You* only wanted? This wasn't about you, Shane. This was about me. But you let me down. You betrayed me; you betrayed the best friend creed. We're through."

Snatching her purse off the counter, she shouldered her way past Farren and slammed her way out of the apartment. All I could do was stand there, tears rolling down my face and heart shattering, as the one person I'd always been able to trust walked out of my life.

A tiny, pitiful noise made me lift my head and look around. There, in the corner, shivering and whimpering, huddled my poor dog. "Poor Lulu. You were almost better off homeless, weren't you?"

As I watched, the combination of emotional upset and the medicine must have hit in full force. Poor Lulu whined and hunched over right there on the floor. In a single day, life had shit on me both figuratively and literally.

How's that for irony?

Chapter 37

At Sensuality the next day, I waited on customers in a daze. Lizzie's worries about "her" store and "her" money might have been justified right then; as I watched a couple of women walk out the door with their purchases, I realized I had no memory of ringing them up.

None.

My heart seemed to be missing every third beat. *Can you develop a heart murmur at my age?*

Annie wouldn't even speak to me before I left for work. She wouldn't let Michel open the door when she heard my voice in the hall. I'd cried a little bit in the elevator, until

Lulu's whimpering had snapped me out of my self-pity. The last thing she needed was more stress, poor furry baby. Her intestinal issues had kept both of us up most of the night.

I made a mental note to call the vet and check on Lulu at lunchtime. She was hanging out there for the day, so they could keep an eye on her and make sure she didn't get dehydrated. For some reason, seeing Lulu sick had been the final straw in my mental stress overload. I'd cried so hard for so long all night that I'd almost asked the vet to check me for dehydration, too.

Instead, I picked up a couple of giant bottles of Evian water on the way to work and spent the morning sipping. Stacking more DreamGlow on the surprisingly diminished display and sipping water. Monotonous but well-hydrated work that somehow kept my brain from an endless loop of mind-fucking.

A woman had answered his phone. He'd been "getting dirty" with a woman. *Another* woman. A woman who was *so* not me. I mean, we'd never gotten to the point where we'd even begun to discuss exclusivity, but I kind of expected that a guy wouldn't be "getting dirty" with some skanky ho mere days after making love to me.

The store phone rang, and I headed over to answer it, not really rushing. I wasn't much in the mood to chitchat with customers or anyone else. I still had to tell Mrs. P. that the bank had rejected my loan application, and that was a conversation I was dreading.

Karma was smashing my philosophy of "all control, all the time."

All to hell.

"Sensuality, may I help you?"

"I knew it!" the voice on the other end of the phone shrieked. Wincing, I held the phone away from my now-tender eardrum.

"Um, excuse me? Are you calling for Sensuality?"

"No, you bitch. I'm calling for the low-rent schemer who went after my boyfriend," she said. But somehow, I was hearing her in stereo. In my ear, and . . . in the back room?

I whirled around just in time to see Lizzie storming out of the back room, cell phone in hand. She pointed at me, still yelling. "You! I knew it was you. What the hell were you doing calling Ben's apartment?"

"What? I—I—you?" I dropped the phone on the carpet and didn't bother to pick it up. "You? What were you doing at Ben's? And what do you mean *boyfriend*?" I asked, stomach roiling around even worse than it had on that all-you-can-eat burrito day experience.

She slammed her razor-thin phone on the counter. "He said Shane. How many Shanes can be running around? Stupid name. You used me to get to him, didn't you?"

I threw my hands in the air. "Yes, Lizzie. That's exactly right. I somehow tampered with your brain to make you call me in the first place and hire me to help force Ben to break up with you."

I crossed my arms and smiled at her. "Wow, all those years of mind-control correspondence courses finally paid off."

She blinked, looking baffled for a moment, then tossed

Alesia Holliday

her hair and sneered at me. "Whatever. Don't try to confuse me with your mind-control nonsense."

"What?"

"Shut up! I'm talking! I'll never work with you. I'm telling Aunt Estelle on you. You can't steal your boss's niece's boyfriend and expect to get a partnership, all happy crappy," she yelled, eyes wild.

Happy crappy?

"Are you on drugs? First, you dumped him! Second, you were the one 'getting dirty' with him, not me," I said, bitterness oozing from every pore of my body. "So it looks like you won, anyway, right? What do you care?"

Before she could say anything else, the door chimes rang and—who else?—Mrs. P. walked in. She pinned each of us in turn with a hard stare, then walked to the counter and stopped. "What is it this time? I thought you two were going to try to get along?"

I vaguely heard the door chimes behind me, but none of us bothered to look. It wasn't like either Lizzie or I were interested in actually making any money for the business we supposedly both wanted.

And I didn't get the loan, anyway.

"Your niece seems to think I'm trying to steal her boyfriend. Except he's not her boyfriend. She didn't want him, remember? She paid me five hundred dollars to get rid of him."

The last voice I expected to hear at that time, at that place, spoke up from behind me. "That's all I was worth? Five hundred bucks? I wondered about that."

Lizzie looked over my shoulder, eyes widening in shock. I stood, frozen, somehow wishing that if I didn't turn around, Ben wouldn't really be there.

Listening to us fight over him like some pathetic losers on reality TV.

Listening to my self-esteem go swishing down the toilet like the contents of Lulu's stomach.

An adult would have stayed to discuss things in a mature fashion. I walked through the doorway to the back room, straight to the emergency exit door, and right through it to the alley.

Maturity was so beyond me right then.

Unfortunately, I hadn't made it a dozen steps down the alley before I heard running steps behind me. "Shane! Shane, wait up. We seriously need to talk," Ben called out.

I kept walking, hoping he would go away.

He didn't. When he caught up to me, he grabbed my arm. "Wait up, please. Please, Shane."

The second "please" got to me, and I stopped, but I never raised my gaze from my shoes. I'd listen to him, but nobody said I had to look at his cheating face.

It wasn't just the part where he'd been with somebody else that was doing a slice-and-dice on my emotions. It was the extra added dollop of hideousness that it had been Lizzie. The Park Avenue princess. The snooty toothpick who had everything I'd wanted all my life: an extensive family who (somehow!) loved her, enough money that she didn't have to scrape and save and eat Ramen noodles in order to afford shoes, and the partnership in the business I'd worked so hard to help build.

On top of that, she had not-so-Awful Ben. At least I didn't have any more tears left to cry, even ones of abject humiliation.

Or so I hoped.

"Shane, you have to listen to me. I'm sorry I didn't tell you," he said, leaning down to try to peer into my face.

"You *did* sleep with her! Oh, God, just kill me now," I moaned, forgetting to keep from making eye contact with him. "You really *are* Awful Ben!"

"What?" he said, grimacing. "Why would I want to sleep with Lizzie? The woman is psychotic. And, more than that, why would I want to sleep with anybody else after I'd been with you?"

Those tears? Yeah, I was wrong. They started up again. "Really?" I sniffled. "But, you didn't call. Then she was at your apartment. And she said—"

"Yeah, I know. But, trust me, there was nothing going on between me and Lizzie. She showed up at the bar—"

"You were at a bar?" I crossed my arms. "What about your sister? Is she okay?"

He looked sheepish. "Yeah, sorry. I should have called you. It was really rough, and I needed to get my head on straight. Then I only got back in town about an hour before our play-off game, and we went out to drown our sorrows after—anyway, this is stupid." He looked around. "And we're standing in a stinky alley. Can we at least walk together?"

I nodded, feeling numb, and walked with him toward the street. "I'm glad your sister is okay. I've had friends who— well, anyway, I know how hard it is."

He nodded, face grim. "Yeah, we finally talked her into seeing a grief counselor. She needs to get past blaming herself. But her husband is great, and Mom and Dad live nearby, and they're all really close. So I'm hopeful that she'll get through it okay."

"That must be nice," I said wistfully. "A close family."

"Yeah, it's great, when it's not suffocating." He grinned at me. "I got some questions about you, believe me."

"About me? Why?" A little tendril of hope peeked through my clouds of doom.

"I think I mentioned you more than once or twice, and Mom's radar went off. Honestly, I think she was desperate to talk about anything but the miscarriage, just for a few minutes." He shook his head, sorrow clear in the lines of his slumped shoulders.

"Ben," I said, putting a hand on his arm. "We really need to talk. I understand if this isn't a great time, but—wait."

Something he'd said back in the alley niggled at me. "What did you mean about telling me?"

"What?"

"You said 'I'm sorry I didn't tell you.' Tell me what? If it's not about sleeping with Lizzie, tell me what?"

He heaved a sigh, and nodded toward the brick corner of the nearest building. We walked over there, and he leaned against the building, looking off into the distance. I waited, and finally he spoke up. "Okay, here's the thing. I knew about you being the Breakup Artist."

I flinched. "What? How? When? Did Michel say something?"

Shaking his head, he held up a hand to stop me. "From the beginning, Shane. I knew from the beginning. Remember when Gleason called you?" He stopped and took a deep breath. "Wow, this is hard. Okay, we planned to set you up. Ream you a new one for being the kind of heartless snake who would help people lie and scheme and play games."

I backed up, mouth opening and closing. "You—you knew all along? And yet you asked me out? You came to my place for dinner?" I could hear my voice getting shrieky, and people walking by were giving me weird looks, but I didn't care.

"You had SEX with me? You bought DISHES for my DOG?"

His mouth quirked up at that last part, and I nearly slugged him. "Don't you DARE laugh at me! How can you talk about lying and scheming and . . . oh, right. Playing games. When you were lying and scheming and playing games the entire time we were together!"

He tried to touch my arm again, and I yanked it away from him. "Don't touch me. Don't ever touch me. I never lied to you. And, for your information, my job is only about helping people get out of relationships they don't want to be in, without hurting anybody's feelings."

I backed up another step. "But you . . . you . . . everything you've ever said to me was a lie."

Ben shook his head back and forth, over and over. "No. No. I mean, yes, I lied, but I didn't lie about anything important. It was only—"

"Nothing important? You're right. It was nothing important. Just my feelings. Just my trust. Just my heart," I said, voice trembling. "And now that you've made me go all melodramatic, like the star of some damn movie of the week, I'm leaving."

I whirled around to leave, but paused for one last moment. "You know what the stupid thing is? I was finally willing to give up a little control. For you. And look where it got me."

"Shane, wait!"

"I hope you and Lizzie do get back together. You deserve each other," I said, trying to hold it together just a little longer.

Leaving my failed relationship and my failed business venture behind, I went to get my dog. The expression really should be "*woman's* best friend."

Chapter 38

As Lulu and I sat on the couch in front of the TV, watching *Pride and Prejudice* for the fiftieth time (well, it may have been her first time; no telling what Hairy Scary Guy had made her watch), my cell phone kept ringing. After I ignored calls from Nick, Michel, and Farren, two from Mrs. P., and four from Ben, I finally turned the damn thing off.

Lulu, clearly having learned nothing from her abdominal problems, was begging for cheese puffs. I gave her the nutritionally correct treats the vet had provided for us, instead.

"Yummy, liver paste," I said, and it must have smelled

great to her, because she snarfed up the three I gave her and pleaded for more.

"No more. You're a sheep, not a pig. I can't take a repeat of last night," I said, curled up and hugging my knees to my chest. Whatever had been wrong with her stomach must have been contagious, because I was going to vomit any minute.

Our apartment phone rang, startling me. Nobody ever called us on that phone; I hadn't realized it was even still hooked up. Curious, I answered it. "Hello?"

"Shane, finally! It's Melissa."

"Melissa? How did you get this phone number? Not that I mind. I'm just wondering."

"Um, I looked you up in the phone book when you didn't answer your cell. We have a big problem," she said.

"You have no idea," I replied absently, still kind of focused on the idea that I was in a phone book. Then I smiled the tiniest smile. "At least you and Tony were my one success. Something to remember when I've disconnected the business line and never, ever, ever involve myself in anybody else's love life ever again."

There was a silence. "Sorry to do this to you, Shane, because it sounds like you're having a shitty day, too, but it didn't stick."

Creeping dread spread through my body. I was afraid to ask, but I had to do it. "What didn't stick?"

"The breakup didn't stick. Tony *forgives* me. He knows I really want to marry him, somewhere deep down beneath my party girl exterior," she said.

"What? No, wait. Whatever it is, I don't have the energy for it," I mumbled.

"Well, you'd better find some energy," she snapped. "You have to fix this."

"Look, you know that expression? About the definition of insanity? We've proven that I am completely worthless to you. Why would you possibly want me to try again? All I do is screw things up."

Lulu jumped in my lap and licked my face. *I love that dog.*

"No, you almost had it this time. Tony is just so freaking stubborn," she said, exasperation in her voice.

"I'm sorry, Melissa, but I . . ." My voice trailed off, as I noticed what was playing on the TV screen. An ad for Michel's *Tomorrow's Designers Today* show.

Which gave me an idea.

A couple of ideas, in fact.

"Shane? Are you there?"

I nodded slowly, then realized she couldn't see me. "Yeah, I'm here, and I may have the beginning of a plan. Trust me, Tony won't forgive you this time."

"Are you sure?"

I looked at the show's teaser, still playing. "Oh, yeah. I'm sure. Let me call you back when I have the details figured out."

For the next week, I called in sick to work, ignored my telephone, and spent my days taking Lulu for long walks and helping Michel in any way I could with his designs. I'd had one very painful conversation with Mrs. P. about the bank loan, and she'd been very sweet.

"I'll try to figure something out, dear. Don't give up hope," she'd said.

But hope, like money, was in short supply for me just then. Annie hadn't spoken to me in eight days, only stopping back at the apartment for her clothes, and Farren and Michel were still refusing to even discuss reconciliation.

But at least I had Melissa. We talked every single day and were becoming more friends than business associates. My plan was coming together, and after initial resistance, she'd finally come around.

After all, what was humiliating herself in front of millions of people, compared to getting out of an engagement to an incredibly hot guy?

Hmmm. When I put it that way . . .

Chapter 39

"I can't believe it's tomorrow, Shane! I am FREAKING out!" Michel sat on the rug in the middle of his living room, surrounded by exquisite creations made from Italian Dupioni silk, silk chiffon, crepe satin, silk velvet, silk shantung, silk organza, silk faille, shot silk, silk jersey, wool silk, silk tissue, *peau de soie*, and (yes, Michel tutored me) silk chiffon degrade.

We're talking about a lot of silk.

There were other fabrics, too, but no polyester. Every single piece in the portfolio shouted quality, murmured luxury, and whispered elegance.

"Michel, you're a shoe-in for landing a spot on the show," I said, carefully folding a shimmery silver lace dress into layers of tissue paper.

He dropped the ribbon he was holding and stared at me in horror, eyes wide. "Don't say that! Don't ever say that again. You'll jinx me. The goddesses of fashion are eminently capricious, Shane."

I rolled my eyes. "Well, as long as you're not superstitious."

"Of course I'm superstitious. I am an artist."

"Okay. Sorry, already." I stood up and stretched. "I have to go get Lulu and take her for a walk. I'll see you in twenty minutes or so, and we'll finish wrapping this up for tomorrow."

"I'm sorry I had to ban Lulu, but . . ."

Laughing, I shrugged. "Hey, even I get that you don't want your designs to be remembered for the coating of dog hair on them."

Lulu and I wandered around the neighborhood for a little while and, as always, thoughts of Ben intruded on my attempts for calm and reflective solitude.

The jerk.

He'd called and called, and even stopped by the apartment and left a note when I'd been out one day. Mrs. P. had called and said he'd come to the boutique, too. But it had been a couple of days since his last phone call, so he was probably finally getting the not-so-subtle hint. Perversely, I wasn't sure whether that made me happy or sad.

Guess I'm a jerk, too.

Lulu finished fertilizing the patches of grass on my street for the night, and we headed back to the apartment. When I opened the door, Farren was there.

"Hey, you're back. How was work?"

"Fine, fine," he said, pulling me into the apartment and reaching down to pet Lulu. "How is Michel?"

"Oh, so now you care about Michel? Where have you been all week? He really needed your emotional support, Farren. This has been the most stressful week of his life."

"I know, I know." He paced around the room, wringing his hands together. "I'm an idiot. A fool. A complete and utter—"

I interrupted his glory of self-flagellation. "Whatever. He needs you now. Why don't you go over there and apologize? Reassure him that he really is a fabulous designer?"

Farren stopped pacing and looked at me, eyes doubtful. "Do you think he'll forgive me?"

Smiling, I unsnapped Lulu's leash and put it on our side table. "I think he'd forgive you anything. Now go! And I'm coming over in"—I looked at my watch—"forty-five minutes, so you'd better be decent. Get out of here."

He rushed for the door, stopping to hug me on the way out. "I love you, Shane. You're the best."

As the door closed behind him, I sighed. "Yeah. If only Ben had thought so."

*   *   *

About an hour later (hey, I was playing it safe), Lulu snoring soundly on my bed, I knocked on Farren and Michel's door. Michel opened it, face glowing, and grabbed me in a huge hug. When he stepped back, he pulled me into the apartment and swept an arm out to show me the sight. Dozens of neatly wrapped tissue-paper bundles were stacked on all available surfaces.

"We're ready," he announced. "My wonderfully talented Farren has a knack for folding clothes in the exactly perfect way."

Farren walked up, grinning, and put an arm around Michel's shoulders. "Yeah, I forgive you, too, you big lunkhead," he said, affection warm in his voice.

I smiled and hugged them both. "Okay, so folding clothes is *so* not what I expected to find you doing. I'm just so happy to see you back together. I can finally have my couch back."

"Hey!" Farren feigned indignation. "I kept your apartment cleaner than you ever have."

"Now maybe Annie will come back," Michel added.

I shook my head, feeling the tears welling up again. "I don't think she'll ever forgive me. But let's not talk about sad stuff. Are we ready?"

Michel looked around, then down at his hands, which were shaking the tiniest bit. He drew a deep breath. "We're as ready as I'll ever be. This is it. My big chance."

"You're going to be great," Farren said, hugging him again. I nodded, but didn't say anything, not wanting to be accused of jinxing.

Michel's cell phone rang, and he walked over to retrieve it from the floor, still beaming. "Hello?"

He listened for a few seconds, and the smile vanished from his face.

I got a sick feeling of déjà vu in the pit of my stomach. The last phone call I'd watched had ruined my love life.

"You what? Are you insane? You can't do this to me, Naomi. I'll be ruined!"

Farren rushed over to him, but Michel waved him off, still shouting into the phone. "I don't care about your freaking Karma. Can't it wait two measly days?"

"Hello? Hello? HELLO?" Dazed expression on his face, he folded his phone closed.

"What happened? Michel? Come on, you're starting to freak me out," Farren said.

Michel looked down at his phone, then suddenly hurled it against the wall. It crashed with a resounding noise and bounced off the lamp, finally skittering to rest on the floor. We all stared at it, as if it held some answers.

I snapped out of my shock first. "What the heck was that about?"

Michel stared at us, hollow-eyed and grim. "That was my model. You know, my model for tomorrow? She can't make it."

Oh, crap. "Where does she live? If she's not feeling well, I'll go make her chicken soup," I said. "I'll bring her in the cab myself. I'll—"

"Phoenix," he said flatly.

Farren gasped.

I was still in "I can fix this" mode. "I'll carry her if I have to—Phoenix? What the hell is she doing in Phoenix?"

"Her Karma wanted her to move to L.A. She's sorry to miss the contest. She's sure I can find somebody else." Michel sank to the floor, boneless, and sat clutching his head. "I'm finished. I'm freaking doomed."

Farren and I stared at each other, gaping. That bitch Karma had a lot to answer for.

"Look, that's . . . what about this? Can we find somebody else?" I asked, kneeling down to touch his arm.

He never even looked up. "Who? Any of the models I know personally, whom I could even hope to convince, are all working with the other designers. Anybody else would want to get paid. Do you see anybody here with the money to afford to pay a model?" He laughed bitterly.

"It's not like your average person walking down the street is a nearly six-foot-tall size two."

"I thought models were size eight," I said inanely.

He laughed again. "Yeah, right. Back in the old days, maybe. Now it's all about the skeletal look. Every one of my pieces is in a size two, and there's no extra fabric to let them out. I'm fucking over."

Reaching deep, deep down into my well of "we can do it," I realized something. I didn't have any "we can do it" left.

"Excuse me for a second," I mumbled, then ran for the door. Once I made it to the hallway, I slid down, back to the wall, until I was huddled in a heap on the floor. My "all control, all the time" philosophy was a pathetic joke. Sometimes life handed you lemons, then it squeezed you through the fucking citrus juicer.

Ha. Bet you won't see THAT on a poster.

Right there in the hallway, I had my own personal meltdown. Only my third or fourth of the week.

Everything I touch turns to garbage. I'm not the "reverse Cyrano de Bergerac"—I'm the "anti–King Midas."

The anti–King Midas. Kind of catchy. I sat there and laughed until I cried.

And that's how Annie and Nick found me. Tears and yuck from my nose running down my face. My head was buried in my arms, my body shaking from the force of my sobbing, and I felt arms go around me.

Considering I was sitting in the hallway, so it could have been some psycho pervert, it should have freaked me out. But I smelled cinnamon, and Annie always smelled like cinnamon, so I leaned into the hug and cried harder.

Then another pair of arms came around me from the other side and hugged, which *did* freak me out. I looked up and saw Annie and Nick. I sniffled and wiped my face on my sleeve, then tried on a tiny smile. "At least you're you, and not some psycho pervert who just happened to eat French toast for dinner."

She sat back on her knees, brow furrowed, looking worried and puzzled all at once. "What are you talking about? Are you drunk? Why are you in the hallway?"

I took a deep, shaky breath. "It's Michel's model. She's in Phoenix, and Farren is back, but we're doomed, and there was all the pretty tissue paper, and Ben is Awful Ben, and the bank rejected me, and I missed you so much, Annie. I missed you so much."

This time, she started crying, too. We hugged each other right there in the hallway for the longest time, until Nick cleared his throat. "Um, wouldn't this be more comfortable inside your apartment? Or Michel's apartment? Or, you know, anywhere but the hallway floor?"

I glanced up at him, then did a mild double take. "Hey, you shaved."

He grinned. "Yeah, I hated that stubbly look. It itched. Plus Annie likes me to be smooth-shaven when I, well, when I kiss her." His ears turned pink, and it was so freaking adorable I almost smiled.

Almost.

Chapter 40

In our apartment, I washed my face and then explained everything to Annie and Nick, from the bank, to Ben, to Michel's model, as they sat on the couch with Lulu. "So, you see, we're screwed," I said, finally wrapping it up twenty minutes later. "Poor Michel. He's worked so hard for this." Then I sighed, trying not to start crying again. I was turning out to be a freaking waterworks lately.

My story done, I figured it was their turn. "So, you two seem awfully cozy. Anything you want to tell me? Wait! Nick said, 'when I kiss her.' What is going on with you two?"

Nick grinned his usual gorgeous and shy grin, and took Annie's hand. She flashed an enormous smile my way, nearly incandescent in her delight. "Well, you may not believe this, given the way I acted with you, but I do actually have some common sense under all this frizzy hair."

Nick leaned over and kissed her. "Your hair is not frizzy. It's curly and beautiful, and I love the feel of it on my skin," he murmured.

She blushed, which fascinated me, since I'd never seen her do it before. Ever.

"Anyway, I realized that you love me, and Nick must love me, to put up with me, and—well—you two never would have cooked up this scheme with any but the best intentions." She touched Nick's face. "Also, Nick and I are *not* my parents."

Nick spoke up. "Yeah, she came in to work one day with full intentions of ripping my head off, and we ended up, um, apologizing, instead."

She laughed. "We put the CLOSED sign on the door and apologized in the office for about an hour and a half. Right there on the desk."

Now it was Nick's turn to blush. I laughed, thrilled for them. "Okay, TMI, but that's wonderful! I'm so happy for you both. Thank you for forgiving me, Annie. I know I don't deserve it, but I'll never go behind your back again."

Annie sat there, smiling at me, and Lulu barked at her. She laughed. "You're right, Lulu. I'm sorry, too, Shane. I was a complete bitch, and I'd completely understand if you want to kick me out." She rushed on. "But please don't, because Nick has three roommates, and I can't stand his dumpy little place."

I held open my arms, and she jumped up and we met in the middle for a big hug. "I'm so sorry I wasn't here for you, Shane. We'll figure out what to do about Ben, okay? I promise," she murmured.

"What we need to figure out right now is a way to help Michel," Nick said.

Lulu wagged her tail and barked at us excitedly, probably happy to have her "pack" back together and happy. Mostly happy, at least.

Annie laughed. "Well, I'm five feet tall, and nowhere near a size two. Shane, you're tall, but—"

"Yeah, also nowhere near a size two," I said. "Try to think, guys. You know a lot of musicians. Are any of them tall, reasonably attractive, and a size two?"

Annie shook her head. "Really not a lot of snooty toothpicks in the gang we hang out with, Shane."

In almost perfect unison, we gasped. "Snooty toothpicks?" she whispered.

"Lizzie!" we both shouted.

All I had to do was find my phone and pray.

Less than an hour later, Lizzie was trying on her first outfit. The chance to be a TV star far outweighed any lingering hatred she had for me, by far. She'd even hugged me when she got to Michel's apartment, which was weird. But I was so happy to see her, I'd hugged her back.

Who says we can't achieve world peace?

"Okay, everybody, here she comes," Farren called out. We all held our breath as she walked down the hall from the bathroom. It was the shimmery silver lace dress I'd loved so much, the centerpiece of Michel's collection.

She looked like an angel in it.

Every one of us burst into spontaneous applause and cheering. Even Michel smiled, although he was checking seams and the fit, poking and prodding at Lizzie like the vet had poked Lulu the other day. I half expected her to bite his head off, but she stood there, radiant, submitting to all of it and never uttering a word of complaint.

Michel made a twirling motion with his finger, and she swung around in a slow three-sixty. The dress fit her like a dream. Lizzie's Nordic blond ice princess look was the perfect foil for the ethereal designs. Michel was going to be a smash hit.

We had Lizzie—at least partially—to thank for it. The idea didn't even totally make me want to vomit.

Hey! Maturity is happening.

Or, exhaustion. Either way, I was so thrilled. For Michel and the show, for Michel and Farren, and for Annie and Nick.

Even, kind of, for Lizzie, who was getting a chance to be on TV in return for bailing us out.

Maturity meant that I was able to repress any twinge of my own unhappiness until three in the morning, when we were all able to finally get some sleep. If my pillow got a little damp after that, nobody but Lulu had to know.

Chapter 41

FINAL RULE: Never, ever admit to being the Breakup Artist to any man with whom you're in a relationship. It's a surefire way to lose him. Forever.

The converted industrial plant blared with jazz fusion and gleamed with lights and polish. The designers ran around the dressing room, making last-minute adjustments, wishing each other well (or not; I could already see a couple of feuds that would make for interesting TV), and generally doing the frantic thing.

I squeezed into a corner and handed Lizzie the first pair of shoes. By some miracle, she and Michel's missing model even wore close to the same size shoe.

"Close enough," she repeated, squeezing her size nine and a half foot into size nine stilettos. "Close enough. We'll make this work, right, Shane?"

I smiled at her and nodded, wondering how we'd managed to morph our vitriol into something approaching camaraderie. Then Michel touched my shoulder, his hand shaking. "This is it. Are you ready? Are we ready? Oh, God why did I ever think I was good enough for this? Oh, God, oh, God, oh, God."

Farren put an arm around him and made shushing noises. "That's enough. No more time for nerves because, in this fashion show, the designers have to strut the catwalk, too. Go out there and shine, baby."

Michel hugged him, then squared his shoulders. "You're right. I can do this. Shane, be sure the bag—"

I groaned. "I know, I know. I've got the bags and shoes covered. We can handle it. Go make us proud."

With one last-second adjustment to the drape of Lizzie's neckline, he rushed over to join the other designers, who were lined up to go out on stage in front of the TV cameras and the crowd.

Speaking of TV cameras . . . I glanced down at my watch. Melissa and Tony should be arriving any minute. The final stages of that plan were in place, too. Tony would break up with Melissa forever, and I could retire from being the Breakup Artist with one final, grand triumph under my belt.

Oddly, I didn't feel the teensiest bit happy about it.

When he realized I was shaking from nerves, too, Farren sent me out to watch the show from the audience and report back. "I'm better at accessorizing than you'll ever be, anyway, Shane."

Lizzie laughed, but not in a nasty way. "Some people have different talents, Farren. You should see the kick-ass layout in Sensuality. That was all Shane."

I stared at her in shock, nearly falling over. "You noticed? I mean, I thought you weren't even interested in the store."

She shrugged, even doing that gracefully. "It's not like I can shop forever. I really like Sensuality, and I hope we can work together some day. But I wouldn't mind it if this modeling gig leads to other things, either. . . ."

I smiled and gave her a thumbs-up, then headed for the front. Lizzie was still Lizzie. The world hadn't turned completely upside down.

Standing at the side entrance to the dressing room, I scanned the crowd, biting my lip. I didn't see Melissa yet, but there was Mrs. P., sitting with Ben, and . . .

Sitting with *Ben*? What?

As I stared, googly-eyed, at the two of them, he looked up and saw me. I saw him lean over and say something to Mrs. P., then he stood up and made his way down the row to the aisle and headed straight for me.

I stood, frozen, as he strode up to me. He took my arm and kept walking, gently pulling me back into a nook behind a stack of extra folding chairs.

As I blinked up at him, he smiled. "Shane, I need to tell you—you need to hear—Oh, hell. I need to do this first," he said, and then he pulled me close, ever-so-slowly, giving me time to say no. When I didn't say no—I couldn't seem to find my voice at all—he kissed me.

And kissed me.

And kissed me.

Somewhere about halfway into all that kissing, I started kissing him back.

My knees were shaking by the time I finally regained enough sanity to remember where we were and pull away. "What—"

No, too breathless. I tried for a steadier voice. "What was that for?"

"That was for how much I missed you, and how sorry I am about lying to you, and how much I hope you can forgive me," he said. "Did I mention how much I missed you?"

I nodded, still stunned.

"I even missed your little dog-sheep," he confessed, laughing. "I found myself Googling 'Chihugapoo.' How pitiful is that?"

Smiling, I shook my head. "That's pretty pitiful," I said, my voice husky. "That alone may be enough to help me forgive you."

His face turned serious. "Shane, I know we need to talk this all out, and I really am sorry. Say you'll give me a chance?"

I nodded, taking my courage in both hands. "Yes. Yes, I will. I—I missed you, too."

He kissed me again. "I'm crazy about you. It was that stupid Breakup Artist thing. I had a big problem with the deceit and lying part of it. But it's my problem. I can work it out. If it's what you want to do, maybe you can help me understand—"

I cut him off. "No worries. The Breakup Artist is officially retired. That's one problem, at least, we can put behind us."

He kissed me again, so deliciously that I almost felt steam rising from my skin. Even my ears were ringing, with the sweet sound of . . . throat-clearing?

I looked over my shoulder and saw Melissa. *Oh, crap.*

"Shane, I'm sorry, but I have to talk to you right now. I'm not sure I can go through with humiliating Tony on national TV. The thing is, I think I might actually want to marry him after all."

Almost in slow motion, I watched Ben look at Melissa, surprise becoming shock, and then disgust, on his face as he turned to me. "You're retired, huh? You're going to humiliate some poor slob on national TV, and that's *retired*?"

His arms fell away from me, and I grabbed at him. "No, you don't understand. This was an old client. I mean, we had to go to extra lengths, and—there was the bassinet, and that didn't work, and the drinking at his family's restaurant, and the cabbie with the needles, and—"

He stepped back from me, frowning. "No, you're right. I guess I don't understand. I've been all torn up because you thought I was such a liar. Well, who's the liar now?"

"Ben, no. Ben, wait. Let me explain," I said, pleading.

But he merely shook his head and walked away. Out the door and out of my life.

Again.

Melissa bit her lip. "I guess this is a bad time?"

Chapter 42

By the time Melissa explained her epiphany to me, promising to invite me to La Cucina for the engagement party, it was time for the auditions to start. Mrs. P. waved me over to sit next to her, in the seat Ben had so disastrously vacated.

"What happened, honey? Are you okay?" she whispered, resplendent in apple green chiffon.

"I'm fine," I lied. But, hey, lying was all I was good for, right?

"I need to tell you some good news about the taxes later." Then the music started, the lights dimmed, and we watched as the hopefuls for *Tomorrow's Designers Today* introduced themselves and their visions. Some were hideous, a few were brilliant, and then there was Michel. The audience actually gasped by the time Lizzie came out in the final piece, the silver dress.

It was the only standing ovation of the show.

I sat in my seat and cried, blaming it on my happiness for Michel when Mrs. P. asked. She didn't look convinced, but didn't have time to interrogate me about it, because the judges were announcing the results.

One by one, they called the names of the designers. Finally, nine ecstatic aspiring designers stood on the stage, hugging themselves and each other.

Michel was conspicuous in his absence.

I clenched my hands so tightly together, I was surprised I didn't draw blood. The announcer said, "Our final name and the tenth hopeful to be selected for *Tomorrow's Designers Today*: Michel Lanier!"

The crowd went crazy, standing up and cheering and yelling. Mrs. P. and I leapt up out of our seats, yelling and screaming. She even put two fingers to her mouth and let out a piercing whistle, which surprised the heck out of me.

Michel walked out on stage, arm in arm with Lizzie, and even from my seat I could see that he was all trembly. A good kind of trembly.

I was so happy for him, I almost couldn't bear it. But as soon as I hugged him and congratulated him, I needed to get out of there.

Fast.

*   *   *

Somehow the days passed. Every night, my pillow was a little less damp. Turned out Mrs. P.'s tax issue had been seriously misstated. She didn't need cash after all, and she was letting me buy into the business on the installment plan. Melissa wouldn't let me give her money back, either, so I wasn't broke for the first time in years.

Lulu got a clean bill of health from the vet, who happened to mention she was dating Jason again.

"Jason who?" I'd asked.

Turned out Hairy Scary Guy had an actual name. *Who knew?*

I'd tried not to cringe. She may have had horrible taste in men, but she was a great vet.

A couple of weeks after the fashion show, I was at Sensuality stocking the last of the DreamGlow on the display. Mrs. P. had pulled some strings at the company, and managed to return fifty of the sixty-four cases, leaving us with only the final few of the sixty-four *bottles* I'd originally ordered.

Lizzie had called that morning from Hollywood, thrilled almost to incoherence. The producer who'd seen her on the audition show and called her to screen test for a bit part in his movie (as the coed who dies early) had been so pleased with her acting that he'd given her a bigger role. She'd be one of the final three who defeat the serial-killing-coed-murdering fiend at the end of the movie, leaving plenty of room for a sequel or twelve.

Since she'd promised to be the "face" of Etheria, Michel's hot new line of clothes that he'd debut next spring, she was thrilled with every bit of her celebrity. Well, thrilled in a subdued way, which pretty much described me, too.

Subdued, but getting on with my life. At least all the people I cared about—and Lizzie, too—were getting their giant happy-ever-afters.

The door chimes rang, and I looked up to see a giant, purple stuffed panda walk through the door. The panda was carrying an enormous balloon bouquet, and he (or, rather, the guy carrying him) was followed by two other guys, both loaded down with the contents of at least two flower shops and what looked like a candy store.

"Um, excuse me? I think you have the wrong address," I said, trying to stop them before they unloaded anything. I was pretty sure it wasn't Mrs. P.'s birthday. Unless it was a delivery from one of Lizzie's many admirers. We'd gotten a lot of that, lately.

Panda bear guy lowered the bear and looked at me. "You Shane Madison?"

I slowly nodded.

He looked back at the other two. "Okay, let's hit it."

After a minimal amount of throat clearing, the guy with the candy said, "One, two, three."

Then they all started singing, right there in the shop.

My mouth fell open, and I stood there, gaping at them like a beached fish.

My Darling Schmoopy Pie
My Shaney Waney

Big Huggie Wuggies

Love,
    love,
       love,
          love,
             love,
Your Benny Bunny.

They finished with a flourish and all held out their flowers, balloons, and other goodies to me simultaneously.

I blinked. "But, but, but, what? Benny Bunny?"

The guy with the bear rolled his eyes. "Yeah, sappy, right? I usually only go with your standards. Your happy birthday, and the like. But the dude made us sing it just like that."

"The dude?" I echoed weakly.

Ben's voice came from the doorway of the back room. "Yeah, the dude. This dude, who is crazy about you. I got this idea from a friend. Calls herself Cyrano. I thought I'd give it a try."

I stared at him, still stunned, while the delivery guys started unloading. "You, what? That was the 'make him think you're crazy' ploy. And it's *reverse* Cyrano, with the four C's," I mumbled.

"Yep. Heard all about it," he said, smiling as he walked around the corner toward me. "Fits you pretty well, don't you think? Cute, cuddly, and completely crazy."

As he put his arms around me, I held my hands up against my chest. "I still don't understand," I said, then I got distracted. "Is that a dog-bone bouquet?"

He grinned. "I'd never forget Lulu."

I shook my head in disbelief. "But I thought you said—"

"I said a lot of things. But that's in the past. Right now, I need to hire the Breakup Artist."

"But—"

"I'm talking here," he interrupted, smiling. "I need to get rid of a woman who's driving me crazy. I can't eat, I can't sleep, and all I do is think about her all the time."

He did look kind of tired and disheveled. He even had black circles under his eyes. But I needed to figure out what was going on. The last time I'd given up any control, look how *that* had turned out.

I tried to push away from him, but he tightened his arms. "Look, Ben, I don't do that any more. I'm officially retired, for real this time. And I never did humiliate Tony, on TV or otherwise, just to let you know," I said.

I'd wanted him to know that.

He laughed. "Maybe you'll make an exception? Especially since the woman I can't quit thinking about is *you*?"

The delivery guys started clapping. One of them whistled then called out, "Yeah, forgive him already, so we can get our tip. Anybody who would do this has got to be nuts about you, lady."

I started laughing. Maybe all that control was overrated. "Well, perhaps we could discuss terms over dinner?"

Ben kissed me, in spite of the cheers and whistles from our peanut gallery. "Or maybe over breakfast? It might be a long job. I think the contract should be open-ended. Months, even. Maybe *years*," he said.

I kissed him back. "I might be persuaded to take on one more job," I admitted. "But the days of the money-back guarantee are over."